Bitter. Broken. Brutal.

Molded since childhood to be the perfect weapon, Gavriel d'Alana (also known as Death's Shadow) has devoted himself to serving Thalia Talfayen. The life of a Noxblade is lethal and lonely, and since the princess has no need of him, he secretly believes there's no reason for him to live—and he should seek a glorious death—but that's before he tangles with a tiger woman who unleashes his darkest desires.

Tough. Tenacious. Trustworthy.

Magda Versai has a reputation for being unattainable—no deep attachments, only discreet amusements. If she has her way, the pride will never learn of her private heartbreak, as she accepted her curse years ago. Now, she focuses on work, which is why she's acting as Raff's bodyguard while secretly hunting for Slay. The search leads Mags to team up with a Noxblade so belligerent that she can't resisting baiting him.

She's the steel, he's the flint, and the sparks they strike together might kindle a fire that could warm them for a lifetime, if they don't kill each other first…

THE SHADOW WARRIOR

Ann Aguirre

Copyright Information
THE SHADOW WARRIOR
Copyright © 2019 by Ann Aguirre
Print Edition

Edited by Victoria West
Cover art by Kanaxa
Print design by Kanaxa
Proofreading by Lillie
Formatting by BB Ebooks

Content warning: This story contains rough sex, dominance and pain play, and suicidal thoughts / ideation.

This is a work of fiction. Names, characters, businesses, places, events, and incidents are either the products of the author's imagination or used in a fictitious manner and are not to be construed as real. Any resemblance to actual persons, living or dead, or actual events is purely coincidental.

All Rights Reserved. No part of this book may be reproduced, scanned, or distributed in any form whatsoever, without written permission from the author except for brief quotations embodied in critical reviews or articles.

To Ms. Beverly Jenkins,
Who writes the most beautiful books
And who once called me a slayer of words.
Thank you for so generously sharing your gift
While inspiring others to strive to do the same.

Acknowledgments

Thanks so much for waiting patiently to read about Mags and Gavriel. He's a been an ass for the first three books, so it was a challenge to make him lovable. I'll leave it up to you, dear readers, as to whether I succeeded.

First, thanks to Karen Alderman, Fedora Chen, and Pamela Webb-Elliot for their beta-reading brilliance. Much appreciation to Rachel Caine, Bree Bridges, Lilith Saintcrow, Kate Smith, Melissa Blue, Kate Elliott, Yasmine Galenorn, Alyssa Cole, Suleikha Snyder, Donna J. Herren, Thea Harrison, and Charlotte Stein for offering advice, support, and commiseration, as appropriate. Thanks to Patrick Weekes for proving that cool guys read romance.

A thousand thanks to Kanaxa for the beautiful cover art. My editor, Victoria West pushed through even past personal illness, so a huge cheer for her dedication as well. Thanks to Lillie for the wonderful proofreading. These books are a team effort!

Finally, thanks to my family, who understand when I'm busy at odd hours. Thank you for being patient with me while I'm lost in fictional worlds, leaving you on your own in the real one. I appreciate your support more than I can say.

Please enjoy this story and look forward to the rest. We're past the halfway point, aiming for an epic conclusion! Thanks for sticking with me and keep telling paranormal romance fans about the series.

The Story So Far…

In *The Leopard King,* Latent shifter Pru Bristow went after the pride leader, Dominic Asher, who had holed up at the seer's retreat after the death of his wife, also Pru's best friend. With the conclave approaching, Ash Valley couldn't afford to let Dom's second, Slay, run the show. It was rocky going, and they were attacked by Eldritch assassins. In the furious fight that followed, Pru finally shifted and saved Dom's life.

In time, she convinced Dom to come back to Ash Valley because the fate of the pride rested on completing the conclave and renewing the Pax Protocols (a peace treaty between supernatural communities). Her success didn't come without a cost, however. She agreed to become Dom's mate and lead the pride alongside him.

Their return startled a lot of people, Slay most of all, because he'd always thought that Pru would wait for him forever. Since he didn't want her when she couldn't shift, she didn't want him once she could, and Pru devoted herself to working with Dom to make the conclave go smoothly.

That wasn't in the cards. Though the attendants all arrived safely, the Pine Ridge wolf pack and the Burnt Amber bear clan hated Lord Talfayen of the Eldritch, and nobody knew what to make of Prince Alastor of the Golgoth. Everything that could go wrong, did, including the murder of an Eldritch envoy. Talks broke down, culminating in treachery, but the Eldritch Lord's plot went awry, as the bombs he'd set detonated too soon, catching his own people in the trap. King Tycho of the Golgoth attacked thereafter and it was all Ash Valley could do to hold.

Meanwhile, Dom and Pru tried to keep things together while falling in love. They did battle with their enemies and each other, before eventually admitting their true feelings. Slay vanished mysteriously and the leading couple finally had a wedding party, once Ash Valley was safe. Soon after, the visiting dignitaries departed, and the Numina prepared for war.

In *The Demon Prince*, Dr. Sheyla Halek reluctantly agreed to take charge of Prince Alastor Vega and work on synthesizing the medicine he needed for his rare illness. Since she preferred research to treating actual patients anyway, she didn't hate the idea, but she was quite annoyed to be saddled with someone she considered an enemy. For his part, Prince Alastor liked the prickly doctor at once and spent a good deal of his time trying to charm her.

They left Ash Valley together—with her ostensibly in the role of company medic—and became closer through an arduous journey to Tycho's likely next target: the unprotected city of Hallowell. Alastor tried his best to woo Sheyla, and while she wasn't susceptible to his brand of charm, she did admire his determination to do the right thing for his people. Slowly, they drew together, because he understood her, and she—without realizing it—quietly partook of Golgoth courtship rites.

Eventually, they decided to embark upon a wartime romance because their passion could no longer be denied. They'd only stay together until Hallowell was safe. Afterward, they'd go their separate ways, because Sheyla belonged in Ash Valley, and Alastor had heavy responsibilities to his people. Since she couldn't have a relationship, even a brief one, with a patient in her care, Sheyla turned treatment over to a colleague and focused on researching Alastor's medicine.

Neither one cared to admit how deeply they'd fallen for one another, and the risky romance only intensified, set against the backdrop of impending doom. When Tycho's forces invaded, it seemed like all might be lost, but Alastor eventually won against incredible odds, mounting a successful defense of a critical foothold in the war effort, though not without painful loss and sacrifice. He also secured the allegiance of Tycho's surviving forces, which was when Sheyla left him, as per their original agreement.

Realizing he couldn't live without her, Alastor chased her down and officially proposed in front of her family, offering to make her his queen once he liberated Golgerra. Though her relatives were skeptical at first, eventually they agreed, and the demon prince was set to live happily ever after with his physician-queen. This decision meant rejecting other marital offers, however, which would have a fascinating impact on the war effort elsewhere.

In *The Wolf Lord*, Thalia Talfayen finally rose to power, but with enemies all around, she realized she needed to make a strategic political marriage to cement her position and claim the Silver Throne. After her first choices turned her down, Thalia was left with the roguish leader of Pine Ridge, Raff Pineda.

About the only thing Raff and Thalia had in common was regard for their people, though they certainly had different ways of showing that care. That led them to pursue a marital alliance, which got off to a shaky start due to Raff's propensity for breaking the rules. When the first activity was disrupted by a vicious attack by House Manwaring and Raff was gravely injured, Thalia acted swiftly and decisively to save his life. On his recovery, Raff committed to the marriage of convenience, pledging aid to House Talfayen in return for their support later when the war reached Pine Ridge.

This wedding was anything but convenient, however. Someone attempted to murder everyone at the head table, a tragedy prevented only by Raff's acute sense of smell. Sadly, Lileth, Thalia's aide, was fatally poisoned. A grief-stricken and enraged Thalia was determined to punish those who helped rival Eldritch leader Ruark Gilbraith infiltrate the fortress. With some help from her new right hand, Ferith, Thalia soon discovered secret tunnels in and out of the Daruvar fortress. Meanwhile Thalia's former head Noxblade, Gavriel, joined forces with tiger shifter Magda to search for both the missing Ash Valley second, Slay, and the insurgents loyal to Thalia's traitorous father.

Unfortunately, Thalia's plan to act as bait to uncover the enemy succeeded a little too well, leaving both Thalia and an injured Raff cut off in the tunnels. They fought their way out and took refuge from a sudden snowstorm in a rustic Animari hideaway. The shared danger heightened their burgeoning attraction and they finally consummated their marriage. Realizing they had an opportunity to flush out the traitor in their midst, Thalia and Raff worked with tiger shifter Titus to retake Daruvar as their feelings for one another deepened.

Titus pretended to be a bounty hunter returning to their bodies, and a bloody battle ensued. Once they won the day, Thalia discovered that her 'cousin' Tirael was a traitor who had staged a coup in Thalia's absence. Just before Tirael's execution, the woman told Thalia that they were, in fact, half-sisters, courtesy of old Lord Talfayen. Thalia silenced Tirael with a personal execution, but her problems were far from over.

The other houses were still in open rebellion, and her own people seemed to be doubting her fitness to lead, as they didn't wish to send children to train as Noxblades until the succession was settled. Thalia tried to talk it over with Raff, but he had a distinctly Animari outlook, which led to conflict between the two lovers. To further complicate matters, a young wolf named Sky awakened as a Seer and required Raff's comfort and attention. Thalia stumbled on an intimate scene and misread the situation, leading her to make a drastic decision.

Thalia embarked on a suicide mission to triumph or die. She witnessed the hardship her people had experienced firsthand and learned more about the growing problem of a strange drug called gray tar. At long last, Thalia discovered her gift during the hunt-kill mission inside Braithwaite, Ruark's stronghold. As she'd left without consulting Raff, he could only help from afar by sending drones to act as a distraction. That feint was enough to save her. With Raff's air support, Thalia and Ferith took on House Gilbraith and won, whereupon Thalia broadcast a message of conquest all over Eldritch lands.

A triumphant Thalia returned to Daruvar with Ruark Gilbraith's head to claim the Silver Throne as the new queen. Other Eldritch houses quickly dispatched vassals to pledge their loyalty and various Animari and Golgoth dignitaries came to pay their respects as well at her coronation. That success gave Thalia the courage to claim her man and she professed her love for Raff, who had been hers all along. But with a marriage of convenience transforming to one of true love, there were still more seeming impossibilities yet to occur...

1.

THIS NOXBLADE WAS begging for somebody to kick his ass and Magda Versai was just the woman for the job.

She'd come to Daruvar—a grim, ancient Eldritch fortress—to guard Raff's back, and this asshole had the nerve to attack on her watch? Not fucking likely. They'd thought they were being subtle by taking the argument to a dark hallway, but everyone knew they didn't get along. She heard Raff say, "Use your words, Gavriel."

The assassin released Raff, spitting an Eldritch swear. Mags understood enough of the language to know that he'd just insulted Raff and his mother. She lingered in the shadows, ready to step in if it became necessary. Dammit, she'd nearly found out something about Slay, too, the whole reason she was here, and now this bastard was wasting her time. He'd pay for that.

Gavriel snarled, "I warn you, wolf. The princess is not for you. Leave this place before something worse happens."

Mags leapt on the Noxblade, seizing his wrist and wrenching his arm up toward his shoulder blade. She put her lips to his ear. *"I'm* something worse. And Raff is under my protection."

For good measure, she twisted harder, digging her strong fingers into Gavriel's wrist bones. He felt fragile in her hold, though she had no doubt he'd enjoy sticking a blade in her, should she show weakness or mercy. Possibly he considered them to be two sides of the same coin.

Raff cleared his throat. "Let him go. We'll use our words too, Mags."

"You brought me as your bodyguard." She pressed harder until Gavriel made a pained, angry sound. It would be *so* easy to break his bones.

Though she was physically stronger than the wolf lord, Mags didn't resist when Raff pulled her hand away and the Noxblade scrambled away from them like they had a contagious disease. She could smell the hatred on him, sharp and acrid. The assassin was breathing hard, unaccustomed to being overcome so easily, and she smiled, enjoying his discomfort.

Gavriel didn't meet her gaze. Of course he didn't. Fucking coward.

Instead, he growled at Raff, "How dare you bring your mistress here!"

She made a fist, taking a step forward. *Is that what you see when you look at me? I thought assassins had to be observant.* "I belong to only myself."

Though Raff set a hand on her shoulder, she grabbed Gavriel's arm again, so tempted to stomp some humility into this insulting war-hole. It was a pejorative term, all credit to Beren. *Damn, I miss that old bear.* Because the wolf was exerting full strength, Mags humored him and pretended to let him haul her back.

"Leave us," Raff said. "He won't hurt me. He respects the princess far too much to violate her oath of hospitality."

She had her private doubts, but Gavriel spoke first, his tone strained. "That...is true. Come with me. Now."

The other two headed for the stairs that led to the ramparts. She pretended to move off and followed in complete silence, a lightness of foot that surprised those who judged her by size and strength.

She caught up in time to hear Raff say, "Go ahead, speak your warning. If I hurt her, you will poison me, so I die in slowest agony, and then you'll carve out my heart and offer it to crows and so on."

"None of that makes any sense," Gavriel snapped. "Slow poison makes it more likely that you'll be caught, an antidote administered. And if you died of poison, why would I feed your heart to innocent birds?"

To her annoyance, Mags agreed with all those points. Raff was laughing, probably not in danger. "You take things far too literally. Didn't you bring me here to threaten me?"

"Much as I would like to, there are more important matters at hand."

"Then, by all means, continue convincing me not to wed Princess Thalia."

"You take nothing seriously and you seem to care only for your own pleasure. You are no fit match for her, and you will only add to her burden in time."

At this point, Mags could have moved off, but she was curious enough to stick around. They didn't know she was listening, ready to pounce if Gavriel made a move, and it might give her some insight as to how the Noxblade thought. That might come in handy later. Opponents rarely expected her to be clever, only fierce; therefore, it was deliciously satisfying when they realized she was both.

Raff snapped, "What the hell are you even saying,

man?"

Only Animari ears could have detected Gavriel's sigh from this distance. "Haven't you considered at all what a disastrous mésalliance this would be? When she's still bright and beautiful, she'll be chained to you, though you'll be a doddering, toothless old hound by then."

Mags had considered that aspect, but she figured they could dissolve the marriage at any point before then. Things weren't normal anymore and there was no reason to pretend the old rules applied. Hell, she never could've imagined leaving Ash Valley to hunt down Slay, who might've turned traitor. When she requested leave, there was one critical fact she hadn't mentioned to Dom.

If Slay had turned on them, she'd put him down. Hers was a three-fold task: Find Slay. Determine whether he was a captive or a conspirator. Take appropriate action. The former Ash Valley second knew too much about cat security for Mags to leave him in the wind, and she had mixed feelings about the mission. She loved the asshole like a brother, so if he'd gone bad? It'd be like losing a limb to take him out.

Raff sounded like he was losing patience. "Unless she asked you to speak for her, shut the hell up. It's embarrassing to see you froth jealousy that masquerades as concern for your lady."

"I'll say one thing more, then." Gavriel paused, maybe thinking about how to phrase what came next. "She may look cold and strong, but she has been alone for most of her life, fighting harder than anyone can imagine. Please, by all the gods you hold sacred, be gentle with her."

Surprise flickered through her at the tenderness of the request. The sincere intensity, from a seemingly merciless assassin, sent a pang through her, not envy, exactly, but wistfulness for what would never be. Mags had long since accepted that the price of her own emotions was too high and she would never again ask anyone else to bear the cost.

She heard Raff say, "I will," and concluded the conversation was over. Lingering might get her caught, so she padded away down the stairs. Though Gavriel doubtless thought he was being silent, she caught the faint hint of his movement behind her, but his own skin gave him up even more, traces of cloves, cinnamon, and copper. Before he could return the favor of pouncing from behind, she whirled on him and slammed him against the wall, one hand on his throat.

"It's unwise to startle me," she said.

This time, however, he managed to get his blades up, nudging them against her abdomen. "It's equally unwise to antagonize me. I'm in no mood to be patient."

"On three, then." Mags didn't explain, but from the terse way he lifted his chin, he understood. She counted out the numbers and they both dropped their hands. Taking a step back, she added, "What's your damage?"

"I just didn't want you to think you got away with it. The wolf lord may not have known or cared that you were prying into our private conversation, but whatever you're trying to do, I *will* stop you, if it harms the Eldritch or my queen."

The fervent declaration startled a laugh out of her, which prompted a ferocious scowl from Gavriel. "What?" he demanded.

"My mission is no secret, shadow warrior. I'm here to keep Raff safe, but I'm also tracking Slay from Ash Valley, and what I found leads here. Old Lord Talfayen's people took him or…" Well, she didn't need to spell it out. "I'll find our lost jaguar, one way or another."

Gavriel stared, unable to believe she'd divulge her purpose so readily, but he read no signs of deceit or subterfuge in her expression. "Is this a trick?"

"You've got issues," she said, shaking her head.

Magda Versai was a dangerous woman; of that, he had no doubt. She stood a few centimeters taller than him, weighed more in pure muscle, and she had combat skills the like of which he'd rarely seen in the field. Even his stealth might not be enough to defeat her, unless he used a fast-acting, powerful poison.

"Excuse me?"

"There's no reason for me to conceal my purpose. You're loyal to Thalia, so you don't know shit about where Slay might be. And if I share who I'm looking for, maybe you won't get in my way out of spite." She tilted her head. "You might even be useful, if you could put aside all that pointless rancor."

The 'pointless rancor' she referenced so easily spiked in a burst of white-hot rage, so powerful that for a moment he couldn't even speak. He hated these Animari *so much,* not for the racial purity reasons Lord Talfayen had touted, but from bitter, personal loss. Gavriel clenched a fist, tucked it behind his thigh to hide the reaction.

"You speak so easily about that which you know nothing," he snapped.

"I know everything. Your brother died at the retreat, after fighting Dom and Pru, and you've hated us ever since. But look, did you ever think maybe you're hating us this hard so you don't have to process your own guilt?

"You were there. You failed to save your brother, you didn't manage to carry out your mission of warning Dom, and you *ran* to save your own ass. Clean your own house before you burn ours down. And once you do that, think about the part your own fucking queen played in that mess. I know you adore her, and you think she's perfect, but she gave the orders, right? It wasn't Dom, or me, so suck it up and stop blaming other people for your loss."

At first, the pain was blinding, and it made him sick to his stomach because she was cool and relentless, but as the words dropped into him like stones in a still pond, he couldn't refute her statements. Though it galled him to the bone, he couldn't admit she was *right,* so he said nothing at all.

She seemed to take that as an invitation to continue, hammering away at him as if he were a sword she must temper. "And Zan, yeah, I heard about him too. I heard everything from Korin. I know you were close, but that's not our fault either, Gavriel. I'm sorry you lost a friend, but I heard that he *chose* to protect Alastor to his last breath. You didn't even order him to do that. He volunteered. It's tough as hell. I get it. But you shouldn't let your pain make you hate the world."

"You know nothing about my pain," he finally bit out.

He wasn't used to anyone coming at him like this, candid and fearless. Everyone in Princess Thalia's lands was terrified of him. They called him Death's Shadow because she whispered her orders and he fulfilled them, quiet as a ghost, leaving no trace. Before, when the Noxblade guild was strong, he hadn't minded so much, but now, most of his sword mates were dead, perished in the Battle of Hallowell or even before. He had no friends or family left, only Princess Thalia, and she—

She did not love him. He would never be more than a blade in her hands.

"Maybe not, but I know mine. And I'm positive of one thing."

"What is that?" he asked before he could stop the question.

In this light, Gavriel could scarcely make out the Animari woman's features, but his own must be well illuminated for her. He hated being on the wrong side of the power imbalance.

"It doesn't help to blame other people… or even yourself. Terrible things happen, and you have to ride them out. When you're hurting so bad you feel like you could die, stay busy. Work until that feeling fades. Since you've lived longer than me, you should know that well enough. Time eases all things."

Gavriel noticed that she didn't say 'cures' or 'heals' and that was the reason he didn't eviscerate her with a few sharp words. It seemed that Magda Versai did know something about sorrow. "I didn't request your counsel," he muttered.

"It was a free consultation. Are you going to help me find Slay or not?"

"What?"

"You didn't think I was comforting you out of the goodness of my heart, did you?" She laughed softly, husky and low, and he…didn't hate the sound. In fact, it was almost pleasurable to his ragged nerves, even knowing he'd caused her amusement.

"Clarify," he said.

"I could use a hand getting these Eldritch to open up.

They're too damned nervous to talk to me. Since you need to stay occupied, help me out."

Gavriel startled himself by chuckling, a rusty noise born of long disuse. "You think *I'll* put the people at ease?"

"Shit. Probably not. You're the would-be queen's enforcer, so you might scare them even more."

"It's unlikely that anyone in Daruvar knows anything about Lord Talfayen's loyalists," he said. "You've most likely wasted your time coming here."

"Well, I needed to be in Eldritch lands regardless. Maybe I can beat something out of one of the enemy patrols who are running recon in Thalia's territory."

"That sounds dangerous."

"For *them*," she said, smiling.

He surprised himself by acceding to her request. "While I can't assist with questioning the staff, I can hunt with you. We share a common goal in wanting to extract intelligence from the queen's enemies."

"You'll patrol with me, help me take out the opposition, and then assist with interrogation afterward? That could be interesting."

"It doesn't need to be that. Only mutually useful." Privately Gavriel admitted that the additional work would provide a welcome distraction from the damned marital alliance that Raff Pineda had to come to pursue.

"Then...I accept your offer. When can we get started?" she asked.

He considered. "Tomorrow, we have some official entertainments planned. After that, I'll be free, or relatively so. Princess Thalia has been distracted of late and has not issued any particular orders since I returned from Hallowell."

She told you to rest.

Relaxation wouldn't drive the demons out of his head, a pity the princess didn't realize that as well as Magda Versai. The tiger woman seemed to grasp that if he retired and closed his eyes, he would see nothing but nightmare scenarios. Guilt would play his brother's death, again and again, and Gavriel would writhe all night on a pyre of failing to prevent the loss, or worse, his flight to save himself. He had never shared that quiet truth—that he despised himself for surviving—yet she knew.

As if she was reading his mind, she said, "Get some sleep before then, or I'll have to save your ass in the field."

Gavriel drew himself up. "Don't cross the line. My cooperation in this matter doesn't give you the right to make personal remarks."

For the third time, she laughed at him, and his jaw clenched. "I can say whatever the hell I want. *You* can ignore me or shut me up. Which will it be?"

Desperate desire for violence flared. Nobody spoke to him this way. He wouldn't permit it from this Animari, either.

"Are you challenging me?" he asked softly.

"Could be fun. Fighting's better than going back to my room, which I'm sharing with a couple of cranky wolf women. Is there somewhere we can go a round or two?"

She didn't seem to take this seriously, her mistake. Gavriel smiled. "Certainly. The soldiers have a training space past the barracks. It's cold and damp, but it should suffice for our purposes. I'll give you the choice of weapons."

"You can use whatever you want," she answered. "I won't need one."

Gavriel gritted his teeth at Magda's impenetrable confidence and stepped around her, choosing the corridor that led deeper beneath the fortress. "We shall see."

2.

As the Noxblade had warned, the practice space was makeshift with gear piled against the walls, poorly lit with a few solar lanterns.

There were no mats to break a fall, but Mags didn't need them. She doubted Gavriel could breach her guard, let alone perform a takedown. No matter how the sparring match went, she preferred this to returning to her room, currently occupied by Skylett and Bibi, who were doubtless complaining about Raff's terrible decisions. While she understood disagreeing with pack leadership, she didn't have time for people who whispered their dissent instead of saying it to the wolf lord's face.

Across the space, Gavriel stretched with economical grace and Mags figured she should limber up too. The chill of old stones had her muscles tight and that was a good way to get injured. Just because she healed fast didn't mean she should skip critical steps. She rotated through her usual warm up, until her body felt strong and loose, ready for whatever the assassin threw at her.

This should be fun.

To her surprise, he stripped out of his shoes and shirt,

removing his belt. He correctly identified articles she could use against him and eliminated them from the equation. For that reason, she took off her top and belt as well. Her shoes were soft, no laces, so they shouldn't offer him any advantage. They studied each other in the wan light; he was lean, muscles so well defined that he must train for hours every day. *Impressive.* Mags couldn't read what he made of her build, but he wasn't disconcerted at the sight of her bare skin, unlike the Golgoth who had been so shocked by Animari ways.

"I'm using a stiletto," he said then.

The blade shone in the dark, sharp and wicked. Gavriel hadn't wrapped it or added protective padding. She studied his stance and judged him more than willing to slice her up.

"Show me your best moves," Mags answered, smiling.

Surprisingly, Gavriel circled her, cautious, probably learning as much from her feints as she did from his. Considering his customary bad temper, she expected him to be impulsive in combat, but he was proving to be patient. When he finally struck, she blocked smoothly and went for an arm lock, but he twisted away, tumbling backward in a move that told her he had skills. He came up in a crouch a few meters away, knife ready to strike.

"That was pretty. Could I see it again?"

His red eyes flashed in the dark, a testament to how little he liked or wanted her praise. "Are you mocking me?"

"No, it's a good move. If I see it a couple more times, I can probably replicate it. I haven't studied Eldritch combat styles, so I appreciate the insight."

With a snarl, he came at her again and she grabbed both his arms, just to piss him off. He was used to hiding in the shadows, not matching his opponent strength for strength.

To salve his pride, she let go instead of forcing a challenge he had no hope of winning. That enraged him more, and he whirled at her in a flurry of strikes.

Block, block, feint, weave, then she lashed out with an open palm, slamming it into his chest. He grunted but didn't stagger, sending a flicker of surprise through her. She'd pulled that hit out of consideration, but maybe he was tougher than he looked. Mags stepped up the pace, and while he couldn't match her for power, his reaction times might even be faster than hers.

She tested him with arms and legs, watching his deadly knife all the while. A few times, he nearly sliced through her defenses, and she was warming up nicely, breath coming quicker and smoking slightly in the cool air. Striking faster, she watched his eyes, his hands, the tightness of his mouth.

He's tiring.

Mags kept him focused on her arms, occupied with matching her furious onslaught so when she shifted and struck at his knee, he wasn't braced, and he went down. She pounced, dropping her weight on his chest to pin him, but she didn't account for his sheer speed. Somehow, he managed to get his stiletto between them and as she pressed down, he increased the pressure, the blade pricking against her chest.

If she relaxed the pressure on his upper arms to knock the weapon away, he'd escape the prone position. For a long moment, she stared down at him, then did one thing he could never expect. Mags bit him on the wrist. Not hard enough to break the skin, but startlement loosened his grip just long enough for her to knock the knife away. The stiletto skittered toward the far wall as she planted herself on top of his hips and held his upper body down with all her considerable strength.

"Get off me," he bit out.

"Not until you admit that I won."

He bucked and tried an escape, but she had her weight balanced and he wasn't physically strong enough to throw her. Even Slay would've had trouble dislodging her once she took dominance. *Stupid bastard. I hope I don't have to kill him.* The former Ash Valley second had been her closest friend, blessedly uninterested in adding her to a list of personal conquests. Mags had a reputation for being unattainable, but it was safer that way.

His mouth sealed in a tight line, as if he'd rather starve on these cold stones than acknowledge her victory. Mags increased the pressure on his arms, hard enough to bruise, but his eyes only glittered with calculation of whether there was still a way to reverse their positions. Gavriel didn't cry out, attesting to a high pain threshold.

"You cheated. Used your mouth as a weapon!"

"*Every* part of me is a weapon," she purred. "Didn't you realize that?"

"It's a sparring match, not a fight to the death. The Eldritch don't fight like—"

"Be very careful how you complete that sentence," she warned.

Her faint amusement faded, and now she was holding him still to keep from venting her temper. She'd swallowed enough outrage back in Ash Valley when old Lord Talfayen called her people 'animals' and 'beasts'. If Gavriel showed he was cut from the same cloth, she might regret not breaking his bones. Hell, this match might take a dark turn, even now.

"Like the Animari," he finished.

"Acceptable. But you still need to—" Even as she spoke, he twisted and rolled beneath her, trying to turn their brief conversation into a personal advantage.

Mags could respect that relentless drive, considering she shared it. He was stronger than she'd guessed from his light build, wiry, tough, and incredibly flexible. Gavriel drove his foot into the small of her back, trying to push her off with his arms, and she lay down on him, equally determined not to be unseated. That brought their faces close together and he snapped at her, proving that he might bite her nose off, despite what he'd said about the Eldritch not sharing Animari viciousness.

"Just admit the loss. It's not the end of the world," she whispered.

She wrapped her legs around his, pinning him further. Now they were completely entwined, her body ruling his. His breath came hard and fast, bitter rage sparking his eyes, driving the churn of his arms and his furious heartbeat. Normally, sparring wasn't like this. Her pride mate would just tap out, leaving her to swagger around a little, and that would be the end of it. She'd never faced off against someone so…obstinate.

Mags tightened her thighs, pulling his legs farther apart to prove that he couldn't get away. Gavriel's breath caught. As he glared up at her, chest heaving, the atmosphere changed. He bit his lip, his arms going slack, and he turned his face away, showing the sharp line of his jaw. His throat worked helplessly as he tried to hide in the tangled mess of his white hair. She registered the warming of his scent first, more cinnamon, and then he swelled beneath her, an unmistakable sexual response. Judging from the tightness of his expression and his ragged breathing, he couldn't control the reaction.

"Oh, shit," she breathed. "You *like* being held down. Does this feel like foreplay?"

GAVRIEL MIGHT DIE of shame.

The heat of it singed his cheeks, burning like red coals. He might have answered honestly—*yes*—or *I'm sorry, it does.* Time had taught him that his parameters for excitement differed from most and couldn't be triggered through soft touches or sweet kisses. His throat closed, and he lay quiet beneath her, feeling her weight against his surging cock. If the Animari woman mocked him, he would perish in a white-hot burst. If she moved, he might do something even worse.

Thankfully, she rolled away without waiting for an answer, leaving him with an imprint of how hot and strong her body was. He could still feel the weight of her on top of him, forcing him to feel as no one ever did—aroused and enraged. His shoulders and upper arms ached from the force of her hold, but that was to be expected. Watching her button her blouse, he had no way to resolve the unanticipated throb of his cock.

"I don't lose. I survive, withdraw, and look for another opportunity to win," he said with a false calm, trying to act as if she hadn't said—or noticed—anything.

"Right, sure. Look, it doesn't have to be a big deal."

He hated that he had no idea whether she was talking about his awkward erection or losing their sparring match, so he simply stared, waiting for her to elaborate.

"I'm undefeated in Ash Valley, that's how I ended up as security chief. Well, that and I'm good with tech, too."

A wave of gratitude suffused him. *Other than her initial, impulsive inquiry, we're pretending it didn't happen. Perfect.*

"I'll bear that in mind. Good evening."

He strode out of the practice room, leaving shirt and shoes behind. With any luck, the cold walk back to his quarters might freeze some sense into him. Gavriel avoided a few guards, hiding in the shadows until they passed because he didn't want to answer inconvenient questions. He was shivering by the time he reached his room, fingers clumsy with cold, and nobody had lit the fire in his hearth.

Unsurprising, he held no tangible rank in Princess Thalia's court, and he frightened the staff, who watched him with wary eyes, as if he might commit murder at the breakfast table. Which explained why he most often chose to eat alone.

It hadn't always been like this. Ironic, that the princess's captivity had been brighter for him personally, but *all* his sword mates were alive then, along with his brother, Oriel, and Zan, always the closest of his companions. The names of the lost gouged at him, excoriating like a dull blade that would hollow him out completely.

First, he kindled the light, one solar lantern because he didn't need it to be bright, just enough to see, then he built a fire, using the last of the wood, and the flames crackled orange and hungry, granting the bare stones some false cheer. His stomach rumbled, but it was too much trouble to go down to the kitchen in search of food. He'd missed more than one meal while working for the princess's ends; another wouldn't matter, and the gnawing discomfort fit his current mood.

He carried that gloom with him to the shower, where it took ten minutes to coax a trickle of lukewarm water.

Despite the lack of luxury, he lingered, trying to scrub away the sensory impressions the Animari woman had left behind, but even when he stepped out into the chilly bathroom, wet from head to toe, he couldn't erase the heaviness in his groin. Under normal circumstances, he didn't lose control of his urges like this, but it had been a long time since anyone touched him, apart from training and violence.

The way he'd felt, pinned beneath her… the sensations came back in a rush. Her body was incredibly solid and strong, powerful enough to hold him against his will. Dark little vignettes flickered in his imagination, where she bound him and did things to him. Against his will, the possibility danced in his head, endlessly humiliating.

A little voice whispered, *Nobody has to know. That's why fantasies exist.*

Gavriel tried—he did try to resist. Tried to turn his thoughts to other paths, but the princess never starred in his fantasies. She'd rarely touched him, apart from a cool clasp on the shoulder, and he certainly couldn't imagine her forcing him to the ground and—

I'm so hard.

Princess Thalia had no place in his filthy yearnings. With her, he'd never bridged the gap between adoration and desire, probably because his secret cravings weren't romantic, no starlight and rose petals. It was better to nip this small tempest in the bud than to agonize over it or let it build into a maddening obsession.

Still naked, he padded over to the bed and got under the covers to keep from freezing. Closing his eyes, he let the mental images come without resisting anymore. For long moments, he only imagined and didn't touch. He relived the brutal strength of her thighs parting his legs. *Powerless, can't resist.* He'd never trusted anyone enough to give himself, but it was impossible for him not to wish to be taken.

Gavriel licked his lips and finally took hold of his aching cock. He hated himself for this weakness, but somehow that loathing only made it better when he yanked on his shaft, hard and vicious. The movement drew out the soreness in his arms and shoulders. Soon, he'd have marks from where she'd pinned him, her imprint on his skin.

Yes.

He opened his eyes and paused, bringing his hand out from under the covers to inspect the place where she'd bit him. Her teeth marks were still faintly visible, red against his pale skin. His lashes fluttered as he fought the compulsion, but eventually, he gave in and put his mouth on the mark, sucking at the forming bruise. The pain was light and gorgeous, making him shiver. His nipples tightened, more excitement than cold. With his tongue, he traced the outline of Magda's teeth.

Nobody else would've dared.

Gavriel shuddered and slipped his hand back down, taking hold of his cock again, faster this time. At no point in recent memory could he recollect being this hard, this ready. Moving his hand slowly, he savored the build, the slippery feel of the head slick with precome. He smoothed it around, pleasuring himself as he'd let nobody else. His thighs tensed, relaxed, and his stomach quivered as more mental pictures flowered, sleek and cruel and seductive. Magda wouldn't be gentle, not even if he begged.

He held his breath as a soft punishment and imagined her arm across his throat, only exhaling in a noisy gust when the pleasure built too hard and fast, and his head went starry with it. With his other hand, he pinched himself, hard enough to bruise, and then he came, hot and messy, all over his hand, smearing on his blankets.

Once his breathing settled, he got up to tidy himself. With merciless eyes, he watched himself in the mirror, washing the semen from his hands, his softening cock. The salty smell of it was both beautiful and terrible. He scrubbed longer than he needed to, then he sponged the stains on his bedcovers. He was so cold that his joints hurt.

The sheet would dry if he draped it, and they'd collect his linens in a few days. Currently, he hated himself, almost as much as he hated Magda Versai for making him feel this way. He knelt, naked, by the fire until the chill and the grief passed, yielding to something akin to peace.

Eventually, Gavriel got in bed and pulled the remaining covers up, letting his breathing even out. Maybe he wouldn't sleep tonight, but he felt calm and easy for the first time in longer than he could recall, so there was some silent gratitude too. It took a lot to provoke him to his point; his control was legendary, but she'd unraveled him in a handful of minutes of close contact and with a few whispered words.

He could happily kill her for that.

3.

After getting dressed, Mags scooped up the personal items the Noxblade had left.

Part of her considered ignoring them, but if a random staffer found the clothes and shoes, he wouldn't know who they belonged to and simplicity was generally best. *I'll give Gavriel a chance to calm down, then return his stuff.* But first… her stomach growled, reminding her how long ago her last meal was. The Eldritch didn't eat nearly as much as the Animari, and she needed more protein, too.

She threaded a path through the old fortress, following her nose to the kitchen. There was only a young Eldritch left, sleepily swishing a mop around, and he didn't protest when she loaded up with bread, cheese, dried fruit, and cold fish. The wolf women might be asleep by now, and she didn't relish the idea of crouching in the dark over her food, trying not to wake them. Mags didn't love being the only cat among wolves and liked it even less when she was surrounded by the Eldritch instead.

Maybe I'll eat on the walls by starlight.

That sounded better than most of her alternatives, but she needed to stop by Gavriel's room first. She found him the same way she'd located the kitchen, tracing his scent through the corridors. The cinnamon scent strengthened, the closer she got, and eventually, the olfactory markers practically glowed before his door. Mags rapped twice.

It took several moments for the door to open, then Gavriel appeared, black shirt hastily thrown on and buttons done up incorrectly. He was barefoot, wearing loose trousers that hung from lean hips. His pallor made his skin shimmer in the dark, so visible that she marveled at his ability to disappear in the shadows. With a face like a beacon, that required real skill.

"What do you want?" he demanded.

"I'm returning this." She thrust the shirt and shoes at him, which he caught with instinctive good reflexes.

His jaw clenched, and Mags could tell that he didn't want to express gratitude. She watched him bite back the sharp retort. Finally, he muttered, "Thanks," instead of what he really wanted to say. Then he started to slam the door in her face.

Funny fact about certain cats, though. They always wanted to sit on the person in the room who least wanted them there, and the more that soul protested, the more cat he got. Mags had that propensity too because she didn't take kindly to the idea of being denied. It was the principle of the thing.

Smiling, she caught the door with one hand. "Aren't you going to invite me in? Since I delivered your stuff, it's the *least* you can do to be polite."

Gavriel's eyes sparked hate, but eventually, he stepped back. "You're doing this to agitate me, but it won't work."

It already has. At least, his scent sharpened, layered with a peppery sharpness that spoke of repressed anger. As she came into his space, she also breathed in the smell of recent sex, but the room carried only his traces, no hint of a partner. He'd hate that she knew, however, so she didn't let on. It was his private business, none of hers.

"Actually, I'm doing this because I heard your stomach growling before. Thought you might like something to eat." She sat on the rug spread before the hearth and set the tray of food beside her.

"It's the middle of the night," he snapped.

She paused in the midst of assembling a strange fish sandwich. "What's your point? Are you hungry or not?"

"Nothing I can say will drive you out?" He seemed astonished by that fact, as if he'd never come across anyone who didn't bow to his bad attitude.

"Nope. Your carpet is soft, and this fire is warm, way better than eating outside, which was my plan before. You can watch or you can join me. Which will it be?"

In answer, he dropped at the far edge of the rug, eyeing her warily. "Your behavior makes no sense."

She raised a brow. "I'm hungry. You're hungry. What could be more practical than eating?"

Screwing with him was fun. Mags knew damn well he wanted to talk about how much he disliked her, but it was hard to do that when someone was offering food. She tried not to smirk as she took the first bite of fish and bread, both fresh and delicious. For all his claims otherwise, Gavriel was clearly starving because he ate his share with gusto and between them, they left nothing on the plate.

"Are you thirsty?" he asked in a grudging tone. "I could make tea."

In all honesty, tea wasn't her favorite drink, but she recognized an olive branch. He was trying to reciprocate hospitality in his prickly, antisocial way. "Sounds good."

To her amazement, he got a copper kettle, filled it in the bathroom, then hung it on a stand near the fire. *So old school.* Then he scrounged up two chipped mugs and mixed dry herbs in graceful motions. When the water heated enough, he added the wire basket to the kettle and glanced up to meet her gaze with an oddly diffident expression.

"Is it strange to see me doing this?"

"A little," she admitted. "I suspect there aren't many who can say they've had a tea party with a master assassin."

For a moment, it looked like he might smile, but he controlled his features, leaving Mags faintly disappointed. "I hardly know what to dispute first, but never let it be said that I balk at conflict. I'm not a master, nor is this a party."

"I don't know, feels pretty festive to me. We just need to get some jugglers in here, maybe hold a knife-throwing competition." She read the shock and reluctant amusement in his face before he strangled it and served the tea.

Normally, she wasn't like this. In Ash Valley, she carried so much weight that she was serious and intense, all the time. There was no space for levity with Raff either, because the wolf lord took so little seriously. The Noxblade, on the other hand, just looked so sad and tragic all the damn time that she couldn't resist trying to see what it would take to lighten him up.

"I don't have the space. You'll have to make do with a hot drink."

Taking her cue, Mags sipped and lowered her mug halfway to eye it in surprise. "This is delicious."

"You sound shocked."

"It usually tastes like weeds. This is different, spicy and complex. Tell me the truth, you got a secret recipe?"

"You're welcome. Drink it and get out." His voice lacked its usual edge, though he was expressing the same hostile sentiments. Something had softened Gavriel's mood, leaving him uncharacteristically gentle.

"Admit it, tonight I made your life better."

"Delusional," he muttered. "I was in bed, trying to sleep when you showed up."

"I didn't knock that loud. If you had succeeded instead of trying, you wouldn't have heard me," she pointed out.

"I *never* sleep that soundly." Gavriel bit his lower lip, apparently frozen in shock over the admission.

It wasn't exactly breaking news so far as Mags was concerned, but the Noxblade seemed to think he'd let slip some deeply personal secret. "Yeah, that's common among people who spend a lot of time in the field. It's worse for Animari soldiers because we fucking hear everything anyway. Squirrels fighting two hundred meters away? Little bastards have kept me up all night before."

"How do you cope?"

That sounded like a genuine question, so Mags gave it real consideration. "You learn to filter. After my first shift, I thought I'd go crazy from the sensory overload, but after a while, you learn what sounds and smells are vital to your safety. Everything else, you can choose to let go, but it also depends on mental strength. When I'm stressed, it's harder to keep those screens in place."

"I never considered that before."

"What?"

"That I could use noise to confuse an Animari foe. I'll have to incorporate this information into my stratagems."

Fury sparked to life as she slammed her mug down. "You're *still* craving better ways to kill us, even as your princess plans to marry Raff? I read you wrong, Gavriel. I thought you had a heart buried deep but you're a monster after all."

"It would be wise to remember that," he said softly.

THAT OUGHT TO be enough to make her go.

Gavriel expected the tiger woman to quit his quarters in a rage, but to his astonishment, she stood and took a step closer to him. "I can smell the lies on you, thick as shit. You act like you hate us *so* much, but the truth is, you hate yourself more."

"Shut up," he bit out.

"Because you're alive, and the people you love aren't. I understand that, believe me, but we live in troubled times. Maybe I can take your venom, but with somebody else, you might start a war, one your people can't win." Her hand curled into a fist as if she wanted to hit him, and fates help him, he wished she would. "You think I don't struggle, surrounded by Eldritch? Old Lord Talfayen blew up my home, killed *way* too many of my people, but I'm trying my best not to blame you or the princess."

"I don't care if you loathe me for his crimes." That wasn't entirely true, but he was accustomed to a certain amount of undue infamy.

"That's not the point. If I hate a whole people for the crimes of one, then I'm a bigot, exactly like those I rail against, assholes who call us names because we can shift. We're still fighting prejudice against the Golgoth in our ranks. Our older folks just won't stop calling them demon-kin, no matter how many times they hear it's wrong."

"Why are you telling me this?"

"Because deep down, you want more for your people, too. You're loyal to Thalia and you're backing her play. Your behavior reflects on her, so fucking *do better*."

He stared at her, unable to respond for a few seconds, grappling with the emotions she stirred, an intricate cocktail of shame, admiration, spiced lightly by reluctant respect. Finally, he said, "Point taken."

"Anyway, I know damn well you just want to piss me off and make me leave. But didn't you ever hear that the more you want a cat gone, the more likely she is to stay? We're contrary that way."

Before he could ask about that strange truism, she stripped out of her clothes and shifted smoothly. Suddenly, there was a tiger curling up on his rug, enormous and ferociously beautiful. There was no earthly way he could move her in this form, maybe not even if she was woman-shaped, so he settled for a verbal protest. "You cannot possibly mean to stay here. What would people say?"

She lifted her striped, feline face from her paws and cocked her head, as if casting doubt on the possibility that a great cat and an exhausted Eldritch could do anything in the night that would be worthy of gossip. *Right, fair enough.* She'd already said that she liked his fireplace and his carpet, so it didn't seem likely that she intended to budge, and it was only a few hours until dawn anyway. Gavriel gave up on a battle he couldn't win. If he continued to protest, it would only make him seem ridiculous, and she'd already gotten the best of him far too often.

There was no way he'd get any sleep tonight, not with an uninvited guest on his floor. Sleep had never come easy, even as a child, but since he'd completed his training and gone into Princess Thalia's service, it only got worse.

Tonight would likely be no exception, just long hours of staring into the dark, only now he had to listen to the weird rumble that proved Magda Versai suffered no such discomfort. For some reason, there was a soothing quality to it, though, rather like white noise, and he focused on her breathing instead of the disordered anguish in his brain.

It was well into the morning when Gavriel woke and the Animari woman was gone, no sign of her prior occupation. He found a message waiting from Princess Thalia, reminding him that he'd agreed to take charge of the afternoon's activities, acting as huntmaster to entertain the visiting wolves. He handled those preparations before going in search of breakfast; it galled him to admit that he was, in fact, indebted to the Animari woman. Her late visit had left him feeling better than he had in days, physically, at any rate.

And healing had to start somewhere.

Well enough, Gavriel understood that it began by sleeping without night terrors, just for an hour or two, eating a few bites without feeling nauseated by guilt. Time would level the field, making the most grievous hurts into old aches and small twinges of regret. That was the best and more terrible aspect of existence.

Probably, he should find Ferith and Tirael and try to comfort them, but he couldn't bring himself to do it. He hid until he had to present himself in the bailey, play his assigned role for the amusement of these cursed wolves. The surviving Noxblades joined him soon after, and he accepted bows from both of them, a silent acknowledgment of seniority.

"You're looking well," Tirael observed.

Somehow, it felt like an accusation, and perhaps Ferith

read it the same, because she frowned. "We owe it to the princess to stay strong," she said, a gentle rebuke.

Tirael offered a half-smile. "Of course. I meant nothing untoward by the remark. We're supposed to entertain these brutes, I take it, and not kill them in the woods?"

He glanced at the woman sharply. "Don't let Princess Thalia hear you talking in that manner. We will do *nothing* to jeopardize this alliance."

"Why pretend?" Tirael whispered. "You hate them too."

"Politics aside, the Animari have exceptional hearing," Ferith cut in.

That was enough to shut the younger Eldritch up. Gavriel had heard such things many times before, even spoken hatred himself, but now he had Magda's words ringing in his ears—about how her own people struggled not to hate the Golgoth and to stop using old slurs. Her conviction—and the empirical rightness of her statement—stayed with him.

The world doesn't get better unless we strive to make it so. It starts with me, with my old grudges and my unjust hate.

The Animari were already assembled, shifted and ready to hunt. A few soldiers joined the gathering, no doubt coerced or persuaded by Lileth. With his vedda beast pawing the ground restlessly, Gavriel waited for Princess Thalia, along with everyone else. Sometimes it felt as if he'd spent his whole life this way, hoping for a glimpse of her.

At last Princess Thalia came, brutally beautiful in her armor, and he had to look away, lest he show something she would not wish to see. More to the point, he sensed the tiger's golden gaze on him, heavy as a hand on his back. Her eyes were the same, woman or cat, a golden brown so light that it was almost yellow, an odd, captivating color. That knowing look told him that she already understood too much about him; it would be foolhardy to let her glean more.

The stable hand brought the princess's mount a moment later and Gavriel judged the time was right to begin. "I will be your huntmaster!" he called. "We will be splitting into teams of two. If numbers allow, our Animari guests should choose an Eldritch partner, as we know the terrain best."

Though he could have predicted this outcome, he still felt a twinge when he heard the princess say, "Partners?" to that bastard black wolf. She even *touched* him, right in front of everyone, as if that was something they should see.

Glancing away, he watched the rest of the Animari pair up with Eldritch, and he didn't realize the numbers were off until he saw Magda sitting alone, tail curled behind her. He'd planned to follow the princess, keep watch over her from a distance, not participate in the hunt, but he already knew what was required of him. Since he'd offered to help Magda hunt down enemy patrols, he might even look on this as a practice run, a test of how well they performed in the field.

Still, he hated feeling as if the choice had been taken from him, so Gavriel made the offer with precious little grace. "Tiger woman, I will take you myself."

4.

MAGS LIKED NEITHER Gavriel's tone, nor his surly expression, so she raked the air near his knees with a sharp claw, not close enough to injure him, but he didn't realize that.

The Noxblade jumped, bringing his legs all the way up to avoid her feint. She couldn't laugh in tiger form, but she did it with her eyes, enjoying his discomfiture. He composed himself swiftly, dedicated to the role of huntmaster. In one hand, he held a curving horn, probably to signal the start of this nonsense. A white and silver drone hovered nearby, painted for winter camouflage.

"Here is your prey," he called. "Bring it back intact or in pieces. The victor will receive a great prize from our treasury and, of course, full bragging rights."

Mags had no intention of wasting her time tracking down machinery. When Gavriel blew the horn and the drone zoomed away, she let the wolves take the lead. They overflowed with energy, exuberant as pups, especially Tavros and Skylett. She and Gavriel left Daruvar last, his vedda beast flanking her.

He cantered out in front of her, leading the way, but she

had other plans. This was her first opportunity to track since arriving in Eldritch territory. She'd collected a few hints in the fortress, time to put that scant information to use. Mags avoided the path Gavriel was following toward the woods, instead setting out for the distant hills. One of the soldiers had mentioned a scouting party toward the border; he didn't know what house had sent them, but she meant to find out.

Might not be an enemy house at all. Could be Talfayen's people, keeping watch.

"Where are you going?" Gavriel called.

She flicked a look over one shoulder. *Dumbass. Like I can answer.*

To her surprise, he wheeled his mount and followed her even without a verbal explanation. Maybe he was committed to keeping an eye on her? Whatever the reason, he rode after her and Mags caught the scent trail half a klick past where the soldier had described the sighting. She focused on the smell she needed to follow, not the wind in her fur or the chill of icy rocks beneath her paw pads. Gavriel was still dogging her steps, his vedda beast quick and sure-footed.

She'd first thought that Slay was running from the collapse of his relationship with Pru. One of the wolf guards said they'd seen him headed away from Ash Valley, but the poor sod died in the explosion and she couldn't get any more intel out of him. Then she spent weeks poring through the wolves' surveillance data, gathered surreptitiously during the failed conclave.

There, maybe she'd seen somebody who *could* have been Slay, leaving with the Eldritch. But the resolution wasn't good, and no amount of magnification could improve a shitty, low-grade image. Failure wasn't something she knew a lot about, and she was dead tired of not finding Slay, no matter where she looked. Ash Valley depended on her to solve this security breach, one way or another.

The scent trail was old, barely discernable even to her enhanced senses. Several times, she lost the thread and backtracked, prowling over rocks and grassy slopes, until she found a whisper again. She'd never run across these Eldritch before, not in Ash Valley and not in Daruvar, so they weren't in old Lord Talfayen's original retinue, nor were they feigning loyalty to Thalia in the fortress.

Good to know.

Eventually, she located an old campsite, but judging by the ashes, it had been a couple of days since these spying Eldritch moved on. Mags snarled and sniffed around, hoping for a whiff of Slay. She nosed everything they'd left behind, just a few scraps here and there. Overall, it was a clean site, and the rain had nearly washed away all traces, but they'd buried something that smelled familiar. *Slay?* She couldn't be certain with the competing odors, the dirt and grass and some Eldritch had pissed nearby.

As she started raking at the cold earth with her paws, Gavriel said, "What the hell are you doing?"

He could only see that someone had made camp here; he probably couldn't tell who. For all he knew, she was checking out one of their patrol stops. Mags ignored the question, as shifting to answer would waste their time. She spared him a look, no more, and kept digging.

A sharp howl split the silence, and her ears swiveled. *That's Raff.* He wouldn't alert the pack for anything less than a severe threat. Reluctantly, she abandoned the search and raced back the way she'd come. *Shit, I shouldn't have left him.*

I promised to keep that stupid wolf safe.

"I hate that you can't answer me," Gavriel muttered, snapping the reins to rally his vedda beast to greater speed.

She guessed he knew why she was running full out, though, because he didn't complain further, only let her set the pace and follow the scent markers she found for Raff and Thalia, closer to the keep. The run took forever, and she heard the battle long before they got there. Her heart thudded like thunder, breath churning in her chest.

They burst into the clearing to find corpses strewn about. The wolves had gotten there first, but it seemed that Thalia and Raff had won the fight without an assist. Gavriel checked the princess first while Magda sniffed at Raff's wounds. They weren't closing like they should, and they needed to get out of the woods. Fast.

Gavriel spoke with a flat aspect, but she saw hell in his red eyes. "Unfortunately, we will not be completing our course. Everyone, head back to Daruvar immediately."

The princess mounted up; everyone else followed her lead. Mags took the rear position, watching as the Noxblade stayed close to Thalia, scanning the horizon for additional threats. On the walls, the guard recognized them, opening the gate with a clank to permit their passage. Overhead, the sky was darkening. Sunset dropped like a hammer on an anvil in these hills, bringing the silent chill of night.

Just inside the greensward, Raff shifted as if he didn't have the strength to hold his form and toppled over. Mags raced to him, slipping from tiger to woman, in the space between one breath and the next. She sealed her palms over his most egregious wound, remorse slashing at her as Thalia barked orders at Lileth and Gavriel.

"I did a shit job of protecting you, I see. What the hell is wrong with this?"

"Not sure. Think it's a special weapon. The Gols have something…" His color was bad, ashy beneath his burnished brown skin, and he was leaning on her *way* too hard.

The princess came over then, offering her other shoulder. Mags glanced at her in surprise, but hell if she was taking her hands off Raff right now. Trust had to be earned, and so far, Thalia wasn't doing a great job of proving she had her territory under control. Together, they moved toward the infirmary.

"We need a doctor!" Lileth shouted. "No, get him inside, you idiots. Move. Now!"

"Just show me where to go," she said.

Mags appreciated all the helping hands, but they'd only slow her down. With a nod at Princess Thalia, she lifted Raff and ran with him, chasing Gavriel who was faster than she was in this shape. He led her straight to the treatment center, where she laid Raff down for the doctor to tend his wounds.

If it's not already too late.

"Why won't the bleeding stop?" Thalia demanded.

The staff sprang into action and Mags backed away, not wanting to hinder their efforts. Someone handed her a robe, which she put on, though it was too tight in the chest and shoulders. Her hands were stained with Raff's blood.

"Vitals dropping," the nurse called.

She didn't recognize the machinery they were using, and the medicines all had strange names too. Eldritch doctors might kill the wolf lord with their attempts at healing, but she didn't know what else to do. Bibi and Skylett were staring at her with desperate accusation. *Yeah, I failed to guard him. I fucked up.*

"He needs a transfusion," Dr. Wyeth said.

If she could, Mags would've given the blood from her veins, but it wouldn't serve as well as from someone in his own pack. Just then, Tavros said, "It should be me. I'm type O negative, universal donor."

Thalia made the call instantly, when the doctor looked to her for confirmation. "Do it. Save him. If there are complications, I'll take responsibility."

GAVRIEL OBSERVED FROM the doorway. Princess Thalia's need might be driven from political necessity, but she was completely focused on Raff Pineda's survival. Quietly, near invisible in the shadows, he rubbed his chest against the ache. And then realized that his actions didn't go unnoticed.

Magda was watching; she *saw* him.

Quickly, he dropped his hand to his side, cursing this momentary weakness, as the medical team filtered Tavros's blood and gave it to Raff. He willed the tiger woman not to approach him, not from mockery or pity, or for any other reason. As if she'd read his mind, she turned away to investigate the bullet Dr. Wyeth had removed from the wolf lord.

She flung it back into the metal basin with a visible tremor. Gavriel took a reflexive step closer. Anything bad enough to frighten her must be dreadful indeed. "This is treated black iron with a beryllium core."

Before he could ask, the princess did. "What does that mean?"

Though Mags answered the other woman, Gavriel had the impression that she was providing the information for *his* benefit. "It's an Animari slayer. Treated black iron prevents wounds from healing. The chemical interaction hinders coagulation. And beryllium is toxic to us, as few substances are. We're resistant to most chemical weapons, most herbal poisons as well." Magda sighed and stared at Raff. "Whoever designed this knows a great deal about Animari vulnerabilities."

Slay.

Gavriel knew she had been hunting the Ash Valley second ever since she left their holding. Could he have conspired with the rebel Eldritch and the Gols to create such a heinous weapon? Magda's gaze met his, holding such shadows that he guessed she must be wondering the same thing.

Dr. Wyeth touched Magda on the shoulder to draw her attention. "Do you have any suggestions for how to treat beryllium poisoning? I'm also unsure if our medicines will help with the coagulation issue."

"One way to find out," Magda said. "Test them on me, first."

As she sliced her wrist, Gavriel stifled a protest. Doubtful that she'd listen to him anyway. But it was harder still to observe in silence when she smeared the tainted bullet across the fresh wound. Her skin reacted immediately, rays of red streaking her arm, and the blood kept flowing. The doctor scowled at this lack of scientific method, but the princess waved him on. A nurse injected the Animari woman, first one medicine, then another, and the reaction began to fade.

"Hurry," Dr. Wyeth said.

Gavriel moved off then. He didn't need to bear witness to the treatment personally or listen to them argue about saving Raff Pineda. His mount was still tethered in the bailey, waiting for him to care for the animal or resume the hunt. Gavriel pulled the drone remote from his pocket and recalled it to Daruvar, then he swung astride the steel-gray vedda beast he had never named.

"Wait!"

"Are you going back to the attack site?" Magda came toward him at a run, hopping a little to cram her foot completely into her boot.

Since she had been naked in the infirmary five minutes ago, a grudging admiration swept over him. He'd never met anyone who could move like she did. Gavriel nodded. "I plan to investigate the assailants and learn what I can."

"I'll go with you."

Before he could refuse that request, she vaulted up behind him, so effortlessly athletic that the admiration from before surged harder and he clamped it down. "Get off."

"Not a chance. I'd go cat, but we won't be able to talk and that could be crucial if there are any stragglers. I intend to participate in any interrogations. Don't worry, I can pull my own weight even in this form."

"That's not the issue." He started when she set her hands on his waist, holding on with such a firm grasp that it brought back fantasies he was trying to forget.

"Are you really wasting our time arguing about this? I thought nothing could stop you from doing your job."

"You are maddening," he bit out.

"So I'm told." She dug her fingers into his sides harder. "Now move."

The vedda beast didn't protest the extra weight, only set off calmly in response to his tug on the reins. That was why he'd chosen this animal; it seemed immune to stress and stimulus, such a placid nature that it didn't react to weapons being fired all around. He'd tested that more than once.

"You risked your life for Raff Pineda. Why?" Gavriel didn't intend to ask; the question emerged on a wave of agitation laced with unwilling curiosity.

"Because I promised to keep him safe. I let myself get distracted, put too much trust in others. I don't take my word lightly, so if I couldn't stop him from being wounded, then I had to do whatever I could to make it right."

"That includes self-harm, exposure to toxins? He's not even your leader."

"He *is* my friend," she said, as if that explained everything.

Would I have done the same for Oriel? Undoubtedly. He was my brother. But for Zan..? Or another sword mate? There, the answer was murkier, for friendship didn't supersede his pledge to Princess Thalia, and if he fell saving someone else, he wouldn't be around to serve.

"You think it's stupid to go that far," she guessed.

It took him a moment to sort out what he did think as they rode down the hill away from the fortress. "More that it must be...gratifying to earn your friendship," he said.

"I don't know which word is weirder, 'gratifying' or 'earn'. Friendship isn't based on merit points. Or is that how it works among the Eldritch?"

Gavriel had no idea why he was even talking to her about this. "I scarcely recall. The friends I made when I was young are all dead and I've forgotten..." He decided against completing that pathetic admission.

But she knew, of course she did. "You forgot how. I hear you. The older we get, the harder it is to believe that someone could simply *like* us, for no reason at all."

"Nobody likes me," he said then. "I have a terrible

personality."

Her laughter rumbled through his back, a sweet little vibration that made him not entirely hate this ride. "No disagreement here. But that's the price we pay as enforcers."

Startled, he glanced back at her, at first shocked by her use of the word 'we', then he processed the implication of her statement. "You think I've donned a persona? To strike fear into the hearts of my enemies?"

"Haven't you? Maybe you didn't notice, but you're not as fierce with me as you used to be. Either you're not as cruel as you pretend or you're starting to enjoy my company. Which is it, Gavriel?"

I hate this damned woman. He'd rather die than make either admission, though the truth was somewhere in between. Magda Versai might be slightly less objectionable than most Animari, and he did perform a certain amount to maintain a reputation worthy of the nickname Death's Shadow.

Avoiding further conversation, he rode the rest of the way in silence. She hopped off the vedda beast even before he brought it to a halt and while he tied the reins to the bare branches of a convenient tree, she crouched to examine the nearest corpse. Anyone else might have been sickened at the way she touched the blood, rubbed it between her fingertips and brought it to her nose for closer inspection. To Gavriel, these abilities seemed more like a portable science lab, filtered through her senses. At last, he had to admit that the Animari had their uses.

"Find anything?" he asked, taking samples of his own.

He would have to wait for machines to analyze the strange-smelling blood, but he wondered what Magda would say, if she'd tell him the truth. She raised somber light gold eyes to his, worry imprinted visibly on her strong features.

"I recognize a chemical tang in the blood. Not sure why they were taking it, but it's an Animari medicine. That seems... strange."

"To say the least," he agreed.

"If you have time, I'd like to head back where we were before. If you don't, I'll go by myself," she added quickly.

"I'd need to know why first."

"Because that campsite had signs of Slay. At least, I was trying to confirm before Raff called, and if it was Slay, then—"

"That was likely a party of loyalists with him." For the first time, Gavriel held out a hand to Magda willingly. "Let's go, we've no time to waste."

5.

TIME HADN'T CHANGED the campsite much.

Fortunately, it hadn't rained or snowed, or Mags might have found it difficult to sift through the detritus to find the trace of Slay she'd caught before. She dug through the rubbish they'd buried and came up with a few scraps of bloody cloth. Even before she carried them to her nose, she was sure.

Slay was here.

Though she didn't know how or why he'd gotten injured, this was his blood. Gavriel was checking the scene in other ways, taking more samples, as he had from where the ambush went down. She rose in a smooth motion, pocketing the fabric. If she had to guess, she'd say these had been bandages.

"Find something?" he asked mildly.

This was a test. Mags was prone to doing the same, especially when she couldn't be sure where someone's loyalties lay. "Yeah. I was right."

"You found the...second's trail?" The brief pause told her that Gavriel wasn't sure what to call Slay.

Traitor and bastard both came to mind, but maybe that

was her own anger talking. People outside Ash Valley probably didn't know Slay's first name since he hated it with a passion and used to fight anyone who addressed him by it. It didn't take more than a couple of ass-kickings until everyone called him Slay instead of Ambrose. She stifled a smile, remembering how she used to taunt him in primary school when they played Hunt Him Down: *Ambrose Cornelius Slater, I know where you're hiding!* That always worked, even when he had a damn good spot. Every single time, Slay would come roaring out and—

Memories *hurt*. The good times had blades attached now, especially when it seemed possible that he'd sold out the entire pride over a woman. It wasn't that Mags thought poorly of Pru; she'd made her choice and seemed happy with Dom. She wouldn't forgive Slay, however, if he'd turned on all of Ash Valley because of a breakup.

"Are you all right?" Gavriel asked.

He was watching her, always watching, it seemed like. "Just thinking about Slay."

"Do you think you can find his trail?"

Mags lifted a shoulder. "At this point, I'm days behind, but I have to try."

"You'll leave the wolf lord after promising to protect him?"

That...was a good question. Her conscience protested, but Ash Valley security had the first claim. "I'll stay until I'm sure he's going to recover. Then I'm hunting Slay down."

"I'll go with you," he said.

Startled, she jerked her gaze to meet his, expecting a sarcastic follow-up, but Gavriel held the look squarely. "You're serious?"

"I need to speak with Princess Thalia and formally

request that she discharge me from her service, but yes. I think I can assist her best from the shadows."

Mags registered the subtext. Gavriel thought his grim reputation could hurt the princess, so he was choosing to distance himself. He'd fight for her that way, silently dispatching her enemies without regard for reward or promotion. That established him as astonishingly selfless...or maybe he had a death wish. This war had taken so many of his loved ones already that it was possible he didn't give a shit about his life anymore.

Well, if Gavriel thought he could go off with her to die like a hero, hell if Mags would let that happen. On that note, she decided to accept his offer—not because she needed help, but she thought maybe the Noxblade did, even if he wouldn't admit it. Taking a breath, she extended a hand, palm open.

"Partners?"

The Eldritch stared for a few seconds before he slowly reached out and grasped her hand. His skin was lighter than hers, but that wasn't saying much. He had long fingers, cool skin, made more so by the chill, but he shook with a firm grip. She had the strange impulse to yank him into a rough hug and wondered what he'd do if she did.

Gavriel cleared his throat, pulling his hand away. He didn't wipe it on his black coat at least. "For now," he muttered.

"Then let's do a little searching before we lose the light." She could hunt in the dark just fine, but she wouldn't leave until Raff woke up, so, for now, she'd content herself with nailing down the direction this party took, so they'd have a better place to start later.

"You won't be able to track as well if you ride with me."

Mags nodded. "I'll go cat from here. Could you take my clothes?"

Before Gavriel could respond, she stripped down and thrust her belongings into his arms. He was usually good at masking his expression, but shock widened his eyes and left him fumbling with her underwear as she slipped into tiger form. She'd been changing so long that there was no pain, only a fluid ripple, and then she roved the campsite, taking in all the disparate smells. Eight Eldritch, all strangers. And Slay.

The Noxblade cursed as he worked to secure her stuff on the vedda beast's back. When she signaled him with a jerk of her head, he mounted up and followed at a slow pace, letting her sniff out the path. It took hours and the sun was dipping behind the hills when she unearthed the next campsite, only a day old and heading off toward the desolate reaches of Thalia's territory. The hunt was in her blood now—she wanted to keep moving—but not yet. Not until Raff recuperated.

Wearily, she dropped out of tiger form and stood shivering in the frosty night air. Gavriel swore again and leapt from his mount, scrambling for her clothes. Though he'd seemed fine with Animari nudity before, he was averting his eyes now, offering her possessions with clumsy hands. She'd never seen him so skittish.

"You're nervous," she observed.

"That's because you're freezing and naked and we're in the middle of nowhere. We don't know how close the enemy is and—"

"I could kill anyone who tries us with my bare hands," she cut in gently.

"Boasting accomplishes nothing."

I'm not bragging. Still, he was right about her being cold, so she got dressed in record time and fastened up her coat. While her people didn't feel the weather as much as the Eldritch, they weren't immune to the elements. Mags blew on her hands, rubbed them together, and then jokingly pressed her palms to Gavriel's cheeks.

"Better?"

His eyes blazed like embers in the pallor of his face, pale hair tumbling like flax. The wind blew it across her fingers, and it felt like the whole world was holding its breath while his chest rose and fell, too rapidly for comfort. Then, so briefly that she might be imagining it, his lashes fluttered, and he turned his face slightly, as if nuzzling into her touch. Nobody expected gentleness from her, and she quelled the urge to push his face away in an abrupt rejection of how the moment had flipped on her.

What's the right move here?

Mags dropped her hands, wondering if she should apologize for teasing him. She hadn't realized it would agitate him so much.

Before she could, he snapped, "Don't treat me like one of your own. I am unaccustomed to your ways."

"Yeah, I got that. Anyway, we should head back. I know which way they're going, and as long as we don't get a storm, I'll be able to hunt them down, after we wrap up our business at Daruvar."

"I've taken images and logged coordinates as well, so I can help retrace our path, even if the weather turns against us." He mounted the vedda beast in a graceful motion, and Mags caught herself admiring his sheer physical agility.

His movements were elegant and perfectly balanced, and his body *showed* that he'd spent years honing it into the perfect weapon. With a faint mental shrug, she bounded up behind him and set her hands on his waist. As before, his spine went rigid and they had been riding for a while before he unbent a little.

He'd probably freak out if she did anything else. Perversely, that made her want to even more. Mags looped her arms around his waist and leaned her head against his back.

"Wake me when we get there."

Just like a cat, she went to sleep in the most improbable spot.

FOR TWO DAYS after returning to Daruvar, Gavriel fought a battle with himself. He was annoyed with Magda Versai, but that low-grade annoyance prevented him from focusing on the thorns in his heart as the princess tended to her betrothed and they made wedding plans. It occurred to him that the tiger woman might be provoking him out of kindness, giving him a target for his ire since he couldn't speak his mind to Princess Thalia.

The trail was growing cold, and they'd waited long enough. Now that it was clear Raff Pineda wouldn't die, he was itching to leave this place, so that he didn't have to witness the wedding. He drew in a soft breath and went looking for Lileth.

The elder Eldritch was near the kitchens, arranging for the hasty ceremony. "Have you seen the princess?" he asked.

Lileth shook her head. "Not recently. Did you try calling her?"

"We've intercepted data that makes me think there might be listeners. Better not to risk it. Could you let her know that I need to speak with her?"

"Where will you be?"

It wasn't an unreasonable question. Daruvar was huge, and they could waste valuable time wandering about. "I'll wait in the strategy room until she comes. Please advise her that it's urgent."

With that, he turned and hurried to the princess's personal office. It was a good size, decorated in style from the last century, lots of burgundy, leather, and old wood, along with tasseled cushions and bits of burnished gold. The most important feature was the huge table, currently covered with a map of Eldritch territory. Markers were placed, showing Princess Thalia's holdings, enemy troop movements based on the latest intel, and probable targets where the opposition might strike. He'd spent more than one night in here, listening to her plans and offering suggestions when invited.

The fire in the hearth was dead, so he built it up with painstaking precision and spread his palms before the crackling flames. Dancing light cast shadows over his hands, so he could imagine the blood that stained them. He didn't regret the dire things he'd done for the princess, but sometimes he felt like a vessel that she'd tapped until there was nothing left, and now that he could no longer serve, he would be abandoned. Gavriel wouldn't permit *that* ending, so he'd make the cut himself, quick and efficient, no looking back, just like the assassin he was.

He'd watched people leaving for so long… well, no more. It was time for the princess to see his back for a change. She probably wouldn't miss him, but possibly, she'd regret the loss of a good blade.

His mood didn't let him get comfortable in her space, so

he went to the window and gazed out, wondering how many more of his own people he'd need to kill before this senseless conflict ended. That was his purpose—the ending he'd chosen. Since he could no longer fight by Princess Thalia's side, he would take the fight to the rest of the world. Eliminate her enemies until he died doing so.

There was no reason for him to live on anyway.

The princess alerted him to her arrival with an intake of breath, a suggestion that she was braced for a difficult conversation. Gavriel guessed that she feared he would kneel and lay his soul at her feet but speaking the words wouldn't change her mind or her intentions. This was only closure.

He turned as she entered, seeing Princess Thalia for what could be the last time. She looked weary, shadows beneath her eyes, and her bearing gave away the wariness that chipped away at his dignity. Her beauty was an icy knife, and it had cut away enough of him. *This is why I must go.* It was less about how he hated seeing her with the wolf lord and more about not becoming a pathetic, seething stain of a person.

Gavriel executed a brief bow, waiting for her to reach the grouping of chairs arranged on a worn antique rug.

"Sit down," she invited.

"I'll be brief. I know that you're busy."

"Go ahead."

"I would like to be discharged from your direct service," he said quietly.

Her pause and the faint widening of her eyes told him that he'd succeeded in surprising her. There was some satisfaction in it.

"Will you tell me why?"

Not the whole truth, but he could offer a small portion of it. "Magda Versai is pursuing an investigation related to the disappearance of the Ash Valley second. I believe the trail could lead us to an insurgent stronghold, where your father's followers are hiding."

"So it's likely that the jaguar cut a deal with my father and is now working for the traitors and the Golgoth?" Princess Thalia tapped a finger against the arm of her chair, running the potential outcomes in her head.

He knew her face like the way home in the dark, but he looked at the hearth instead, watching the flames gnaw at the firewood. Yellow, orange, blue, white-hot, the colors of destruction were beautiful, but the logs couldn't survive them.

She was waiting for a response, but he couldn't draw conclusions based on what he knew. "She picked up a hint of him from one of our patrols, but everything was in such disarray that we can't be certain if he was a captive or actively cooperating."

"What I'm gathering is that you would like the freedom to pursue this on your own?" The princess sat forward, watching him carefully.

He thought about night and starlight and the chill winds that swept in from the sea. Though she knew him well, the princess wouldn't glean anything from his face that he chose not to give. And he'd closed the door on her while he waited for her arrival. A bit of a poem fluttered in his head, something he'd read during a rare moment when he wasn't training. Literacy hadn't been prized by the mentor with whom he'd apprenticed, but Gavriel had always loved words and had stolen them as treasures to be hoarded.

Bitter sorrow hides Her face
As Time sweeps me from this fair glen.
The only certainty is our farewell
And that I shall not see you again.

He held Princess Thalia's gaze; he wouldn't look away first. "Exactly so. Will you release me from your service?"

To his surprise, her eyes dropped. She studied the ornate carpet for a few seconds, as if she had some regrets about this parting. It was more than he'd expected.

Finally, the princess sighed softly, then nodded. "Follow your own path from here. Send word if you learn anything important."

This is it, truly.

While his heart burned in his chest, just like logs in the hearth, there was also an unprecedented lightness in being liberated. Now he was no longer obligated to serve as her right hand. Someone else would do this going forward, and it meant he could choose his own course for the first time in his life. Freedom had a sweet and inviting ring, no matter what awaited him outside these walls.

Gavriel rose, ready to end this meeting. There was nothing further to say. "Thank you, Your Highness."

"When are you leaving?" She stood with him, acting as if she would walk him to the door.

A flare of irritation, when he considered that he would be traveling with the woman least likely to give him any peace. "As soon as the tiger woman is ready."

"Then be safe." Princess Thalia offered a smile, the studied one she presented on difficult occasions, so perhaps this wasn't easy for her, either.

But she'd chosen her path and it led away from him.

Gavriel inclined his head. "You as well."

At the door, she paused to ask, "Could you do me one last favor?"

"What is it?" Wariness sharpened his voice. *This better not be some final mission.* He was done following her orders.

"Recommend your successor of the two who returned with you from Hallowell."

That was easy enough. "Ferith, definitely. She has the most experience. Tirael is too young and is impulsive in the bargain. Was that all?"

"Yes, thank you. Take care, Gavriel."

6.

MAGS MET GAVRIEL at the gates just after first light, all her belongings slung over one shoulder. The sky was heavy with charcoal clouds, the sun only a flutter of faint brightness. She smelled rain or snow in the air, but it wouldn't come for a while yet. The worst of the storm was still well out to sea, beyond the cliff that guarded Daruvar.

"Are you ready?" Gavriel asked.

"Yeah. I already talked to Raff." Not for long, admittedly.

She'd been curt in her leave-taking, partly because she felt guilty. After all, she'd used the wolf lord as a cover to go hunting for Slay, hoping to keep the worst of the scandal out of the wind. If times weren't so uncertain, people would be talking more, discussing the decline of Ash Valley.

The gray vedda beast was tethered nearby, and Gavriel mounted up. "Are you running or riding?"

That was unexpected, almost like an invitation. "Riding, if you don't mind. I should conserve my energy until we get to the most recent site and I need to start tracking."

"Would it stop you if I declined?" he asked with a touch of bitterness.

Fair question, since she'd done as she pleased to bait him since her arrival. "We're partners now, and I don't plan to piss you off on purpose anymore."

She waited, eyes on his, until he reached out a black-gloved hand, the first time he'd done anything like that. Though she didn't need help to climb up behind him, she allowed the pull and settled in, feeling like things had shifted a little. They were both dressed in black, layered against the early spring chill.

"I'll believe that when I see it." Before she could respond, he called, "Open the gate!" and the guards on the wall complied. As they rode out, Gavriel added, "Don't use me as a napping station this time."

Mags quelled a smile. "Did that bother you?"

He made a faint sound of annoyance, one that wouldn't be caught by an Eldritch passenger. "What do you think?"

"Since you brought it up, yes. I guess you're not used to being somebody's bed."

He shot her a baleful look over one shoulder. "That is possibly the most nonsensical statement anyone has made in my hearing."

"Really? You should spend more time with Raff."

"Pass," Gavriel said at once, and when Mags laughed, she felt him relax a little in the saddle.

Not enough to let his back touch her front, but she saw his shoulders drop. Physical contact wasn't a big deal among the Animari, but he made her feel self-conscious about it, like she needed to calculate the value of every touch. Mags took care not to lean against him as they rode, bracing herself with hands behind her instead.

It was strange to think that they'd be relying on each other for a while. Nobody from Ash Valley even knew where she was, and Raff had his own problems. She couldn't expect backup from her pride and there wouldn't be an assist coming from Pine Ridge either, if things went sideways out here. Mags didn't trust Gavriel, and she was sure he felt the same, but as long as he didn't flip first, she'd respect the truce.

"He's not that bad," she said. "You just hate him because he's marrying your perfect, dream princess."

"Don't talk about Princess Thalia," he snapped.

"If you go around showing your weak spots that way, it's like asking somebody to poke at them. I'll teach you how to be inscrutable. I'm really good at it."

Gavriel shot her another malevolent look, before quickly gazing forward again. "I'll have you know that—never mind. Why am I even talking to someone like you?"

"What's that supposed to mean?" Mags jabbed her thumbs into his spine, not hard enough to hurt, just enough to be annoying. Or so she thought.

He jerked and twisted, making a strange sound. "Stop it at once!"

"Does that *tickle*?" She tested her theory by digging her fingers into his back and he exploded with incredulous, infuriated laughter, flinging himself forward to avoid her hands. "Oh shit, you're so ticklish. I'm selling this information to the highest bidder. Which of your enemies will it be, I wonder?"

"I despise you," he said, catching his breath. "And all my enemies are dead."

Mags smirked as she pulled her hands away. "I'm right here."

"You are not my enemy. At the moment. We're allies, remember? But if you tell anyone about this, I will reconsider our status. You do *not* want that."

"I'm terrified," she mocked.

"You should be. Why aren't you?" He sounded honestly perplexed, which brought a reluctant, sincere smile to her face.

"You're not my bogeyman, Gavriel. The only thing you could do is hurt me physically and I heal too fast to care about that."

"Does that mean you've been hurt emotionally?"

Her smile faded, weight settling in her chest as bad memories tried to surface. She tried to play it off, glad he couldn't see her face. "Hasn't everyone?"

Mags didn't want to talk about what she'd heard from Arran, the first time she went to see him about a prospective mate. Not with Gavriel, not with anyone. And she didn't want to think about it, either. She'd made peace with the fact that she had to live her life in the shallows. Terrible things would happen if she got in deep with anyone; she wouldn't make that mistake ever again.

"True enough. I've input our coordinates and we should reach the site in a couple of hours, if we don't encounter trouble."

"It sounds like you wouldn't mind," Mags pointed out.

Gavriel hesitated. They rode for a few moments in silence as the vedda beast carried them deeper into the forest. Finally, he answered, "Violence solves nothing, but sometimes the adrenaline reminds me…"

"That you're alive?" Whatever he thought, the Nox-blade was easy to read.

Still, he tilted his head as if he was surprised by her acuity. "Exactly. But it might bode better for our mission if we didn't encounter trouble so close to Daruvar."

"We already know there are enemies creeping inside the border. The attack, while we were hunting, spoke to that."

"True enough. I'll stay sharp."

"You always are," she said.

"Is that a compliment? Flattery has no impact on me."

"Just an observation. From what I've seen, you live on high alert. That must be fucking exhausting."

"I suppose. I don't remember how to do anything else," Gavriel responded.

That struck Mags as sad. Even she could relax when she was among friends in Ash Valley. Right now, not so much, but he should have been at ease in Daruvar. "There's nobody who helps you relax or makes you feel at home?"

"They're all dead now." His flat tone warned her not to push.

Not to ask about his brother, Oriel, who died at the retreat, not to mention Zan either, the Noxblade who sacrificed himself to save Hallowell. Gavriel was one raw wound, and someone with a softer heart than Mags might have wanted to console him. For an instant, she let herself consider the possibility; she could wrap her arms around his lean waist and rest her head against his back, hold on until he relaxed. But that wasn't her style, even among her own pride. Instead, she let the sentence stand as a wall between them, one that discouraged further conversation until they got closer to the campsite.

They rode for over an hour in silence, and she was starting to stiffen up when the bare trees yielded to a small clearing. "We're here," she said.

Mags didn't wait for him to rein in the vedda beast, just dropped off the back with the agility that made her a dangerous foe when combined with her great strength. The weather had been kind while Raff recovered, or she might not have been able to pick up Slay's traces after so long. A cursory check assured her that there was still a path to follow and she struck a victory pose.

"Still viable?" Gavriel asked.

Mags nodded. "I'll go cat from here. Is your mount okay for a bit longer?"

"He's fine right now, and if he tires, I'll run. Don't worry about me. I'll keep up with you." Gavriel's grim expression suggested that he would, or he'd die in the attempt.

As Mags stripped and shifted, she had the unsettling thought that might be true.

GAVRIEL WAS STARTING to enjoy watching the tiger woman's transformation.

That realization aggravated him. He still hadn't worked out exactly how it happened, and it was so fast that his brain couldn't process the change. She prowled the site, digging here and there with razor-sharp claws. Soon she'd unearthed more discarded bandages. Their quarry must be injured seriously, as Animari wounds tended to heal quickly, or perhaps they were torturing the Ash Valley second for information. Gavriel wondered if that possibility had occurred to her.

He knelt, collecting her discarded clothing, and as he crammed her things into a bag, he scowled. The tiger met his gaze with golden, unblinking eyes, then she tipped her head, silently asking if he was ready. That had to mean she'd locked onto the trail.

Nodding, Gavriel mounted up. His vedda beast remained steady despite proximity to a dangerous predator, responding to a flick of the reins. Magda was careful in choosing her path, staying to ground open enough that he could follow without getting slapped in the face with a rebounding branch. Honestly, it was more consideration than he would've expected.

Half an hour after they left the campsite, Magda stopped. Gavriel started to ask if she'd lost their prey, but she sent him a sharp look that demanded silence. He closed his mouth and waited, dismounting in case she'd scented an enemy.

He held still and listened, finding the woods eerily silent. And that was precisely the problem. There should have been some noise from the wildlife, unless they were frightened by the tiger woman. It was possible, he supposed, but not likely. From what he'd seen traveling with other Animari, they registered outside the usual predatory chain, and they didn't alarm the local fauna unless they were actively hunting, as Sheyla had done for the Golgoth prince on the way to Hallowell.

He didn't hear the enemy as much as sense them, a cold prickle on his spine that drove him to draw his knives and spin, narrowly avoiding a blade in the back. Five opponents, all Eldritch. They weren't wearing house symbols or colors, but from their robotic movements, they were on the same stuff that the attackers from House Manwaring had taken. None of them spoke as they rushed. They didn't have guns or heavy weapons, so they must be a recon team, possibly the remainder of the one that failed to exterminate Princess Thalia and Raff Pineda.

Three of them went after the tiger, which might have

offended Gavriel, if he wasn't already fighting for his life. These Eldritch were lightning fast and incredibly strong. He blocked a strike that rocked him back, numbing his arm to the elbow as the second foe charged. He barely dodged that attack, using a tree to cover his retreat.

From that better vantage, he rolled and struck low, eviscerating the first opponent in a smooth strike. That left him open to another hit and he simply took the wound and tumbled backward to keep the dagger in his shoulder. Now the other enemy was unarmed, not that it seemed to trouble her. Her eyes were dead, blank as an untouched page. She ran at him with complete disregard for her own well-being. Gavriel kicked her ankle, her knee, and when she stumbled, he cut her throat. Dark, viscous blood stained the earth and the dry leaves, leaking out of her so slowly that it seemed to be made of treacle. Winded, he turned to see how Magda was doing.

She stood in a circle of bodies, claws stained dark. As he watched, she pawed one and then cocked her head. Gavriel thought he knew what she was asking.

"They're the same as the others. You said they're on an Animari drug?" When she nodded, he let out an angry breath. "I don't like what it does to my people. They act like the living dead."

Magda nodded again, and he wondered if that could be true. That was absurd, wasn't it? Briefly, he imagined a whole army of these silent, relentless warriors and his flesh crawled. Perhaps he was worrying before he had all the facts, but they'd run into two parties using the same drug in less than a week. Though that hinted at a widespread problem, he'd make damn sure of his facts before he reported this threat to Princess Thalia.

This is exactly why I asked to be released from the princess's service.

"I'll search the bodies," he said then.

Magda took a step back, giving him access to her kills. The first two corpses he examined yielded nothing of interest, not even currency or identification, but the third one carried a peculiar obsidian stone with a sigil carved into it.

He held it to the light, then showed it to Magda. "Ever seen anything like this before?" he asked.

Yes or no questions should be fine while she was shifted. She studied it, then shook her head, ears swiveling. Her whiskers twitched, then she padded over to the two he'd defeated.

He checked the bodies quickly and found a small, bloodstained picture of Princess Thalia. If there had been anything more specific, he would have sent a warning, even if the channel wasn't secure, but the princess already knew she was a target and he had no new information to convey. That was simply confirmation that she had enemies, and they'd known that since long before her father turned traitor and allied with a power-mad despot.

Grimly, he crumpled the photo in his fist and then tore it into pieces, giving the remainder to the wind. He had closed that door before he left Daruvar. Next, he got some supplies from his pack and removed the dagger from his shoulder with a wince. The wound wasn't too deep; he bandaged it quickly. If the blade had been poisoned, he must be inured to the effects.

Magda studied him, and he was glad that her tiger form prevented her from commenting so he could understand. Her silence felt almost like a balm because it gave him peace, but he also wasn't alone, as he had been for much of his adult life. Novel not to be stalking in solitary silence, avoiding detection and sliding away like a ghost.

"I'm ready," he said, mounting up.

She set off at a faster pace than before, and they barely reached a new campsite before nightfall. His vedda beast was tired, moving slower and with a recalcitrance that said he'd pushed the animal hard enough. If she didn't suggest they rest here, he would.

As Gavriel dismounted and scattered some fodder for the gray, Magda prowled the perimeter, checking signs he couldn't detect. Then she shifted and calmly walked past him to fetch her clothes. It was impossible not to notice the smooth play of muscles beneath her skin, the way her impressive deltoids flexed when she lifted the bag. Her shoulders were broad, her build stocky, and he had never beheld such a strong, round butt.

I shouldn't be looking.

He didn't look away.

"We'll catch a few winks here," she told him as she got dressed.

"My thoughts as well. Is this one of the sites they used?" Gavriel didn't see a need to be more specific. They both knew who they were hunting.

"I think so, but I didn't find any sign of Slay's blood. No bandages this time. So…"

"He's healed or they got the information they wanted, no further need for torture," he finished.

She lifted a shoulder in half a shrug. "As guesses go, it's a good one. If they'd discarded him along the route, however, I would have found the dump site."

"They have some use for him, if they haven't killed

him."

"Or he's collaborating."

The open pain in her expression startled him, making Gavriel take a step forward, though, for what, he had no idea. Offering comfort was alien to him, and he'd been reared with the expectation that he would hide his emotions and desires; if he let them slip, it would shame the guild and besmirch his honor. A Noxblade wanted nothing but the next kill order, nothing but the next successful strike.

For the first time, it occurred to him that this was a terrible way to live.

7.

Mags stared at Gavriel, wondering at his conflicted expression. Normally, he showed only enmity or hostility. He extended a hand, then let it drop, and whatever was on his mind, he didn't speak of it. His shoulders squared, his features reverting to his usual impassivity.

"We should set up camp," he said, tying the vedda beast to a tree where the snow had melted enough to offer some forage.

Mags normally wouldn't have bothered, but she didn't think the Noxblade would be willing to curl up with her and share body heat. A pity, since that would be the most practical solution. She couldn't blame him, however, since he didn't have the fur or sufficient body weight to resist the elements as she did.

That was why she assisted when Gavriel pulled out a small tent. He had a few creature comforts stuffed into an impressively small bag, and she silently praised his decision not to build a fire. His tent was silver and white, and it blended well with the wintry landscape. A plume of smoke would give away their location to anyone who might be hunting nearby. In this situation, it seemed best to assume that they were surrounded by enemy patrols.

He also set up a few sensors around the perimeter. Mags knelt, examining them with great curiosity. "Will these be triggered by wildlife?" she asked.

"Only if the animal weighs more than fifty kilos."

She laughed. "We'd want to know if something that big was prowling around anyway. I'm a pretty good danger detector as well. I sleep light out in the field."

"You expect me to trust you with my well-being?" Gavriel asked, raising a brow.

Until he put it that way, she hadn't thought about it, but… "Yeah. We're partners, and if I let anything happen to you, it makes me look bad. That means you can trust me, as long as our truce holds."

He cleared his throat. "I'll bear that in mind." Kneeling, he parted the tent flap and crawled inside, then he added, "Aren't you coming?"

Mags cocked her head. "Am I invited?"

"It will be warmer with two of us in here. It will be cramped if you shift, however."

She smirked. "You saying you prefer me as a woman, Gavriel? And you want me for my body heat?"

"As a tiger, you might destroy my shelter. So yes. And honestly? Yes to the second query as well. Unless close spaces bother you, we'll both be more comfortable."

"I thought you liked a certain amount of…discomfort." That was too personal, and she regretted letting the question slip the second it came out.

He froze for a few seconds, then withdrew into the tent, but he didn't fasten it, leaving the decision up to her. It was damn cold after nightfall, so it wasn't a tough call. Mags knee-walked into the tent and zipped it behind her. Gavriel had laid out thermal sleeping bags and he'd cracked a chemical light stick so the space wasn't completely dark, but the eerie yellow glow gave the interior a strange atmosphere, akin to a cave where mysterious rites might take place.

"Sorry, I shouldn't have teased you," she said then. "There's nothing wrong with enjoying certain things." That was vague enough not to offend him further, she hoped.

"I don't want to talk about it."

That was clear enough, but the barely concealed shame in his voice made it hard for her to leave it alone. "Then just listen, okay? You shouldn't torture yourself emotionally over what gets you off. Everyone's different, and as long as nobody hurts you without permission, it's all good. I like it rough, and that's fine. Give yourself a break, all right?"

He was silent for so long that Mags was about to give up on the conversation. Then he finally said, "It's so easy for you to talk about."

"What is?"

"Your…inclinations."

She laughed softly. "You don't have to whisper. We're the only ones here. And yeah, I don't have any issue discussing what I like in bed."

"It's not like that among Noxblades. We're not a monastic order, but we're encouraged toward an ascetic lifestyle. Excess desire could cloud our judgment, make us want something more than—"

"Killing on command?" she finished.

Irritation popped in the back of her head. The Eldritch had abused their children long enough, making them feel like they should be honored to be murder machines. Gavriel seemed to have existed for much of his life, devoid of warmth or joy. He'd lost everyone he loved in service to Princess Thalia, and now she'd cut him loose. The injustice of that made Mags want to set fire to something.

"Not how the guild masters would put it, but essentially, yes. If we're allowed to feel things fully, there could come a point when we're ordered to take out a target, only to find we have an attachment to that person. Conflicting loyalties are not permitted."

"That's bullshit."

"I've begun to think so."

Maybe it was the forced intimacy of their shelter, but she'd never witnessed Gavriel so willing to talk. She risked a personal question. "Have you always liked the rough stuff?"

"As long as I can remember," he whispered.

"Me too." Maybe a personal story would make him trust her more. "I was always the most aggressive one in my training class, the first to shift, the first to strike. Before I was old enough to know what I was feeling, I knew that I liked getting the jump on my opponents. It gave me such a good feeling when I had someone under me."

"It sounds like sex and sparring are intertwined for you." Gavriel's voice was deeper, and she could hear that his breath was a little uneven.

Really? Just from hearing that little bit? Mags decided to test it. "You could say that. The first time I came with a partner, it was after I beat her in the practice room. We were both sweating, and I was holding her down. She started struggling, but playfully. I bit her. She bucked against my hips and whispered, 'don't stop'. I didn't."

His breath hitched, and she smelled the warming of his scent. Not the same as when she brought his clothes back, but close. Probably she should stop provoking him, but it had been a long time since she'd taken a lover. Emotional entanglements were neither simple, nor safe, and she couldn't risk it a third time.

Gavriel responded in a deep, dark voice that sent a shiver through her. "Back when I was in training, I failed an exercise badly. The instructor caned me and…"

"You liked it," she guessed.

His breath caught audibly, revealing the power of the memory. "It was the first time I ever felt….excited."

Mags could picture the scene with a clarity that startled her, as she wasn't given to fantasies, but the images filled her head. A slender, young Gavriel bearing the strikes with silent, bewildered arousal. Did he slink away and masturbate afterward, biting down on his hand to increase the intensity? Those were questions she couldn't ask, and now she was remembering the smell of his sex after they fought, after she held him down.

I shouldn't think of him as a potential partner.

Still, if she could mitigate some of his shame, she had to try. Mags silently marveled that he was opening up to her this much. "I hope the instructor didn't—"

"No," he cut in quickly. "Nobody ever knew. I kept the revelation to myself."

Wait, that can't mean what it sounds like.

"For how long?" she asked.

"What do you mean?"

"There has to be someone you trusted with this before now. A friend or a lover…?" Gavriel couldn't be a virgin, right?

"This isn't the sort of thing that comes up in conversation," he said stiffly. "You found out on your own through the most awkward circumstances imaginable. Otherwise, we wouldn't be having this discussion either."

Oh, goddess.

Suddenly it felt like the tent might go up in flames. Nobody had ever given him what he craved; he was all skill and discipline, needs subsumed in his work. She could be the first to show him that there was nothing bad or wrong about his hidden desires.

I definitely should not do this.

GAVRIEL COULD HARDLY think for the way his heart thundered in his ears. This was the most intimate conversation he'd ever had with anyone, and it registered on all his senses as seduction. He had to remember that the Animari were different. They were frank about sexual matters and they stripped down casually in front of whoever might be watching. That openness was never meant as an enticement.

"Are you trying to shut me up?" Magda asked.

He'd lost the rhythm of the conversation. People didn't tend to chat with him in any event. Most of his relationships were adversarial, even more so since Zan's passing. He didn't *know* how to simply talk to someone, couldn't remember if he'd ever known. And the insistent thrumming in his head made everything feel fuzzy, similar to indulging in too much wine. Not that he'd done that often either.

So many things I haven't done.

He was starting to regret how austerely he'd lived, how much he'd allowed the Noxblade guild to dominate his existence.

"You're quiet," she said. "Did I make you uncomfortable?"

"I was reflecting."

"On what?"

"Everything," he said wearily.

"I had no idea our exchange was that deep."

"Maybe not for you. Most things appear to come easier for the Animari." He was surprised at the flicker of envy that supplanted his customary bitterness.

"That sounded almost like a compliment."

"You can take it that way if you wish."

He turned his back on her then, thinking that if he couldn't see the curves of her face, he would stop feeling this maddening compulsion. Even now, he was wondering about her strength. Imagining how hard her hands must be and how soft her hair must feel.

Gavriel wrapped up in his sleeping kit and that should have ended the conversation. Another Eldritch would certainly have taken the hint. Magda lay down behind him, close enough that he could feel her body heat, radiating like a furnace, even if they weren't touching. It shouldn't feel so good, being this close to an enemy.

He wanted to roll over and ask more impossible questions. Somehow he kept quiet.

She didn't.

"You're punishing yourself again," she observed.

"What are you going on about?"

"I'm wise to your ways now. You're always denying yourself something you want."

"The only thing I want right now is to sleep," he snapped.

"That's a lie. I can smell it on you."

Smell what? Deception? Or... he cringed, shoulders pulling inward. Surely she couldn't sense that she'd stirred him with her candid talk? That would be mortifying, as the urges still lingered, and he was half-hard, throbbing with no relief in sight. He certainly couldn't handle it here, as he had in the past.

"Why are you doing this to me?" he whispered, hating the touch of a plea that escaped when he meant to be all stoic resistance.

"Somewhere along the line, your people convinced you that there's merit in self-sacrifice. And I agree, to a point. But not when you never allow yourself anything good."

There was no rebuttal to her words because he'd made the princess's will his world. Now he had freedom and precious little else. More to the point, he had no idea what to do with that liberty. Mostly, he felt that he'd outlived his usefulness and he wanted to die. Sobering, to permit that thought to form fully without choking it back. It was a frail little thing, that self-realization, and it trembled at being exposed to her scrutiny.

"My whole life, I've focused on killing and hoping that I'd earn a good and worthy death. Never once did I consider how I'd like to live." Gavriel spoke softly, the words like water overflowing a broken dam.

He couldn't see her. Could only see the flutter of the tent wall, trembling against the wind.

"You don't need to know the answer right away," she said. "It's enough that you're asking the question."

"It feels like you're being kind to me. I don't understand why."

Her hand settled in the center of his back, firm enough to settle his galloping heart. "We're partners. Isn't that enough? You can say anything to me, and I won't judge you."

For the first time, he understood the wolf lord's obsession with conquering Magda Versai. What wouldn't a person do for this sort of acceptance? But this didn't seem to be a merit that could be gained by force or valor; from his observations, Magda offered it on her own terms. Certainly, Gavriel had never done anything to deserve it. He'd only treated her with rancor and icy disdain.

Before, he might have thought this was a trap, some trick to get him to reveal his weaknesses. She'd already told him enough to make him feel sure they were talking as equals, not playing an Eldritch power game. The Animari didn't seem to do that.

He didn't roll over, but he did speak. "You're right about that."

"I usually am," she said, laughing, "but what in particular?"

"How the guild trains us. We're taught from an early age that success is all that matters. It doesn't matter if we hurt, if we're lonely, if we suffer as others don't."

It was easier, now that he'd started. The words came freely, no longer as if pulled through thorns in his throat. "Most of my people don't eat meat. You know that, I remember you complaining about it. But in the field, my sword mates and I ate it raw and bloody. Whatever we had to do, we did—to survive, to complete the mission."

Gavriel still recalled the awful hardships before they reached Hallowell. The snow, the scarcity of food. It was necessary, but he'd been so sick afterward, wanting to throw up, but he couldn't. He needed the energy to keep moving and he couldn't lose face in front of the Golgoth prince. More agonizing, the sense of being tainted and impure, less than the rest of his people. They had the freedom to uphold their principles because of what the Noxblades did to protect them.

"I don't understand because my people see it differently. We respect the animals we consume, and we know one day we'll be eaten too, even if it's less directly." She talked a little about Animari funeral rites, until the pressure lessened in his chest. "Anyway, I don't think you should blame yourself for doing what you had to, even if you broke some rules."

Gavriel didn't want to get into Eldritch religious practices with her, so he pretended to accept her words. It was easy for an outsider to say it was no big deal to consume flesh, but according to their beliefs, he would never be pure enough to take his place in paradise, no matter what he did going forward. There was no penance sufficient to atone.

"Do you plan on letting us sleep tonight or not?"

"That depends on you."

"Now what?" he growled.

"We have a lot in common, shadow warrior. If you want to take it to the next level, I'm interested and willing."

That was so shocking, he rolled over in reaction. Her face was very close. She smelled of the wilderness, fresh pine, and bracing wind. Part of him wanted to put his face in her neck and breathe deeper, and he missed the feel of her hand on his back.

"You want us to…" The right words wouldn't come, because nobody had ever propositioned him before.

They wouldn't dare. Not Gavriel, Death's Shadow.

"Don't be delicate. I want to fuck you. I want to make it hurt in all the best ways. If you're good with that, we'll have some fun. If not, no pressure. I won't ask again."

"But you don't even like me."

Magda laughed quietly. "Is that necessary? You hate my guts and *I* get on your last nerve, but I promise you won't hate what I can do to you." Her smile held countless secrets. "That lack of affection will make it simpler for both of us when we decide we're done."

"No emotional entanglements? Just sex for its own sake."

"Now you're getting it."

"How do I know you won't use anything that passes between us against me later?"

She sighed. "Have you ever heard a whisper about anyone I've been with?"

While prowling around Ash Valley during the conclave, he'd learned that she had reputation for being unattainable, an unscalable mountain, and Raff Pineda had failed to seduce her as well. If she'd had partners before, she didn't speak of them afterward. That made her perfect for realizing the dark fantasies he'd nursed in secret and in silence. Afterward, he wouldn't have to see her or deal with awkward, knowing looks.

"I take your point."

Magda went on, "If we work together long enough, I might eventually manage to become your friend, but I'll never love you. And I'll never meddle with your heart, either. Does that deal work for you?"

Surprisingly enough, it did.

8.

Though Gavriel hadn't verbalized his agreement, Mags could tell he was tempted. He wouldn't hesitate to reject an offer that held no appeal yet he hadn't responded. That meant he was considering it.

She didn't push. Patience might deliver what aggression couldn't. There would be time for that part later.

Finally, he said, "Let's say, hypothetically, that I agree. How would we proceed?"

"I won't pounce you and tie you up, if that's what you're asking. Right now, you barely trust me to touch your back. We have to work on that before we take it further."

"Trust? Really?" He sounded so surprised that she smiled. "I thought you weren't interested in my emotions."

With the faint, yellow light from the chemical torch, Mags could make out his skepticism easily. Now that she was looking at him as a potential partner, she let herself admire the sharpness of his jaw, the autocratic arch of his nose, and the contrasting softness of his mouth. It also helped that his expression wasn't contorted in a scowl and his white hair wasn't hanging half across his face like a veil.

"Not in a romantic way, but a certain level of rapport is

required."

"Clarify."

"You need to be comfortable with me and with being touched. Given how high you've built your walls, that might take some time. It might sound counterintuitive, but you have to trust me not to hurt you for real before we can play together."

In some ways, Mags felt like she was gentling a wild animal, a genuinely feral wolf that might chew his own leg off to avoid personal contact. She reached out slowly, watching for the flinch, however slight, but Gavriel didn't move, not even when she flattened her palm on his chest. His heart was thumping too fast, but she'd sensed his reaction earlier and tried not to reveal that awareness. He'd hate for her to know what he felt before he was ready.

"It's not that I think you're going to assault me," he muttered. "I can protect myself. I'm simply not used to being touched."

"Well, that's step one. You have to change your mindset and embrace the idea that it's okay for me to put my hands on you. Do I have permission now?"

"Is all of this really necessary?" he demanded.

Gavriel put his hand over hers, possibly to pull it away, but he hesitated, and she held still, letting him feel the contrast between them. His hand was cool and lean; she could feel the scars and calluses from his years of training. Her own hand was hard and hot. She hoped it felt like the promise of spring after a long winter.

"It is for me," she said simply.

"Then...I'll try. No promises." His voice dropped, so low that even with enhanced senses in close quarters, she could barely make out his next words. "I might be too broken even for this."

"I don't think that's true. Nobody is shattered beyond mending. All it requires is enough time and patience. As it happens, I have both."

"Why would you bother?" This vulnerability wasn't like Gavriel, a sign that she was succeeding at storming the walls she'd mentioned.

"It will be worth it. In the end, we'll both get exactly what we desire."

He stroked his fingers down the back of hers, still resting on his chest. "I'll put myself in your hands then."

That first softening, first submission, sent a quiet thrill through her, a pleasurable spike that curled her toes. The next step was a test to see if he meant it or if he was simply saying what she wanted to hear. She slid her hand up his chest, over his shoulder, and brushed the hair away from his face. He still didn't move, though his lashes fluttered.

"This is a good start. You're not yelling at me when I do this anymore."

"Before, you were baiting me," he snapped.

"Sometimes. More often, I was treating you like I treat my pride mates. Which pissed you off something special." Mags stroked his hair, mostly testing whether he'd let her—slow, sweeping motions that startled a strangled sound from him. "Are you uncomfortable? Be honest. I'll stop anytime you say the word."

A little shudder ran through him, and she couldn't read the complex play of emotions that twisted his mouth and led him to squeeze his eyes shut for a few seconds. Then he shook his head. "No. It actually feels…good."

"But it seems wrong to let yourself enjoy it," she guessed.

"A little."

"We'll work on that. Come here." His quick compliance brightened her smile. Maybe this wouldn't take as long as she feared; then they could have some real fun. She pulled him to her, so their bodies were touching, but she didn't hold him. "Is there anything you've ever wanted someone to do for you?"

"You mean…like a fantasy?"

"Not a sex thing. I like having my feet rubbed for example. Sometimes when I've had a long, shitty day, I wish there was someone to do that for me."

"Ah, I see. You want me to…share."

"More or less. It's like a rehearsal for more intimate requests. If you can't tell me something easy like this, how are you going to ask me to bind you with rope and use my teeth until you come?"

Gavriel sucked in a sharp breath, reaction vibrating through him palpably so she could *feel* his response. He was already half-hard and trembling, just at the mention of the possibility. Playing with him later would be pure delight.

His voice was hoarse when he finally answered. "When I think about my responsibilities, I get headaches and the tendons in my neck are so often tight that they hurt, not in a good way."

"So you'd like a head and neck rub, easy enough. Do I have your permission, Gavriel?" That was a much deeper question than it might initially seem.

Because if he said yes, it was the first step down this road together, and even if it was slow-going, she wouldn't turn back.

"Yes. Please."

The 'please' evoked a sudden rush of surprising tenderness because he sounded so bewildered, eyes shut again, as if he couldn't watch what was about to happen, some sin of self-indulgence too great to bear. Smiling, she curved her right hand around the back of his head. He hadn't been kidding about the tension; the knots had knots, and she worked with brutal determination. Gavriel wouldn't mind a little pain. It might even make this better.

A groan escaped him, and he pushed his head against her fingers. She dug in with firm fingertips, until she heard the soft hiss of tension releasing. There would be soreness afterward, but not the kind of pain that led to debilitating headaches. Gradually she eased up, stroking the sides of his neck to smooth out the last of the stiffness. To finish, she sifted through his hair and scratched lightly all over his head, alternating pattern and pressure according to what pleased him best. Mags gauged that by the unconscious sounds he made and the way he leaned into her touch.

Eventually, she was only playing with his hair and he'd shifted close enough that his head was almost resting on her shoulder to give her easier access. He wasn't aroused anymore—his scent had cooled—but he was more relaxed, pliant against her as she could never have imagined before this strange night. In fact, it seemed like he was about to drift off to sleep.

"How did that feel?" she whispered.

"Incredible," he said sleepily.

His head drooped; he rested it on her shoulder, and she slid an arm over him, another little test to see if he would withdraw. But there was warmth and ease between them, a good foundation, and he only shifted to get more comfortable. *Nobody would believe it, if they saw us now.* The other Eldritch would be shocked; so would her pride mates, but

Mags had never been one to publicize her personal business. She would protect Gavriel's privacy as fiercely as she did her own.

"It's easy to get what you want. You only have to ask." She was stroking his hair again, so silky that it almost made her want to grow hers out, only she didn't have the patience to care for it.

"That's never been true before," he muttered.

Mags smiled. "Then your life's about to change."

GAVRIEL WOKE TANGLED up with the tiger woman, who had thrown an arm and leg over him as they slept. The weight didn't trouble him, but the intimacy did. Her pine and icy wind scent lingered all over him, and the feel of her body, well, she was just as strong as he'd imagined, firm and muscled and so hot that he'd shoved the thermal blanket off in the night. Her right breast nestled against his chest, her thigh spread across his like a sly enticement. He didn't roll away.

He half-regretted the things he'd agreed to the night before, half-wished he could take back the way he'd allowed her to handle him freely. Yet the fresh pleasure lingered.

Even now, he could feel the tenderness where she'd worked away aches he had nursed for months. She could well be a witch because magic might be the only plausible explanation for what had passed between them. He wasn't susceptible to soft words or sensual blandishments, but she'd made everything sound so reasonable—

"Doubts already?"

He started, ignoring the question. "You're awake."

"Since you are also, we should get moving. I'd kill for a

hot bath and a warm meal." She got up before he could, crawling over to gather her gear. There was no delicacy or elegance about her, presenting her backside like she wanted to be mounted.

And now he was thinking about sex, something he did all too often around Magda Versai. She drew it out of him like poison from a wound and left him shivering in the aftermath.

Why does she want me? Why me? He couldn't ask. The answer might unravel him. She had the knack for doing so without half trying, and he was barely keeping the pieces together, like an ornament stitched of tattered thread and bits of broken glass.

"You'd do that anyway," he said.

"Not without provocation. Let's see if your beast is still around. What's his name?"

"He doesn't have one."

This conversation seemed remarkable—that she could act like nothing had changed—when for him, everything had. Gavriel hardly knew how to behave around her, now that he'd given her permission to touch him. He was constantly braced for her to do something outrageous, but she was acting as she always had, like they were comrades.

"Well, he should." She edged out of the tent, still talking. "He looks like a Gray. How does that work for you? Who's a good Gray?" From the nonsense she spouted, she must be talking to the vedda beast, not him.

Gavriel took a moment to compose himself and once he was calm, he packed his belongings. Maybe she could truly keep things separate. During the day, they would focus on work and not discuss what happened at night. That suited him perfectly.

"I hope we find something today," he said. "And not another damned empty camp."

The tiger woman nodded. "I'm with you. I wish had a clue what these assholes are looking for, roaming around Thalia's territory."

"They could be making contact with other insurgents."

Magda shook her head. "That doesn't feel right. There would be more signs if larger groups had passed through. I'm only finding traces of the group that had Slay."

"We'll know when we catch up to them. How are you moving today?" As a tiger, he suspected, but he didn't want to assume.

"I have to be a cat to follow the trail. Are you going to miss having me up behind you or something? Now that we're…involved, I could cuddle up behind you and whisper dirty things in your ear as we go."

"Don't be ridiculous," he snapped.

She removed her shirt, indifferent to the cold. But her golden gaze held his as she wriggled out of her pants. "You still hate me, got it. Then will you give my stuff to Gray? He says he doesn't mind porting it for me."

Gavriel bit his lip against a reluctant smile as the vedda beast puffed out a sound that could be taken for agreement and stamped its hooves against the frosty ground. Magda scratched the animal between his horns, and he recalled the feel of her fingers on his head and neck, stroking him into a stupor.

"You'll freeze to death, standing around in your underwear." Annoyance made his voice sharp. "We have no time to waste."

"It's not that cold," she said, petting his vedda beast until Gavriel started to wish he had horns and a shaggy mane. "You're right about the last thing, though."

His faint aggravation faded as the rest of her clothes hit the forest floor. No matter how often she did this, it would never be commonplace for him. Her people might bare their bodies casually but his didn't. The Eldritch were simply better at hiding their emotions than the Golgoth, who had gawked like peasants at a penny carnival.

He admired her in tiny, stolen glances, unable to let his gaze simply feast. Too hungry for that, he might give himself away if he looked as long as he wanted. Certain parts of her burned into his mind's eye, the broad curve of her hips, the thickness of her thighs, and the dark hair that curled between her legs. Her skin was beautiful, coppery warm, and perfect like most of the Animari. Most bore no scars, no matter how often they fought, due to their accelerated healing. Heat prickled at the edges of his self-control as he remembered how she felt on top of him.

Now is not the time.

The next time he checked, she was a tiger, pacing in impatient silence. Gavriel fastened her things to Gray, then his own, and mounted up, letting her set the pace. This morning, the vedda beast was jumpy, as if it sensed danger. But surely if there was something to hear or smell, Magda would be aware of it too. Sobering to realize that he trusted her enhanced senses and furthermore, he'd seen enough of her battle prowess to have no hesitation about following her.

Is this what she means about building trust?
Enough of this. We have work to do.

The ride freed him from the need to think, though he did stay alert. Normal forest noises accompanied their movement, nothing that should alarm him. The trees were dark and bare, brittle with the ending of winter. He heard only the sounds of their passage, Gray's hooves moving over a carpet of dead leaves and broken branches. Yet Gavriel couldn't prevent the chill that rippled down his spine as they moved out of the woods. Perhaps it was only the suggestion of being exposed to the enemy, now that they'd lost the trees for cover.

But he didn't think so. And he hadn't survived as a Noxblade by doubting his instincts. He was the last of his sword mates, and he wouldn't die easily. If the rebel houses thought they could weaken the princess by attacking him, he'd spit on their corpses. And even if they succeeded in eliminating him, she still had the wolves at her back. Odd that he would find some reassurance in that after opposing the alliance so fiercely.

"We're close," he said.

She growled in response and lifted her head, a gesture he took for agreement. It would be helpful if they could communicate more than this, but no use wishing for the impossible. Dismounting, he drew his weapons and signaled to Gray that he should wait. The beast was well-trained and didn't make a sound. If Gavriel didn't return before dark, the animal would head for Daruvar on his own, taking all their belongings with him.

Better not to risk it.

He pulled each of their packs from the saddlebags and slung them across his back, then he dropped to a crouch, moving so slowly that it would take a bird of prey to spot him. Or possibly an Animari. Daylight wasn't a friend, and his dark clothes didn't blend with the brown grass. *Nothing to be done about that now.* Magda prowled ahead, a lean and feline threat to whatever they had finally tracked down.

He used the scrubby evergreen bushes for cover when possible. The tiger's ears swiveled; clearly, she was hearing something up ahead.

Ready for anything, Gavriel crested the hill and braced for battle.

9.

MAGS RAN IN ready for a fight, but she skidded to a stop when a little Eldritch girl shrieked at the sight of her and tumbled backward. The kid scrambled up and didn't stop running until she got to a woman Mags figured must be her mother. The little one grabbed the lady's filthy skirt and hid her face in it.

Well, damn. Now I have to add frightening small children to the list of shit I did before dinner.

In a glance, she took in the dismal scene: makeshift shelters built of sticks and tattered fabric, a hole they were clearly using as toilet facilities, and no potable water. She didn't see any food in the empty containers scattered around. Five families at least—Mags did a quick headcount. Over twenty displaced Eldritch. These people were starving and scared to death. It didn't take a genius to realize that this was a refugee camp. She shifted quickly and got behind Gray so she could dress. There was no way to help as a tiger.

Gavriel dismounted, his customarily impassive features awash in horror. "What's happened here?" he demanded, his tone so sharp that nobody wanted to respond.

In fact, he radiated such authority that a couple of people were already edging away, ready to run in case they got punished for trespassing. Mags got her shirt and pants on in record time, no time for the underwear—otherwise, this situation might go bad. It wasn't that she had great people skills, but she'd give herself the edge over Gavriel. She tapped his arm to get his attention and silently shook her head when it seemed like he was about to go after the ones shying away.

"Let me try," she said.

At his curt nod, she took a few steps toward the cowering little girl and dropped to one knee in front of her mother. "Sorry I startled you. I wasn't expecting to find anybody this cute roaming around out here."

A pair of wide, gray eyes peered at her around the edges of ragged, dirty ruffles. Mags held the look, trying to seem harmless, which wasn't easy as the acknowledged pride badass. She didn't move or reach out. Gavriel stayed still too, letting her work.

"You were a monster cat and now you're a lady!" the girl finally said.

"I'm a tiger when I want to be."

"I want to be a cormorant."

Mags had a vague idea that was a bird of some kind, so she answered, "Flying would be pretty amazing."

"And I could peck people who are mean to my mater!"

Ah, that was information she could use. "Is someone giving her trouble?"

"They're bothering all of us!" She risked a longer look at Mags, then added, "You could eat them when you're a monster cat. Would you—"

"Leena!" The Eldritch woman slid a hand gently across

her daughter's mouth, eyes anxious. She bit her lip, trembling visibly. "I'm sorry. We won't cause trouble. We'll move along soon. Please don't report us to the Talfayens."

Damn, so these people feared Thalia? But who—or what—were they running from? Gavriel stepped up beside her, holding Gray's reins, and she hoped his presence wouldn't set them off again. At least nobody was running and screaming. Yet.

This isn't your problem, a little voice said.

While she understood that, she couldn't shrug and move along. Even if it meant losing Slay's trail, if she could do something to help here, she had to. Otherwise, all her talk about building bridges and doing better when she was lecturing Gavriel was so much bullshit. And Mags wasn't a damn hypocrite.

"We don't work for the princess," Gavriel said then. "And we won't be returning to the stronghold anytime soon. Please tell us what's happening."

The woman took a steadying breath, then flicked a look at someone else, an Eldritch woman of indeterminate age. From the authority she radiated, Mags guessed she must be the leader or at least someone whose opinion mattered. Despite the rags she was wearing, she had a stately air, and she gave a gentle nod, granting permission.

"The town we called home is no more," Leena's mother said. She paused, as if that statement gave her so much pain that she couldn't breathe for a few seconds. "Or rather, the town still stands, but it is no longer safe."

"What changed?" Mags asked.

"There have been conflicts between the houses as long as anyone can remember, but they used to be more covert. It was a business for Noxblades, not normal citizens. Now, they fight in the streets. They burned our houses the night we fled. Ancalen used to be a such a safe, beautiful place. Since the conclave, however..."

"So there's a civil war in Ancalen...what houses are fighting?" Maybe that didn't make a difference, but it might explain why these folks were scared of the princess.

From across the camp, a lean man with silver-blond hair caught up in a messy knot spat in disgust. "You're fucking beast-kin. You'll probably cut our throats and drink our blood the minute we let down our guard. Why should we tell you?"

Sickness and shock silenced her for a few seconds. It wasn't that she didn't know some Eldritch felt this way, but hearing it spoken straight out instead of in whispers, that was like suddenly taking a fist in the gut. Before she could respond, Gavriel closed the distance and jerked the asshole forward by his shirt front.

"Keep a civil tongue in your head, or I'll cut it out. The tiger woman is my partner, and I will brook no disrespect."

Well, damn. That's kind of hot. Mags could absolutely have thrown the pissant through a tree on her own, but it was nice seeing Gavriel riled up for her sake. *I can't believe this is happening.*

The man glared. It seemed that privation had driven him well beyond caring who he provoked. "Beast lover."

"Don't say another word, worm. By speaking about her so, you've offended *me*."

"After what I've seen, I'm supposed to be scared of you? Why? Who are you?" The man spat again, all hopeless defiance.

In answer, Gavriel knocked him down and stepped on his chest. Mags suspected she should intervene, but she didn't want to, considering the shit the asshole had said. *I fucking hate being the voice of reason.*

The Noxblade's smile was all winter chill, knives carved of ice. "I am Gavriel d'Alana, Death's Shadow. Perhaps you've heard of me."

From the Eldritch swear that the man on the ground let out, Mags guessed he had, indeed, heard of Gavriel. His already pale face dropped into ashen territory, and he plucked at Gavriel's pant leg with trembling fingers. "Forgive me. Please. I had no idea. I don't know why you're with the tiger woman, but please overlook my—"

"You should be groveling at her feet, not mine," Gavriel snapped.

Mags finally decided to speak up. "This is entertaining and all, but let the jackass live. I'm still waiting to hear the end of the story that Leena's mother was telling."

With a silent snarl, Gavriel stepped back and the Eldritch male scrambled to his feet. He skidded all the way to the far side of the encampment, eyes flickering like he feared his skin might be peeled from his flesh. Leena, on the other hand, was beaming at the Noxblade like his pockets were filled with candy.

Guess she doesn't like that shit-stain either.

The girl's mother was saying, "Apologies, I should have introduced myself. I'm called Keriel. Now, where was I?"

"You were about to tell me what houses were fighting," Mags prompted. At least, she hoped so.

Keriel sighed. "The truth is, I'm not entirely sure. They didn't bear sigils or colors before the conflict started."

The leader spoke for the first time. "They were truly the least of our troubles. The real, unavoidable danger came when the Dead-Eyes descended on Ancalen."

Dead-Eyes? She shot a quick look at Gavriel, wondering if he was thinking along the same lines.

Dammit, I have a bad feeling about this.

RAGE STILL POUNDED in Gavriel's skull like furious drums, thudding against his temples. His guild master had always said that he had anger issues and that controlling his temper was key, but he'd rarely snapped like this. There was no explanation for why he'd erupted like a volcanic island when he'd nursed bitter sentiments in the past, blaming the Animari for all he'd lost. Regardless, nobody would be permitted to speak of Magda Versai that way in his hearing. She had a fierce, brave, honest heart, and he'd die before letting some wretch dishonor her name.

He sent a final glare at the caitiff, then forced himself to attend to what was being said. *Dead-Eyes?* Magda made eye contact and seemed to be asking a silent question, but he lacked the ability to fill in those blanks. He had been able to do that with Oriel before he died, never with anyone else.

"What are Dead-Eyes?" he asked.

"They've taken a drug that steals their souls," Keriel answered. "After the first dose, they change, stop caring for friends and family. They only exist to fight, maim, and kill. We tried to resist at first, but they don't seem to feel pain. There's no talking to them either."

Now he understood Magda's look. She thought the Ancalen Dead-Eyes sounded like the strange, silent Eldritch they'd fought from House Manwaring, and he had to agree. Gavriel gazed until her eyes met his, then he offered a slight nod, earning a half-smile from her. That quick exchange filled him with peculiar warmth.

"I think we've encountered them already. Are there many in Ancalen?"

Keriel sighed, her shoulders slumping. The little girl tucked her hand into her mother's, trying to offer comfort. "The town is overrun, Dead-Eyes and dissidents. We fled in the night with bits and bobs from our former lives. We came from Gilbraith territory, and we've crossed the border, so we have no rights in Talfayen lands, but please—"

"Don't beg," Magda cut in. "If we can't help, we definitely won't hurt you." She crossed to Gavriel and set her hand on his arm. It surprised him that he didn't have the urge to shake off her touch. "Can we talk?"

He turned to the Eldritch leader and said politely, "Would you give us a moment?"

"Of course. Take your time."

Magda dragged him past the outskirts of camp, still holding his wrist, and Gavriel didn't wrench away. "We have to help them," she said.

"That's not our mission. I'm searching for the hidden loyalist stronghold and you're looking for…" What was his name? "The Ash Valley traitor."

"We don't know that Slay's turned for sure," she snarled. "Besides, this is the right call. They won't survive if they run into a Dead-Eyes patrol. We've fought two small ones, wouldn't have fared as well with larger numbers, and there are probably more. We need to liberate Ancalen and then we need to hunt down whoever is supplying the stuff."

Her earnest sincerity startled a rusty laugh out of him. "You think we can stop a civil war in enemy territory *and* eliminate drug trafficking? The two of us. We're more likely to die."

When she flashed a cocky grin, he noticed that she had

dimples, faint ones; she rarely smiled broad enough for them to show. "You're an army of one, right? Death's Shadow and all that. And *I'm* a one-woman wrecking crew. Together, why can't we do the impossible? It's not what we intended when we left Daruvar, but I'm not okay with saying 'good luck' and leaving these people to starve or get butchered."

"It could mean losing the trail for good," he warned. "If we do this, you may not find Slay before it's too late."

He was being generous by not contesting her assertion that the cat lieutenant hadn't yet been proven to be a turncoat. Assuming that was true, however, also meant giving up the chance to save him in order to help random strangers. In all honesty, it wasn't the sort of thing he would normally do. Noxblades didn't receive love from the common folk, and they wouldn't expect him to step up, not like this.

I'm an assassin, not a fucking hero. I kill people; I don't save them.

But with her gazing at him with expectant, golden eyes, he wished that he could. For once. Princess Thalia would consider this a colossal waste of time and resources, as these people had no strategic value.

Magda let go of his arm then, expression somber. "Whatever's going on with Slay, he's not waiting for me to save him. I guess you already know that I'm hunting him, just in case. But a potential security threat to Ash Valley does not take precedence over clear and present danger."

This woman constantly astonished him, making him reexamine his principles and his priorities. "They're not even your people. Why do you care so much?"

"Maybe you should ask yourself why you don't care enough." That was a deflection, though, and she seemed to acknowledge it with the twist of her mouth.

Gavriel waited, arms folded.

"Fine. The truth is, because everyone matters. I'm trying to walk the talk, okay?"

"In other words, you're trying to live up to the high ideals you lectured me about. We all do our part to build a better world." He meant those words to sound caustic, but somehow the tone was humiliatingly sincere.

Her smile was pure sunshine. "You get it."

"I think you might be ruining me," he muttered.

"Or saving you. The jury is out. So are we agreed? We're doing this."

Gavriel sighed. He ignored the cynical voice telling him that this was a terrible idea, one that he would certainly regret. "Fine, what's your plan?"

"It would be a stretch to say that I have one yet," she said. "We need more information. First, we have to get these people somewhere safe. Any suggestions?"

He considered. "Not Daruvar. They don't have the supplies to take twenty more with a dubious ability to contribute to the war effort."

"Oi! What did I just say?" She poked him in the chest.

"Everyone matters. I suggest we escort them to the nearest Talfayen settlement. I should have enough authority to assure them a civil if not warm welcome."

"Where are we headed, then?"

Before answering, he checked the map. "Kelnora. It's twenty kilometers west, closer to the sea than the border. Hopefully, it's far enough from the fighting that it will offer a quiet respite, after all they've been through."

"How big is it?"

"Two hundred, give or take. Our towns aren't large. There aren't many of us, especially in comparison..." He stopped himself.

The Animari weren't to blame for low Eldritch birth rates. Neither were the Golgoth. Sometimes Gavriel wondered if his people were a relic from times past and they ought to dwindle into nothing, become a footnote in history books about the Numina.

"All the more reason for us to save as many lives as we can," she said. "I'd like to be known for doing something other than kicking ass. I'm good at it, yeah, but nobody is only one thing. And maybe I had to leave Ash Valley to get that chance."

"To change your brand? Why, are you hoping to go down in the annals of Eldritch lore as a heroine of legend?" he asked, gently amused. There was that strange, unwanted softness again, pervasive and insidious, growing through him like a parasitic vine.

"Like Annwen? Sorry, I don't know any Eldritch heroines. I'd bitch at you, but honestly, it's fun that you're teasing me. I didn't realize you even had a sense of humor."

For a fleeting moment, he imagined sitting with her, sharing one of his favorite stories. He…wouldn't hate teaching her about Eldritch history, if she truly was interested. Some things, they could learn together, as his studies had been stunted when he was pulled from scholarship and shoved down darker, deadlier paths.

"Neither did I." Gavriel offered that deadpan, and he wasn't sure if he was joking. His existence hadn't given him the space to seek levity or light; he'd lived in the shadows so long that the sun felt like a threat or a myth.

Magda burned with that same brightness—courageous, incandescent, honest to a fault—and he feared she might burn him alive.

10.

THE TWENTY-KILOMETER TREK to Kelnora veered away from Slay's trail, and Mags stifled a frisson of guilt.

Part of her felt like she *was* letting down Ash Valley, choosing strangers over kith and kin, like Gavriel had said. But if Slay came back with more Golgoth invaders, Dom and Pru would have to handle it without her. Leena's eyes would haunt her until her dying day, if she abandoned this child in the wilderness.

Now, she was running point as a tiger with Gavriel watching their backs, riding with Leena in front and two more children up behind him. The rest of the refugees were on foot, so she couldn't set a bruising pace. They were all carrying more than they could easily manage, the wreckage of lives shattered by a war they neither wanted nor welcomed.

Distance she could have covered in less than hour stretched to nearly four with frequent rests and stops. She ran ahead multiple times, scouting to make sure the path was clear. Fighting Dead-Eyes with refugees in tow could be a disaster. The strain of constantly circling back to check on them started to grate on her, rubbing her nerves raw.

This was different than hunting, more intense and burdensome, but she didn't regret the course she'd chosen. It was no surprise the refugees had agreed so readily; they were lucky to get this far unprotected, and they had nowhere else to go. Now it was on her and Gavriel to shepherd them to safety.

Around the halfway mark, she smelled trouble, a hint of the camphor she'd scented on the Dead-Eyes. There was no time to signal Gavriel. If the odor was this strong, they were close, and one was wounded. *Can I take them before the others catch up?*

Really, it depended on how many there were.

Crouching low, she slunk through the tall, dead grass toward her prey, ears swiveling for any signs of movement. She caught a flicker of sound at the edge of her range but checking it out would mean leaving the convoy vulnerable for a while, as it was off the road to Kelnora. *Worth the risk,* she decided. *I'll be quick. And Gavriel's there to protect them.* He could play defense while she went on the offensive.

She stilled when the Dead-Eyes came into view; they weren't talking, even among themselves. What was the drug doing to their brains anyway? There were four of them, and one was holding a gun. Safest to assume it might be full of Animari-slaying rounds like they'd used on Raff. *I'll kill that one first.*

Wait, if they have Animari-stopping rounds, that means they're hunting my kind. Did that mean Slay got away from his captors? There could be others in Thalia's territory, she supposed, but it seemed significant. Too bad she didn't know all the players on this stage; lack of awareness impaired her ability to make quick judgment calls.

What the hell. She'd already decided to fight when she

deviated from the path. *Let's get this party started.*

Mags leapt from the underbrush with a lightning fast, predator pounce, and only that speed saved her from a point-blank shot in the head. The Eldritch with the gun moved so fast that his arm blurred, snapping two shots with a celerity that sent a chill down her spine. The second bullet grazed her neck, and the burn started immediately. She hoped to all good gods that the cure she'd tested on herself to save Raff was still in her system, or she might be in trouble.

No time to worry about that.

Mags struck her target with her full weight and knocked him flat. When he hit the ground, the gun bounced away as she tore out his throat. The sticky, tainted blood clung to her teeth and tongue and she wished she had a spare second to clean her mouth, but the nearest Eldritch was already grabbing for the weapon.

I didn't plan for this. I should have.

She leapt and managed to knock the gun down the hill with one swipe of her paw, so now it was lost in the brush. Three more to deal with, and it was unnerving when they came at her in silence. No trash talk, no threats, just violent determination. It didn't matter to these Eldritch that their former comrade was gushing blood and choking on it in noisy, gruesome fashion.

They came at her from all sides, and she was damn lucky they were using blades because her skin and fur offered some protection, but their knives were razor-sharp, and sliced into her flesh when she couldn't dodge. Mags took the hits with a snarl and pushed forward to topple her next opponent. In tiger form, she killed the same way in repetition: rush, overwhelm, teeth and claws. It was messy, not much technique to it, but few could stand up to her for pure strength...actually none, since Slay disappeared.

The Eldritch tried to get his knife up, but he didn't have the raw power and she broke his arm in the leap. His bone made a satisfying snap, but it was even more unnerving when he didn't cry out as his arm bent at an unnatural angle. He hit the ground under her, and she raked her claws across his abdomen. That left the others free to attack her back, so she rolled across the bastard's thrashing body and shuddered at the feel of the hot, treacly feel of the blood on her fur.

I can't let them surround me. That's how wild dogs win against larger prey.

That might be the wrong analogy, but it was accurate, and they gave her no time to think further, relentless and silent. Thankfully they didn't have the quickness of mind to go searching for the gun in the undergrowth. Now that it was out of sight, it also seemed to be out of mind. She got why the refugees called them Dead-Eyes. Even with his guts half-spilled, the one beneath her was still slashing with his blade.

She bit down and severed his hand at the wrist and spat as best she could, letting saliva run out, frothy and pink. Disgusting. Two left. Any reasonable foe would have second-thoughts, considering the possibility of a tactical retreat. No such doubt showed in their blank faces.

The poison was in her blood now, though. Not enough to kill her, but she *was* starting to feel woozy and weak. Mags fought the tremors and faced the survivors with a snarl, showing teeth. The remaining Eldritch were fuzzy about the edges; she had to be fast. If she didn't take them out quickly, she might not win this.

Using treated black iron bullets infused with beryllium was a shitty trick. Yet Raff got shot multiple times and he made it. *I'm stronger than the wolf lord, and this is just a scratch. Come on, get this shit done.* The mental pep talk did nothing to clear her vision. More knives sliced across her back, wounds taken because she was getting slow and careless.

They'd heal soon, but the loss of blood wasn't helping. She lunged low and bit off a foot, though that still didn't prompt a sound from the Eldritch she'd attacked. The lack of balance made him stumble as he tried to run at her for another strike, and she bounded behind him, pushing him forward in a mounted attack, where she dug all four claws in and gouged, then she finished with her teeth.

Nausea clawed at her stomach. It might be the poison, could be the bad blood she'd taken in. Either way, this was the worst fight she could remember. Breathing hard, she whirled on the last one and rallied her strength. Not easy when she could feel the jitters in her legs, and her tongue was numb.

Why is this so hard today? The answer hit her like a fist in the skull. *I'm used to Gavriel having my back.* That awareness pissed her off enough to permit one last pounce and she went at the final Eldritch in a fury. She took a knife in the chest, but he didn't have the strength for a killing blow. Mags savaged him with all her remaining strength, and then she didn't have the reserves left to hold her form.

Amid all the corpses, she dropped to a self-protective crouch—a naked woman covered in blood, wondering if she could get back to the group.

GAVRIEL HAD NO idea how he wound up in this position.

When Magda didn't circle back on time, he kept riding, herding these poor souls toward Kelnora, but after a while, it became clear that something had gone wrong. What, he couldn't imagine, as the tiger woman was incredibly fierce in a fight. The people hadn't noticed yet or they wouldn't be walking with such confidence.

There were probably only three kilometers left, and if he abandoned the refugees, they might not make it and even if they did, without his introduction to the town elder, they had no assurance of being permitted to stay. Word wouldn't have gotten around that he was no longer Thalia's right hand, and he felt sure that the princess wouldn't begrudge him using her name to do some good.

What he wanted to do and what he *should* do—those impulses were wildly at odds. Over a lifetime of following orders, obedient and unquestioning, he'd never indulged in the weakness of wishing he could follow another path. What the princess required, she received of him. Now, things were different, and Gavriel wanted like hell to leave Gray for the children, to tell these people to keep going, and then go search for Magda. He'd promised to serve as her partner while they traveled together and his blood chilled when he imagined letting her down, as he had so many others.

There's a reason I'm alone. I'm meant to be. I always have been.

This was more of the same, and if he believed in such nonsense, Gavriel could imagine he radiated such malevolence that nobody could bear to stay close. They left or they were taken. Of the two, terrible options, it was better they went willingly, he supposed. Better than being claimed by death to walk among the sunlit lands no more.

His chest tightened with these grim reflections, and his expression must have given something away because Keriel was trotting anxiously beside his vedda beast, shading her eyes against the scant spring sunlight. "Is something wrong? It seems like the Animari lady ought to be back by now."

Yes, she should be. And there was no question at all about what she'd want him to do. Stifling a sigh, he lied without blinking. "She sent a message. Though she's been detained, the path is clear to Kelnora and she'll catch up with us there. You needn't worry. I'm here if anything happens. I'll stay until I get you settled."

Keriel beamed up at him; he had never received such a warm smile for deceiving someone. The tightness in his chest intensified to the point of pain, but he ignored it, and he could almost count the cost worthwhile when Leena rested her head on his sternum and whispered, "You're not as scary as I thought at first."

"Is that right?" he muttered.

Talking to children seemed strange, even sacrilegious, because he had no idea what to say. They hadn't permitted him to play since he went to the guild and started his training. His memories were full of austerity, discipline, and constant awareness that if he disappointed his mentor, he could be discarded like yesterday's rubbish.

"Mater said you know a princess. Is she *really* a princess? Does she have a crown and a sparkly gown?"

"I have no idea." Since the conclave, he'd only seen Princess Thalia in black, dressed for war, not a ballroom gala.

Leena lost interest in his conversation quickly, thank the fates, and she went to sleep in his arms with so much trust that he worried for her future. His nerves prickled as he rode, scanning the route ahead, but everything seemed quiet. No movement startled his vedda beast, and the refugees kept moving at their excruciatingly sluggish pace. He wished they had wagons to transport what little they'd managed to save from the fire, but that was a selfish thought. especially when directed at those who'd lost all but their lives. Funny, how Magda Versai had become the voice in his head, pointing out when he was terrible.

I'm often terrible.

The day felt endless, but they reached the outskirts of Kelnora before nightfall—and without incident. Gavriel noted when the road widened with the spread of humble buildings. This was a fishing town and he inhaled the fresh salt of the nearby sea. The air smelled of fish and seaweed too, smoke from the houses that had built fires against the storm that seemed to be threatening. Rain or snow, the heavens hadn't decided.

It had been years since he'd visited a place like this during the day, not coming to kill someone in silence, but simply…here. Gavriel tried not to show how out of place he felt as he rode forward, leading his motley band to the center of town. It seemed wiser not to mention that these Eldritch hailed from Gilbraith lands.

There, he dismounted and whispered to the elder, "Do not contradict anything I say. Do you understand?"

The older woman nodded.

Then he got the children down from the vedda beast one by one. Leena hugged his leg for a moment, leaving Gavriel frozen in shocked bemusement. Keriel pulled her away with a shy smile. "Don't worry, she doesn't bite."

He answered, "It's fine, I've had my shots," and the small group nearest to him burst out laughing, as if he'd intended to be humorous.

He tried a smile and it tugged strangely at the corners of his mouth.

Just then, a man came out of the largest structure—everything was built of stone that must have been quarried nearby, and by the look of it, most of the homes had been standing for hundreds of years. It was sobering to realize how much the people had suffered under Lord Talfayen, how little of his own prosperity and technology he had shared. In a way, this was like stepping into the past.

"We rarely get visitors," the town elder said, with a worried look.

"Not visitors," Gavriel corrected. "Princess Thalia has sent these people to Kelnora under my protection. Do you recognize me?"

Stories of the red-eyed demon who murdered in the night had a way of getting around, so he was surprised when the man simply shook his head. "I've not spoken to a stranger in almost three years, good sir. It'd be easier if you tell me."

"Understood. I'm Gavriel d'Alana, and these people have been displaced by the war. I'm tasked with helping them get settled here."

The headman took another look at the refugees, expression softening. "I'm sorry to hear that. The fighting hasn't come this far yet, so you must've traveled a ways."

"That's putting it mildly," the refugee leader replied. Her voice was gentle as a summer stream and just as musical. "I'm Irina. Thank you so much for taking us in. You'll find that we're not unskilled. I'm a brewer myself, and we've a cobbler among us. Keriel is a seamstress and—"

"No worries, my lady. We don't have a lot here, but

what there is we'll share gladly. Ah, I'm Haryk. We can talk more later. Let me send a runner to spread the word." He grabbed a boy gawking nearby and whispered in his ear. "First off, we'll need to find families to take in guests while we see about permanent lodgings…"

Gavriel stared as things unspooled without him needing to drop Princess Thalia's name again. For the life of him, he couldn't recall ever meeting such kind people who did things without asking what was in it for them. He didn't think fear was driving this aid effort, but maybe the headman was hoping to be rewarded later for his generosity? Probably not a good idea to suggest that aloud.

It's the right thing to do. That was Magda's voice in his head again, damn her, and worry surged forth, twice as strong as before. He'd discharged his duty by getting these folks to safety, and it didn't look as if his presence as an enforcer would be necessary.

"I'm going now," he said abruptly.

I have to find her. Not because it was right; because it was *necessary*.

"Are you sure?" Haryk asked. "It's a poor idea, sir. The weather's about to turn, and if you're still out in it, well, that mistake could mean your life."

"So be it," Gavriel said.

11.

FOR A FEW moments, Mags stayed down because getting up was too hard. Eventually, she got her head together enough to search the bodies with trembling hands. This time, she found a picture of Gavriel, not Thalia. *So he's been targeted as well.*

That might explain why the group had been carrying an Animari killer, if they knew Mags was traveling with him. Four seemed like a small number for the two of them, though. They'd already taken out more than that—

Oh.

Those groups didn't have the poisoned bullets. *If they'd gotten the drop on us, I get taken out in one shot, then they finish Gavriel.* Their knives were probably poisoned also, which accounted for her unusual weakness. *I'm probably fighting multiple toxins here, including one that's usually fatal to the Animari.*

Working that out made Mags feel a little better about her weakness, but it didn't alter anything about her shitty situation. Worse, she was feeling the cold as she normally didn't, so much that her fingertips were numb, and her bones hurt. She clenched her jaw to stop her teeth from chattering as she forced herself to stand.

Sparks popped before her eyes, but there was nothing to hold onto. If she fell over, she'd just have to get up again. The air smelled too crisp now, stinging the inside of her nose with the promise of snow.

She took one step, then another.

I can do this. Kelnora is that way, right? Hope the group's doing okay.

Doggedly, one foot after another, she pushed forward, barely noticing when her sole sliced across a sharp stick half-hidden in the dead leaves and dry grass. Her blood smelled off, likely a result of the poisons her system was trying to filter. More concerning was the crimson trail she'd left behind, an easy way for the enemy to track her. While the Eldritch couldn't hunt by scent, they had excellent eyesight, and there was no telling what gift one of them might possess. She guessed if an Eldritch had the ability to track down a specific person, they'd already have made their bones as a bounty hunter, however.

Those thoughts kept her knees from buckling as she forced herself on. The shivers came nonstop, a result of both sickness and cold. With bleary eyes, she surveyed the terrain and she found nowhere that would work for shelter. They'd left the forest behind hours ago, and now the land was all rolling hills, sparsely covered in dry grass and scrubby bushes.

A convenient cave would be nice, but not if she had to fight a bear to hole up for a while. Time would solve her problem, but exposed to the weather like this, Mags didn't have much of it. If she froze to death, it would be such a humiliating way to go.

How far am I from town?

Mags couldn't think for the fizzing in her head, but she had been staggering toward Kelnora for what seemed like a long time. Sometimes her legs wouldn't hold her, and she dropped to all fours. It would be faster if she could muster enough strength to go cat, but she had nothing left.

The Eldritch sure lived in desolate lands. Their settlements seemed to be few and far between, and they weren't large. It rankled to see how the common folk lived while the so-called ruling class lived it up with staff running about to boil hot water for their tea. That injustice should have filled her with a fortitude born of indignation but instead of flames for her engine, there was only a sad puff of smoke.

For the second time in as many minutes, she tumbled to her knees, slicing the left on a rock. *Hell, I'm doing more damage to myself than the enemy managed.* In trying to get up, she pitched forward and landed on her face. Mags rolled over and let out a long stream of curses; she wasn't used to failure, but her body just would not fucking cooperate. She balled her hand into a fist, and with great effort, she hauled herself to her feet.

I can get there. I can.

Before she took another step, she heard the tell-tale thud of vedda beast hooves over the ground. Coming toward her, fast. There was nowhere to hide, so she didn't bother to try. If this was to be her last fight, she'd go out with blood on her hands.

"Finally." It was Gavriel's voice, but with a much rougher edge than usual.

He leapt from Gray's back and reached her in two steps. At first she thought she was hallucinating and that he was fighting the urge to hug her. His look warmed her from head to toe, a visual ravishment, and he reached out one hand, only to drop it before he made contact.

Wait, shouldn't he be with the refugees? Mags tried to ask the question, but when she opened her mouth, no sound came out. At some point, her throat had swollen.

"Here, take some water if you can."

He set the bottle to her lips and she got down a few swallows. She didn't enjoy playing the damsel in distress, and she was a little pissed that he was out here instead of protecting the helpless Eldritch yet a small part of her was also glad that he'd come looking. Her pride mates would've, but she hadn't expected such kindness from the Noxblade, even if he'd defended her.

"I tried to call you." He ran a hand through his hair in visible agitation, making the white tufts stand up like dandelion fluff. Maybe it was the poison fogging her brain, but his dishevelment was kind of cute. "You don't know how annoyed I was when your phone rang in *my* pack."

She wheezed out a laugh. "Tigers don't have pockets, genius."

"I know that," he snapped. "According to the local experts, we're in for some rough weather. Hurry and get dressed."

Over the years, Mags had read a few romantic stories and at this stage, the hero always took off his jacket to offer it to the heroine. But Gavriel's wouldn't fit; she was broader across the shoulders, and somehow, it touched her more when he chucked her clothes, starting with the underwear, though his pale face went scarlet and he couldn't make eye contact afterward. He even knelt to help her get her shoes on when she had trouble keeping her balance.

"I'm ready," she said huskily.

He rose slowly. "We should go. You can tell me what

happened later. I gather it was nothing good."

"It's a win for our side." She offered a lopsided smile, twisted by the swelling she could feel in her face.

Probably from when I fell on it.

The damage would heal fast, once the poisons left her body. Her wounds weren't closing properly because of the beryllium, so she looked like shit.

"Mount up," Gavriel ordered.

At the moment, she was so happy to see him and Gray that she didn't even mind his attitude. Using the last of her reserves, she hauled herself up, and to her surprise, Gavriel mounted behind her, just as he'd ridden with Leena.

I'm not a kid. The protest hovered on the tip of her tongue, but in the end, she said nothing. Not even when his arms came up around her so he could hold the reins. She tried to hold herself upright, knowing how he felt about casual physical contact, but it was too much effort. Gavriel didn't say a word when she sighed and leaned back against him. Actually, to her muzzy mind, it felt like he was holding her, but that couldn't be right. Gavriel hated all Animari, especially her, and this had nothing to do with the bedroom games they might eventually play for mutual amusement. Before they set off, he tucked a blanket around her, and she mumbled in exhausted expression.

"Is everyone else all right?" she asked quietly.

"They're settled in Kelnora. I ensured their safety before I came looking for you."

A startling burst of joy crackled through her. She captured one of his hands and gave it a warm squeeze. Mags was already fading as she whispered, "Thanks. You did the right thing, Gavriel."

IT WAS STARTING to alarm Gavriel how far he'd go to hear those words from this woman. People didn't praise him. In the guild, they assumed he would complete his missions. The princess certainly hadn't gone out of her way to offer positive reinforcement; you would never encourage the knife in your hand, after all.

His temper chewed at the edges of its tether as he fought the urge to shake Magda awake and demand to know what Animari witchcraft she was using on him. Since she was sound asleep in his arms, that would be cruel and irrational. She made him both. She also made him want to be better, to be something else, although he wasn't altogether sure what shape that change would take.

Gray was moving slowly, a sure sign that the beast was tired. He hadn't covered that much ground today, but he'd carried more weight than usual, and he'd gotten slow and indolent from all the time in the stable. Gavriel clicked to the beast softly and nudged with his heels.

"We'll be in soon. If you don't move it, we'll be caught in the snow."

In response, Gray quickened his step, as if he understood that a warm stall and tasty fodder were waiting for him. The weather had turned already, dropping from spring chill to winter ice in a flash. Already, fat, wet flakes were flickering down, melting against Gavriel's cheeks and sticking to his hair. Gently he pulled the coverlet up to shield Magda's face. Whatever she'd fought had left her in a hell of a mess.

She did it for us.

The conviction came fully formed. Even if he didn't know the exact circumstances, he felt sure she'd risked herself to make sure the convoy could pass safely. It was exactly the sort of reckless, big-hearted idiocy that drove him wild. While he was starting to come around to her notion of 'caring more', he couldn't accept how lightly she took her own well-being. Yes, the Animari could heal grievous wounds, but that didn't mean they were immune to pain.

He sucked in a sharp breath, fighting the disquieting memory of finding her stumbling, naked, liberally smeared with blood. He'd never seen her dazed and helpless before, would rather not see it again. It felt as if the shock took twenty years off his lifespan. He tightened his arms on her. There was no harm in it since she was out cold. Her steady breathing reassured him that she was in no danger.

Little by little, the heart-stopping fear that had exploded in his head and raged like a wildfire died by increments, until there were only sparks and embers. As they rode, he held her full weight, and it occurred to him that since his brother died, nobody had trusted him this fully. To show someone your sleeping face, that was no small matter. He might dump her off Gray's back or take advantage of her weakness. This unexpected confidence felt like a gift he'd neither earned nor deserved.

The storm worsened as they approached Kelnora, blinding wind and stinging ice mixed in with the snow. His eyes were nearly frozen, and he could hardly blink for the accumulation of frost. Gavriel couldn't feel his fingers and Gray was stumbling with exhaustion. Fortunately, the stables were in sight and the beast made for them with single-minded intent. A young Eldritch could barely hold the doors open long enough for them to stagger inside.

Outside, the gale howled like a devil from the old stories. He gestured to the stable lad. "Hold him steady."

Once the boy took the reins, Gavriel slid off Gray's back and braced, because it didn't look like Magda would rouse. He caught her, staggering with her weight. The fall woke her, thankfully, as he didn't know how he would've transported her.

"We made it?"

The smile softening his mouth felt almost like a kiss. "It seems so. Can you stand?"

"Yeah, I'm fine."

Since she was shaky as a newborn vedda beast, that was clearly an overstatement. He chose not to question it. "Let me care for Gray, then we can see about finding accommodations."

"I can do it," the stable boy offered.

Gavriel shook his head. "He's mine. I will look after him."

"That's sweet," Magda said.

His mouth compressed on a wave of faint embarrassment. "You're mocking me."

"Definitely not. I approve of taking care of your own stuff. Not that you need my approval or that Gray's a thing."

Her earnest response hit him like a key turning in a lock. Somehow, with that witchery he'd noted before, she made him want to tell her things. "I don't have much, so I...treasure what belongs to me."

To his astonishment, she joined him in caring for the animal, using brush and comb according to his terse instructions. Gray preened beneath the attention, stamping his hooves and tossing his mane. When they got to the horn-polishing, the vedda beast radiated satisfaction and was ready to munch on the fodder Gavriel scattered, then take a long, well-earned rest.

"He's rather a vain creature," he said.

"As he should be. What a lovely boy," Magda crooned, scratching the sweet spot between Gray's horns. "Thank you for saving me."

Against his will, Gavriel recalled how good her hands felt. *I can't believe I envy the damned vedda beast.* He choked the urge to protest that she was giving the animal too much credit.

What is wrong with you? Do you truly wish she'd rub your head and sweetly thank you in the same fashion?

Fates help him, he did.

Stepping away from the stall, she glanced around, then asked, "Where are we staying?"

Gavriel shrugged. "I've no idea. I went looking for you before all the arrangements were made."

"Master Haryk is waiting for you at the public house," the boy volunteered from a nearby stall. "He said to send you as soon as you returned. Well, actually he said if, but he said not to—oh."

Magda laughed. "It's fine. Thanks for passing along the message. Where's the public house?"

The stable lad gave precise directions, and once Gavriel gathered their worldly goods, they set off through the blizzard on foot. If not for the lights in the windows, it was bad enough that they might have gotten lost even in town.

She would've died out there tonight. *I really did save her.* Hell, he'd saved the refugees too because this storm would've done for them as well. Gavriel tried not to be an ass, even in his own mind, but there was more pleasure in playing the hero than he could have guessed.

I could get used to this.

He was practically frozen solid by the time they stumbled into the tavern. Half the town seemed to be assembled there, and there were pallets laid before the fire. Probably there wasn't enough housing for the newcomers, so they were making do.

"You made it and you found your friend. This is good news," Haryk called. "Come, you must be starving. Do you like barley vegetable soup?"

At this juncture, Gavriel would have gladly eaten raw caribou, even if it meant more damnation for his soul. He gave a grateful nod. "I do and thank you for it."

Keriel leapt up to get food for them and soon she was back with hot soup, fresh bread, soft cheese, and warm mugs of spiced wine. These modest comforts were so delicious after the terrible weather that he could've melted in delight.

After accepting her meal, Magda plopped down on the rug next to the children, who made room for her with beaming smiles. Leena touched her injured cheek with a small hand. "Did you fight?"

"Indeed I did."

"Did you win?" the little girl asked.

Magda leaned in as if to impart a confidence, golden eyes twinkling. "I'm here, aren't I?"

"Would you teach me to fight?" Leena gazed up at Magda with wide, shining eyes.

Belatedly, Gavriel realized he was watching the tiger woman with such rapt attention that his spoon was hovering in midair without him taking a single bite. A hot flush washed up his neck, onto his cheek, and ears, and he hunched his shoulders, lowering his gaze to his bowl.

What the hell is wrong with me?

12.

"IS THERE ANYTHING else you need?" Keriel asked.

Mags glanced around the small space and shook her head. They'd sent her and Gavriel to the eaves, a cozy nest above the public house with a sloped ceiling that seemed to be used for storage, as there were boxes piled all around. She'd shoved them back to offer enough room for them to lay their blankets, and the walls were sound. Heat from the hearth rose up, leaving the attic toasty and comfortable.

"This is fine, we're out of the weather. You don't work for us. Please just look after yourself and Leena."

"It's because of you that we're alive at all, Mistress. So if there's anything at all you'd like…" The woman trailed off, but clearly, she'd be happier if Magda just asked for something. Anything.

Since she hated being indebted to others, she got that. "Then… if it's not too much trouble, a couple of buckets of warm water? I should wash the blood off before I mess up my bedroll."

"Of course. Right away!" The Eldritch woman hurried off with such alacrity that Mags felt bad for not asking sooner.

Maybe she was too much of a hard-ass about requesting help. Damn did she miss the bathhouse in Ash Valley, though. The facilities at Daruvar were ancient and basic, so for a few seconds, she fantasized about soaking for an hour in steaming hot water.

That fantasy puffed into nothing when Gavriel came up the stairs a bit later, lugging the pails he'd likely snagged from Keriel. Haryk, who ran the public house, had given them some candles earlier, and the attic was strangely...romantic, all shadows and flickering golden light.

"Your bath, my lady." His tone was caustic, but she didn't even mind that anymore.

She couldn't hate him when she knew how many wounds he was hiding. His history of loss made her see why he did everything in his power to keep people from getting close. And hell, didn't she do the same damn thing? She just didn't think she was quite so abrasive about it, though maybe her pride mates would disagree.

"Thanks. One of the containers is for you, though."

That startled him so much that he stumbled on the last step and nearly spilled the water. Mags had recovered enough to put on a burst of preternatural speed, and she steadied his hands on the bucket.

"You think we're bathing together?"

Time to go for it.

"It's on offer. We talked about certain shared interests, but there hasn't been an opportunity. And now, I owe you, Gavriel. That means I want to level the scales."

"I don't want sex that springs from obligation," he snapped.

She smiled slightly. "It wouldn't, I promise. I value

myself too highly to offer this deal without desire."

"And what is 'this deal'?"

"First, we tend to each other. That sort of care-taking builds trust. We talked about that before. Maybe by the end, you'll feel safe enough with me to want to take things to the next level, but we won't do anything unless you want it too."

"You're saying...you want me." The doubt in his voice echoed the shadows of his face, and even in this faint light, she could see that he was biting his lip, tempted but hesitant.

"Yes. Even more after today. I want to give you what you crave, whatever that might be. Say the word and I'll make your fantasy come true."

"Anything?" His voice rumbled so deep and low that it gave her the shivers.

"As long as we can manage it up here. I'm lacking certain specialty equipment." She smiled as his breath caught, but she went on as if he hadn't reacted. "No shame, Gavriel. No judgment. Just what we enjoy. And if you want to stop at any point, you make the call. Pick a word so I'll know you mean it and aren't feigning reluctance."

He stared for a few seconds in silence, then he asked softly, "Is that...customary?"

"It's the best way to avoid misunderstandings. You like the idea of being overpowered but this way, you still have control. You're safe, because I stop as soon as you ask me to."

"I feel so strange."

"What's wrong?" A touch of concern flickered through her. If he couldn't handle even this much, maybe it was too fast.

"Just talking about this is…exciting me a little."

Mags laughed. "Ah, well, I've never been in your shoes, but I think it's understandable. Why wouldn't it feel good, knowing you're about to get what you want?"

"When you put it that way, I feel almost normal."

"That word is overrated. You'll break your own heart, trying to be like everyone else. You're good as you are, Gavriel."

"Ah." He made a quiet sound, like she was already touching him, and a silent thrill worked through her, escalating her excitement.

She'd raised the subject because she wanted to give something back to him, but really, the talk of paying off what she owed was an excuse to get her hands on him again. The poison must be mostly gone because other than a faint weakness, Mags felt recovered after food and rest.

"The stopping word is 'caribou'," Gavriel said then.

"Should be safe enough. That's one thing you'd never say to me accidentally during sex. Unless you've got some very interesting tastes." That was a joke, but it surprised her nonetheless when he laughed, a shy sound that made her feel like she was starting to get to know the real Gavriel, behind the hostility and bitterness.

"My thoughts exactly," he agreed.

"Before we begin, do you want to draw any definite lines now?"

"Like what?"

"No penetration, for example, or no kissing. It's all personal preference. If you're not sure, we can see how it goes."

"Part of me can't believe I'm having this conversation with you," Gavriel said, shaking his head slightly.

"Better me than someone who might gossip about you," she pointed out.

"Without a doubt. This first time, I'll just...trust you."

Warmth blossomed in her chest at that simple statement because she knew damn well it wasn't simple or easy for him. This was the feral wolf finally taking food from her hands. She resisted the urge to hug him.

"We'll start by getting naked. You wash me first, then I'll do you."

"Is that—"

"Yes, it's necessary. Trust, as I mentioned before, and frankly, I don't want to roll around with you smelling like this. I'm gross and covered in blood." She cocked her head. "Wait, is that—"

"No," he cut in sharply. "Blood isn't my thing. Fine, we'll bathe."

She shivered once she stripped out of her clothes. Though she'd done this in front of Gavriel so often that she'd lost count, it was different. This time, he would touch her body while thinking about pleasure to come.

The water had cooled to lukewarm while they spoke and he was a little too efficient, washing off the blood with impersonal hands. Oddly, that briskness endeared him to her because she could tell so clearly that he'd never done this. More, he had no idea how to. Unlike most, he avoided touching her breasts and he only washed where she had been wounded, like he was a battlefield medic.

I'll be teaching him everything.

She didn't criticize his performance. That would only make him more nervous at this stage. Later, when he was more comfortable, she'd take him in hand, show him what to do and when to serve her well. Baby steps now, at the beginning.

"There," he said finally. "I think I got all the blood. It's hard to be sure in this light."

"If you did your best, that's enough."

A lover would have lingered, but he wasn't that, not yet. He would be, before the night was through.

Smiling wickedly, Mags wet her cloth in the other bucket and closed the distance between them. "Take your clothes off. It's my turn to do you."

Under Magda's watchful gaze, Gavriel flushed painfully hot but he didn't demur. He removed his clothing slowly, one piece at a time, trying to regulate his racing heart. He was already half-hard and that was so far from usual that he feared he wouldn't be able to control himself.

In silence, she washed his whole body with humiliating thoroughness, lingering in places nobody had ever touched. His cock went rigid as she cleaned it, and he groaned when she slid the cloth up his backside and even massaged in between his cheeks. That was the last place she touched.

"Lay the blankets," she said.

That was part of it, he thought. Doing as she bid without protest, so he got the bedrolls from their packs and spread them out, his for the bottom, hers for the top, and now they would smell of each other. Part of him understood the excitement the Animari must feel, knowing their scent would be all over their lover's skin, announcing their relationship to anyone with the senses to discern it.

As he bent to pull back the blanket, she hit him from behind, a surprise attack that nearly made him come, because she was so hot and so strong and so naked. A spurt of fluid jetted from the end of his cock, and he snarled a challenge, fighting with all his strength. It wasn't enough; she wrestled him down, so that his chest scraped against the blankets, his stiff cock too. Magda bit down on his neck, so hard that he cried out. The pain zipped down his spine and swelled in a delicious rush, cascading through his nerve-endings.

"Be quiet," she whispered in his ear. "Unless you want them to know what's happening. Or is that your thing? Do you want everyone to watch me have you?"

He shook his head, silent as she'd demanded. The effort hurt his chest, because her teeth were back, on his shoulder this time, and she was digging in with her nails, making marks all down his sides. Gavriel couldn't keep from pumping his hips, once, twice, and that earned him hard hands on his thighs in punishment.

"It's too soon for that. Don't get carried away."

Having that growled with sharp teeth on his nape only made it harder to keep himself in check. This was everything he'd ever wanted, in his deepest, darkest dreams, and it felt like his whole body might explode. That euphoric pleasure was so alien that he fought it—and fought her—with all his strength. He managed to roll beneath her and shoved, eyes snapping resistance. It was just like that time in the sparring room; her raw physical power let her slam his hands against the floor and then she was on top of him. Shit, he'd fantasized about this, jerking himself to an agonizing orgasm, and currently, they were both naked.

Gavriel could feel the wet slide of her body against him, and it was both glorious and terrifying to know she liked this; she wanted it too. His head went fuzzy when she leaned down to kiss him, but it wasn't the soft kissing he'd seen in others, more of a ravaging, with vicious press of mouth and invading tongue, and she used her teeth again, savaging his lower lip.

His cock jumped beneath her, pleading, demanding, and he whimpered into her lips. Hated the sound. This was terrible and glorious and—

"You can speak now," she whispered.

"I hate this. And I hate you for making me like it. And I hate myself for wanting it." The words came out in a furious rush, like the lancing of a wound, and his whole body eased, even as his cock got harder still.

She bit him again, almost hard enough to draw blood. "You hate this, Gavriel?"

His answer was a shuddering groan and to close his eyes, silent resistance since he couldn't move his hands. He bucked upward, trying to unseat her or get inside her, or maybe both. Soon he was fighting in truth, not caring if he hurt her—she wouldn't let him anyway—she was too fucking strong, and then she was straddling him, rubbing her slit back and forth across his aching cock.

"You want to come, don't you? I could make you do it this way. Just helpless and spurting and—"

Jerking beneath her, he came. The words were too much, and he lost to her husky voice and the hot glide of her glorious body. An evil smile curved her mouth as she reached between their bodies. "I don't remember letting you do that." Then she smeared his fluid across his lips. "You'll pay for this."

When she let go of his hands, he dropped them onto the blankets, no more fight left, but she wasn't done, and before he could take more than a shaky breath, savoring the aftershocks, her thighs went across his face, and her pussy was hovering right against his mouth.

"Lick me properly, Gavriel. If I don't get off, you don't sleep."

Somehow, that crude order sent a glow through his cock and it tried to rise, but there wasn't quite enough fuel for the fire yet. He'd use his mouth instead. She gave precise, illicit instructions as he tasted her, and she showed him with rough hands exactly what he was meant to be doing. Mags moved on him and used him, until he could barely breathe for the rapid shifting of her hips. Her wetness smeared his face and her scent filled him up until she became his entire world, delicious and demanding.

She liked it when he alternated lips and tongue, but never teeth, and a soft pressure on her clitoris made her cry out, head thrown back. He licked her through two orgasms before she finally shivered and slid off his face, legs trembling.

"That was good. You're a quick study."

"I should wash up."

She put a hand on his arm to stop him. "The water is dirty, and I want you to sleep, smelling of me. It won't hurt you. But… it's your choice. Say the word, if you prefer."

Somehow it felt like failure if he yielded already. This wasn't a huge deal, and she was apparently going to sleep with his semen on her belly. Thinking about that sent a low-level shudder of arousal through him. "I think you've created a monster," he muttered. "I cannot seem to be satisfied."

Her tone was gentle, surprising him after she'd just been so fierce. "You're just making up for lost time. Come here."

Gavriel didn't question, and they curled up together as

they had that one night in the tent. "Are you not…disappointed?"

"In what? Your cock isn't the only good part of you. That was some great work with your mouth, especially for your first time."

"How do you know it was?" he demanded.

"It's obvious. You mentioned that I'm the first person you've talked to about sex. It didn't take a genius to put the pieces together, and…I'm glad you chose me as your first."

"First what?"

Magda didn't answer, but the question haunted him. They weren't lovers, but he felt at ease when she was close by, and she understood his desires better than he did. Though he was a bit sore, she hadn't done any lasting damage. He traced the bite marks on his shoulders with a dawning sense of wonder.

He wanted to do it again. To do more.

If he wasn't careful, this sexual obsession could distract him from his goal of destroying the loyalist stronghold. Already he'd taken one detour and now he was snowed in, unable to act—

On behalf of the princess.

Holy hell.

Gavriel realized he hadn't thought of Princess Thalia in—well, he wasn't sure how long, at least not more than in passing. And remembering her didn't summon the usual sorrow and despair, possibly because Magda Versai was all over him and the smell of her was about to drive him out of his mind.

"You can't sleep," she said then.

"What?" He started, illogically certain that she could see inside his teeming brain. It was all he could do to swallow his bewildered questions.

"Do you need another round? I can use my hand and make it hurt a little."

"Ah, no. I was just thinking."

"About what? You can talk to me."

He considered that, before shaking his head. "Not tonight. But…possibly soon. And thanks for asking."

"That's what friends do," she mumbled.

"Is that what we are?"

Friends who fuck. The answer didn't seem entirely wrong, but something about the definition troubled him as well. Gavriel couldn't put his finger on what was bothering him, but he *could* touch Magda. He did so stealthily, so as not to wake her, learning the softness of her skin and the sleek feel of her hair.

These stolen moments felt fragile and infinitely precious, but like the rare spring snow, they would soon vanish.

13.

Judging by the milky light trickling through the round window, Mags awoke just before dawn. While she couldn't say she felt 100% better, she'd recovered most of her strength. She was tender with a few still-healing wounds, but time would take care of that.

That was all happening according to expectations, but what she didn't figure was that Gavriel would still be sleeping deeply, curled up next to her as if this was something they did regularly. He didn't sleep much, and she had reckoned that he'd catnap, then slink off to hide out among the refugees, unable to face her in the light of day.

She took this opportunity to study his sleeping face, assessing each of his features like she might need to sculpt a statue of him from memory. Like most Eldritch, his features were sharp but delicate, with hollows beneath his cheekbones and a jaw sharp enough to shave glass. As she gazed at him, his pale lashes fluttered, so light as to be nearly invisible, then he was staring back at her.

"What?" he snapped.

Yeah, that was more like it.

She made up something off the top of her head. "I never

told you what went down yesterday."

"Ah, yes. We did leave matters unfinished."

Quietly, she summarized what happened, finishing with, "And they were carrying your picture, Gavriel. That worries me."

He didn't seem alarmed. At least his features didn't shift, and his posture revealed no tension. "It's to be expected. I've been the princess's right hand for many years. Tactically, it's a sound decision. If they can eliminate me, they weaken her position significantly."

"But you're not even working for her anymore," she protested. "At least not directly. Yet you still have a target on your back. That's some absolute bullshit."

"Are you worried about me?" he asked.

"Would that be so weird?"

He rolled onto his back, gazing up at the beams that framed the ceiling with an air of bemusement. "It is...novel."

"Your life seems like it's been lonely." Mags blurted that out before thinking, and like usual, she regretted it.

Raff had told her once that she had no filter and she should work on not making people feel like shit. In all honesty, most times she didn't care how others felt and it was better for her to speak her mind. This wasn't one of those occasions; Gavriel had been injured enough by his own folks, and she had the odd notion that she should be careful with him, when she wasn't fucking his brains out.

The long silence got awkward, and just when she was about to blabber anything to break the tension, he finally sighed. "It started that way, and it's become so again, but it wasn't always."

"Oh?" That was as casual a prompt as she could manage, because she was interested, and there was no pretending otherwise. Mags wasn't good at push-pull games, never had been.

"How much do you know about the Noxblade guild?" he asked.

On the surface, it seemed like a topic change, but she went with it. "Not much. You start training young and they teach you to become the best killers possible."

"Then you don't know that many of us are orphans. Eldritch birth rates are low, so there aren't too many unwanted children, but it does happen. A high-ranking person dallies with a servant, and they can't afford to keep the child, or the reverse—and the noble can't permit a scandal."

"Is that your story, Gavriel?"

He nodded. "One or the other. It's how I came to the guild. Oriel, he wasn't just my brother...he was also my twin. Incredibly rare among my people. So rare that they must have taken us as a bad omen, especially when it became clear that I was different."

"You mean your coloring?"

"Precisely. He wasn't like me, so I sometimes wonder why they didn't keep him. But they sent us both away, and I'm grateful for the time I had with him. Growing up in the guild, I wasn't lonely because I had Mistress Alana and Oriel."

"Mistress Alana?"

"My mentor, I take my surname from her. As an outcast with no family willing to claim me, I have no other."

"Ah, I did wonder about that. Sometimes I've met Eldritch with a 'D' before their name. Does that mean they're orphaned too?"

"It can, but not always. If you're speaking of Lileth, her name refers to a region instead. There are those who simply call themselves after where they're from, if they don't have a family name. It's more common among the lower classes."

"You know you sound like an ass when you talk that way, right?"

"I don't make the rules."

"No, but you support a system that keeps your people living in the dark ages. I can't believe this town doesn't even have running water!" It was too early to pick a fight, but if Mags didn't aggravate him this way, she might piss him off by being too sympathetic. This was the better move.

Surprisingly, Gavriel sighed. "I'm aware. Believe me when I say, I had no idea things were this bad in rural areas. Lord Talfayen cared only about his own consequence and not all for his people."

"You think Thalia will do better?"

"I know she will, given the opportunity."

Okay, that was a bit depressing—to confirm that Gavriel still had that woman on a pedestal. He seemed to think she could do no wrong, even though she'd basically wrung him dry, then cut him loose when it turned out she could use Raff next. For once, she held her tongue because this wasn't a fight she could win.

Mags made a noncommittal noise and changed the subject. Or rather, refocused it. As long as he was in a talking mood, she'd learn all she could. "So you were happy in the guild?"

"Early on, yes. You judge my situation by your standards, but I knew no different, so I was happy to train, happy to learn what they taught. I had Oriel, and I wasn't lonely."

"When did that change?"

Gavriel sighed. "These questions are becoming bothersome. Are you writing a treatise on my life?"

"I'm just curious. Eldritch ways are very different, and Noxblades are legendary among the Animari."

"Like the bogeyman," he guessed in a bitter tone.

"Sort of, I suppose. But there's an element of admiration. We respect great hunters, Gavriel, and there's no doubt that Noxblades can stalk with the best of us."

"I will accept the compliment, but I'm starting to feel a bit…exposed. You dig into me, yet you share nothing in return. Why is that?"

A flicker of guilt started deep in her chest. "Habit? Among the pride, people know all about me already. At least, they know what I let them see. The rest is private."

"If I asked personal questions of you, would you answer?"

She thought about that, then said, "Sure. It would be bullshit if I talked about building trust while refusing to let you in. What do you want to know?"

A frisson of discomfort crawled down her spine. Probably she should have foreseen this. Gavriel wasn't one to permit a power disparity, at least outside of the sheets. Now she knew too much about him and he was taking steps to get inside her defenses.

When he spoke, the words were a dagger thrust to her heart. "Why are you alone? As I understand it, your people usually take a mate. Can you not find someone who is…compatible?"

Memories came at her, hard. She had never spoken of this, and in fact, she'd even sworn Arran to secrecy after he uttered the warning. She didn't want to be the pride's tragic heroine, the story that could never have a happy ending.

And at first, she hadn't even believed Arran. It seemed so improbable, so absurd. Why *couldn't* she fall in love?

Though most gave the Seers credit for a certain accuracy and prescience, Mags thought she knew better. She didn't listen.

Until it was too late. Until she'd crossed the bridge, and then had to watch while it burned behind her.

"Well?" Gavriel prompted.

She swallowed hard. "You want to know my sad story? Fine, I'll tell you. Not because I want to, but because it's fair."

ONCE, AS A child, Gavriel had been tricked into kicking a beehive—Oriel at his best—and he had the same feeling now; the buzz of imminent danger set all his senses alight. Odd, because Magda wasn't moving.

"I'm not sure how much you know about pride dynamics, but each Animari settlement has a Seer, not as powerful as the leader, but sort of...adjacent? Most leaders worth their salt consult their Seer before making important decisions, and the same is true for individual pride members as well."

He didn't see what this had to do with her personal life, but he nodded. "They're shamans or something, yes? They see portents and read auguries."

"More like, they dream the future. They don't read bones or entrails these days."

"Right, so..." He drew the word out, encouraging her to continue.

"When I came of age, my mother sent me to Arran. That's our Seer's name. She thought he could give me a hint as to where I should search for a mate." Sighing, she closed her eyes, and he sensed that this was difficult for her to discuss.

What could possibly cause the tiger woman so much pain? At this point, he regretted asking, but there was no way to disavow the question.

"Is that customary?" He'd never had parents, so he had no idea if they usually interfered in such matters.

"It depends. In my family, yes, because my mother was vehement about my passing along our good genes. Ideally, she wanted me to find another tiger and settle down." At his questioning look, she explained, "Tigers are a bit rare among the cats. She was proud of that heritage and wanted me to preserve it."

"I had no idea there were such intricacies of lineage among your people," Gavriel said, surprised.

"It's not the usual thing. People don't ordinarily make it some big issue if an ocelot marries a lynx, like with Pru's parents. My mother is a bit…special."

Her tone implied 'obsessive' and Gavriel nodded. "To please your mother, you went to visit the Seer, and then…?"

She took a breath, and he heard the unsteadiness, so startling that he reached out, only to stop, because he had no clue what sort of touch would be appropriate for a pain he didn't understand. Gavriel gathered his nerve to complete the gesture and finally settled for touching her shoulder. *Don't make me regret this.*

She didn't.

Instead, she put her hand over his, completing the circuit, and suddenly there were fireflies in his veins. It didn't even matter if she stopped talking because there was this instead, and it made him feel that stinging sweetness, like the day of the beehive when Oriel was alive and brimming with mischief.

"Arran said I must resign myself to being alone. That I would be a good friend to many, but I must never love."

Her pain came to him so clearly that it was like taking a blow. "What the hell kind of prophecy is that? It sounds like Arran has his head firmly up his ass."

She laughed, but there was no humor in the sound, only bitterness and regret. "I thought so too. And when I met someone special, I pretended I hadn't gotten that warning." Her face was blank, like a wall of ice, but when he leaned closer, he saw the burning in her golden eyes, a hell she still hadn't escaped.

"What happened?"

"He died." Flat tone.

Gavriel didn't press, positive she wouldn't say more. "That could be a coincidence. Terrible things happen, and you're not to blame, just because you—"

Loved him.

Somehow, he couldn't even say the words aloud. They would cut his mouth to shreds, as did the thought of her loving someone, someone precious whom she'd lost. He had no idea why his chest hurt. *This is abominable.*

"We think more alike than one might suspect," she said softly. "Because once wasn't enough for me. I still didn't believe it could be true, not really. Then it happened a second time."

Gavriel swore. "Is it…may I hug you?"

"If you want," she muttered, like he wasn't dying to do exactly that.

He wrapped his arms around her, fearing that she'd bite him, and then he'd be inappropriately aroused instead of suitably supportive. Offering comfort was all strange seas to him because Oriel had been the gentle one, the kind one, as if their unknown mother had split tenderness and rage in the womb, giving the entirety of one to each of her sons.

Her breath gusted hot against his neck when she tucked her face against his shoulder. Perhaps it was easier to speak with her face hidden. Whatever the reason, he didn't discourage it.

"What happened after that?"

"I stopped letting people get close to me. When I went to see Arran, he didn't say 'I told you so', but he was so grave and sad. He actually said, 'the signs are clearer now, Mags. There's a shade on you and only death could stand against it'."

"…A shade?"

"It's a bit complicated, but my people believe in past lives. The gist of it is that I must have done something pretty terrible to be punished like this now."

Gavriel hadn't known that, and he filed it away under interesting facts about the Animari. "Is there no way you can atone? A ritual or…" He gave up because his religious training was inadequate for Eldritch purposes, let alone for giving cross-cultural advice.

She touched his cheek gently. "Unfortunately, no. Or I would've done it already."

"It's still not your fault," he said.

"It is, though. Because that was my fate, and if I'd respected Arran, if I'd listened, those I loved would have been safe. But I was selfish, I wanted…" Magda sighed. "You know what I wanted."

"The warm and happy home, little tiger cubs running about," he guessed.

"That, and to please my mother. She wouldn't shut up about our family line, and we fought so hard over it that she left Ash Valley. I haven't spoken to her in two years. Last I heard, she was living in Hallowell, and I don't even know if she survived the battle. I haven't been able to work up the nerve to call. She said not to unless I was ready to 'do the right thing'."

"I know very little about families, but you're certainly more than a gene packet. Your mother should see that."

"I wish she did," Magda said softly. "But she thinks I'm being stubborn."

"You haven't told her what the Seer said, or what you've already suffered."

She shook her head against his shoulder. "It's better that I carry it alone. Nobody else needs to know."

"Yet you told me."

"I thought it might reassure you. This way, you can be sure I'll never ask more of you than you want to give. We can enjoy each other and when the time comes, part with no regrets or repercussions."

Her words should fill him with elation and relief, so why did it feel as if she had dropped a brick on him instead?

"Thank you for trusting me," was all Gavriel could manage to say.

"You've told me some deeply personal stuff as well. It must be the setting." She raised her face enough for him to glimpse a half-smile, as she gestured at the dim room.

"It does feel as if we're the only ones in the world at the moment."

"Probably the storm...and the early hour. Later, the inn will be bustling."

Since she sounded better, more level, he should withdraw, but he couldn't make himself pull away. Not while she was content to stay in his arms.

"Little as I like it, I suspect we have no choice but to bide here for a few days."

"Better than freezing to death," she said in a philosophical tone.

A sudden thought occurred to him, and he couldn't hold the question. "Is that why you're so focused on doing the right thing? Because you didn't in a past life, and you're trying to make up for it?"

"Could be, I suppose. I never thought of it like that, but...it would be nice if I got to be happy in my next life." Her wistful tone twisted his heartstrings.

Though Gavriel wasn't prone to wasting his energy on useless fancies, a small part of him wished she could be happy in this one.

14.

AT SOME POINT, Mags must have gone back to sleep. Surprising, because she never did that. In Ash Valley, she'd get up at dawn, throw herself into a brutal workout, then spend the next twelve hours busting her ass in the security office. This morning, however, she stretched and lazily assessed the slant of light creeping across the floor. Late morning, she figured.

There was a plate of food with tepid tea on top of a box nearby, and a bucket of cold water waiting by the stairs. In all fairness, it was probably warm when it arrived. Gavriel was gone.

She washed quickly and started to get dressed when she realized all her clothes were missing. *Hell, what's this about? If he thinks I'm up for playing these sort of sex games, well, he'd be right, only he needs to be the one waiting for me naked.*

With a shrug, she ate her breakfast. Afterward, she gave thanks for her short hair and slicked it to her head with the clean water, then she fashioned a wrap out of her camp blanket and went to see what the hell was going on downstairs.

The room went silent when she tromped down, and

that was saying something, considering the packed bodies and the din of cheerful conversation. Forty Eldritch eyes—or more—locked onto her, and they were all staring like she might suddenly burst into flames. Or hell, her hair might already be on fire from the intensity of these looks.

"Hey," she tried. "I couldn't find my pants. Did you ever have a day like that?"

Haryk rewarded her with a snort that could've been a laugh, and then Keriel was chuckling. Like a bad cold, a good laugh was contagious, so pretty soon the whole room was chortling. That was a nice change, not being the serious-as-hell Magda Versai. Since these folks didn't know what to expect of her, she could leave some of that pressure behind.

"We laundered your things," Keriel said when she caught her breath. "Gavriel brought them down earlier, but I don't think they're dry yet. I doubt we have anything..."

To fit me. Mags mentally finished that sentence and she didn't flinch over it, though it was exhausting to be the biggest. Though she didn't regret her strength, sometimes she did wonder what it was like to be a fragile, petite woman who made people want to protect her. Too often in the past, others had assumed her size meant that she didn't also have feelings, that she could suck it up through anything and remain tough as nails.

She played it off with what she hoped passed for a gracious smile. "I don't mind the blanket if you don't. What's the weather like out there?"

"Still wild as a pagan feast," Haryk answered.

Mags wasn't exactly sure what he meant by that, but when she went to the window, the snow was fluttering so thick, clinging to the half-frozen pane, that it must be fucking miserable out in it.

"Are the stables warm enough?" She was thinking about Gray, but Keriel flashed her an amused, knowing look that startled her.

"Gavriel's fine. No need to worry. And yes, the stables have heat, just as we do. We can't leave the animals to freeze."

She guessed that meant Gavriel was out checking on the vedda beast; that struck her as strangely sweet. The Noxblade was gentle when nobody was looking. Hopefully, he'd taken some precautions, however, and wouldn't get lost on his way back.

As if Haryk read her mind, he said, "We've strung lines between the main buildings. If he doesn't return soon, I'll check on him."

Just then, the door banged open, revealing a windblown and shivering Gavriel. Two Eldritch nearby helped him slam it shut, and then they barred it for good measure. *Guess nobody else is out in this.*

"Did you fear I'd freeze to death two meters from shelter like a fool?" he asked, instead of 'hello' or 'good morning'.

Part of her got pissed over the fact that nothing had changed between them, despite what was said in the wee hours, but on the other hand, it should mean she could trust him not to focus on her sad story. That was what she feared most of all, the moment when she stopped being Mags and became a tragic figure that people tiptoed around, whispering about her misfortune.

Smiling, she took verbal aim at him. "Well, you're not likely to freeze, but I may end you if you steal my clothes again."

"They were filthy."

He swept past her to crouch by the fire, extending his hands toward the crackling flames. The children were playing on the rug with little carved tokens. The game pieces reminded her of the dark stone carving they'd found on one of the hunting parties. This might be a good chance to see what the others made of it.

It should still be in my pack.

Without another word, she rushed back upstairs to rummage in her pack. Gavriel followed, much to her amusement. He stood by the stairs, arms folded.

"You have nothing left to wear, if that's why you're digging like a rodent."

"Do they burrow? I don't know that much about wildlife, except what's most delicious." That was probably more than his crack warranted, but it was still fun to watch his fastidious shudder.

"You are horrifying," he declared.

"Thanks. And I'm looking for the rune thing we found. Someone here might know what it means. It's worth a shot anyway."

"Good thinking."

As her hand closed on the stone, she registered those two simple words of praise and stared at him in mock amazement. "Did you just compliment me? Oh shit, we're in the end times. Hell truly has frozen, that's what this spring blizzard means."

"Shut up." But a smile was pulling at the edges of his mouth, and it even reached his eyes, warm and soft as they never were.

For a few seconds, they just stood and smiled at each other.

Oh God, this is weird. I have to stop.

"Anyway, I'm heading back down. Take your time."

Mags rushed past him down the rickety stairs, wooden skeletal things that bent a bit with her weight. She'd long since lost her taste for telling people, 'it's muscle, dammit', because frankly, even if it wasn't, it was nobody else's business. In some ways, it sucked to be surrounded by so many slender, ethereal types, who lived off mushrooms and sunlight, or so it seemed.

Her stomach growled. She'd already eaten more fish and vegetables than she ever had in her life, and there was no break from it in sight. Hell, she'd do her own hunting if it was feasible, but not in this weather.

Whatever, no point in pouting over what couldn't be changed.

This time, her appearance didn't stall out the chatter, and she slid up to where Haryk was discussing drainage methods with some farmer who'd gotten stuck when the storm broke sooner than expected. The proprietor cast her a questioning look.

"Anything you need, madam?"

She'd never been called that in her life, and she grinned. "That's all kinds of wrong, makes me feel like I need to open a brothel and buy some red velvet drapes. Please, just call me Mags."

Haryk rewarded her with a shocked look, then a belly laugh. *Yeah, I got jokes. I could do this all day.* Kind of strange how at ease she felt here, considering how many Eldritch nursed prejudices about her people.

"Mags, then. What can I do for you?"

She produced the dark stone with the unusual carving and showed it to him. "Ever seen anything like this?"

The innkeeper shook his head. "Sorry, no. Where did you find it?"

She wasn't ready to spill that, but while she was considering her next move, Keriel dropped the tray she was holding, spilling spiced wine all over the wood floor. The red liquid trickled outward, seeping into the cracks, while the other woman shivered, eyes locked on the token. Keriel never had what Mags would call good color, but now she was white like a dead fish belly, ashen and quaking like a sapling in a storm.

Rushing toward her, she deftly leapt the puddle. "You recognize this? Tell me what you know."

GAVRIEL REACHED THE common room in time to hear that question, to see Magda give the Eldritch woman a little shake. Some of the men stirred, like they might intervene to protect their own, and he fixed a dagger stare on them, until they subsided in their seats. This scene would play out without interruption because he wanted to know too.

Keriel cast a desperate, fearful look at the other Eldritch, and then she put her hand on Magda's arm. "Can we speak privately?"

Belatedly Gavriel recalled that he hadn't told the others that the refugees hailed from Ancalen, a town situated in Gilbraith lands. "That's a good idea," he said, and thankfully, the tiger woman could take a hint.

She let Keriel pull her into the kitchen, and Gavriel followed. The room was even warmer than the common area, likely because it was smaller, and there was a fireplace in here too, along with a stove that ran on wood, not solar power.

"Sorry, I didn't mean to scare you," Magda was saying.

"It's all right. I just wasn't expecting to see that in your hands."

"What is it exactly?" Gavriel cut in.

"I'm not entirely sure, but I saw the Dead-Eyes flashing them before they bought...whatever it is they take. To make them like that."

"So it's a ticket to ride," Magda said thoughtfully. "They can't buy the drug without one of those? Somebody must be handing them out like permission slips."

"That's really all I know," Keriel said quickly. "I should go tidy up the mess I made or the children will track it everywhere."

Gavriel nodded. "Go ahead."

Visibly relieved, Keriel rushed off and Magda stood staring at the rune in her hand. "I would love to know who's responsible for selling our meds to the Eldritch. Their asses need kicking."

"Agreed."

"But I have no idea. Could be Ash Valley, Pine Ridge, Burnt Amber, Hallowell, or some little satellite settlement that badly needs the revenue."

"Would you blame them less if they did it out of desperation?" Gavriel asked.

She cocked her head, seeming startled by the question. "I guess so. As motives go, greed and survival are poles apart."

"You don't believe in moral absolutes, then. The end justifies the means. Perhaps there's more Eldritch in you than I would've guessed."

Her golden eyes snapped at him, and oddly, the unease that had plagued him since her confession that morning dissipated. He was used to her anger, not her vulnerability.

"Screw you, shadow warrior. It's still wrong, don't twist this around. I'm just saying I'd feel a bit sorrier about the ass-kicking, that's all."

He didn't hate the nickname she'd bestowed upon him. It was far better than most names he'd been called, including murderer, devil, bastard, and demon. Now he feigned annoyance because it had almost become a game they played, one that left him hiding a smile in his heart instead of seething anger.

To provoke her, he said, "Seems saving these people wasn't a waste of time. We learned something anyway."

"Just when I think you're less of an ass, you come out with a comment like that. Are you trying to piss me off?"

Yes. Of course I am.

Because the crackle of outrage suited her much more than the shadow of a broken heart. He couldn't mend the wounds that the Seer had inflicted on her by pronouncing her curse, but he could distract her from it. Perhaps this was the first time he was glad to have such a rotten personality, a disposition so sour that only his twin had ever been able to tolerate it.

Love, not tolerate.

Oriel had been the only one. And his death was a wound that would bleed until Gavriel finally managed to die himself. Sometimes he tried to stop the tide, but mostly he held onto the pain like it was a knife clutched between his palms, because that anguish was better than nothing at all. In a way, he could understand Magda Versai since he wasn't destined for a cozy home or a loving mate, either. Now he was a ghost or an echo, slinking from shadow to shadow, because the light would burn him alive.

When she started berating him, he laughed. Nobody else would dare, and it was absolutely, exquisitely endearing. Magda feared nothing, not his bad temper, his vituperative words, or his potential retribution.

"What's so funny?" she demanded.

For a bit, he couldn't catch his breath to reply. Gavriel couldn't recall ever laughing like this, not until his sides hurt. "Our situation," he finally gasped.

"What a crock."

Her mystification only amused him more, and she came at him in a fury, ready to beat to his ass. When he caught her wrists, he could tell that she let him stop her, and that felt like... well, he didn't know what.

"Careful. You shouldn't start what you can't finish. We're in the kitchen, you understand. They won't understand if you do indecent things to me on the food prep table."

With a snort, she flung his hands away and took a step back. "My fault. I forgot that combat feels like foreplay to you."

But her tone was matter of fact, not mocking, and it eased him for that to be something she understood, not an inclination that filled him with shame.

"I didn't mean it," he said, surprising himself. "When I said that about saving them. They were worth it, even if we didn't unearth a clue."

"And I like you again," she told him, smiling.

"You're so capricious and easily moved." He wanted to touch her then.

Not for sex, not to be held down or taken, but to trace the curve of her cheek, to see if the cinnabar roses there were as warm as they looked. To press his fingertip into the dimple peeking at him with the hint of her smile. And those eyes, did she always have lashes so dark and thick, like little fans flirting with each blink. Exactly when did her golden eyes get those green flecks anyway? They couldn't have always been there, waiting for him to notice.

Sweet hell, it's warm in here.

Gavriel took a single step, but thank the fates, Keriel stopped him from yielding to whatever impulse was driving him, when she rushed in with the messy tray and red-stained rags. Right, she was cleaning up the wine she spilled.

He could breathe again, but each inhalation tasted faintly of regret. With a mumbled excuse, he hurried out of the kitchen and joined the others. Yes, safety in numbers. Hiding among his own kind would shield him from this Animari enchantment.

Please let us leave here soon.

If the weather didn't break by tomorrow, maybe he'd brave the storm. Otherwise, he'd lose the last of his good sense, and he'd say something he couldn't take back.

Worse, he might give himself to Magda Versai in ways she didn't want, and he'd had quite enough of being rejected by those who couldn't love him. The word drew him up short, and he shook his head, angry at himself. There was no emotion in what they were doing; that was the whole point.

It was only because he'd never done this before. Her acceptance must be confusing him, making him entertain absurd fantasies. This one topped the list, and he'd—

"Tell me a story!" Leena plopped herself into his lap, a welcome distraction from the wild humming of his thoughts.

Everyone was watching as if they expected him to shove the child onto the floor. Instead, he snuggled her close and said, "Very well. What sort of a story?"

"With a princess and a dragon and a very sad curse." Some little girls knew exactly what they wanted, it seemed.

"No handsome knight?" he asked.

Leena shook her head. "Handsome knights don't need a story because people love them wherever they go, but people scream and run away from dragons, so they need a princess even more."

Gavriel stared at her, wondering if he was unhinged to take her remark personally. "You'd rather love a dragon?"

She patted his head with the fearlessness of the very young. Gods, Leena was starting to remind him of Magda. "Definitely. He'd always protect me and take me flying and let me have some of his gold."

He swallowed hard, hating the sudden twinge in his withered heart. "Yes. He would. All of it, most likely, if you asked."

15.

As Mags soon discovered, it was impossible to keep people at a distance when you were snowed in with them.

Before the day ended, she had played four children's games, read eight stories, crafted a makeshift dartboard, and won a drinking contest, which frankly wasn't fair, given her accelerated metabolism. The drunken Eldritch on the floor didn't seem to mind. Haryk was bellowing some folk song at the top of his lungs, despite all attempts to shush him. All things considered, she felt almost at home.

When she got up to pour herself more wine, as alcohol wore off too fast for her to enjoy it, a powerful thump shook the whole door. Most of the Eldritch were bosky, and she snickered as Haryk tried to wobble to his feet, then tipped over. Gavriel had abstained and he went over to call out.

"Who's there?"

"A nearly frozen trader. Open the damn door!" came the bellowed response.

Since the Noxblade didn't seem inclined to show mercy, Mags slid back the bar and the wind howled into the room, carrying whirling snow and bits of ice and an extremely large Animari male. And for *her* to take note, the man was immense.

Like he'd said, he was dressed as a trader, loaded down with pelts and skins, though some of that might be his own gear. His beard was black and silver, needed a good trimming, and he wore his hair long with a silly ushanka hat jammed down so that the fur flaps covered half his cheeks. Not handsome—he had a face like a rugged cliff, ravaged by wind and rain. His gray eyes were sharp, and he seemed surprised to see her. Oh, he covered it well, but he'd already clocked her as Animari and the lowering of his brows in conjunction with the flaring of his nostrils told her he recognized her as a tiger also.

Interesting as hell, because she was doing the same. A tiger man in the flesh, after all this time. *Wouldn't Ma be elated?* That bitter thought made her smile. But she'd never run across the stranger's scent trail before; he'd never been to Ash Valley, and he must avoid other Animari like the plague because there were no other scents on him, just vicious cold and wildlife.

Wonder why.

The newcomer might've guessed she was wondering about him because he pulled off his hat and shook himself like a wet pup. Not much feline grace about this one. Maybe living outside of a pride had done it, or possibly he was never a good cat in the first place.

Haryk managed to get to his feet, unsteady but upright and he beamed at the new arrival. "Titus! I wasn't sure you'd make it, lad. The weather took a nasty turn."

"As I was nearly done in by it, I'm well aware. Make way," he said brusquely, and Eldritch children scattered around his legs like falling dominoes.

He sank down in front of the fireplace with an audible groan and dropped his pack beside him. Leena crept closer, quick as a trained thief, and soon she was peeking in various pockets and compartments. Though Mags couldn't get a good look from where she was standing, it seemed like in addition to his skins and furs, the trader also had statuettes carved from wood and bone.

"What're you looking for, little rabbit?" Titus reached out to tousle Leena's hair with a big hand, but she ducked away, eyes wide.

"Are you a giant? Do you *eat* rabbits?"

"No, and yes."

That probably wasn't the best reply because he'd just called the Eldritch girl a bunny. Unsurprisingly, she shrieked and took shelter behind her mother.

The stranger sighed, closed his pack, and directed his attention to the innkeeper.

"We've got a full house," Haryk was saying. "I can't give you the usual room. In fact, I'm hard-pressed to figure out where you can sleep at all. You take up a lot of space."

Mags stifled a chuckle. It was the sort of tactless thing people had been saying to her for years, but Titus appeared to be used to it. He would be, she guessed, if he made regular supply runs to this Eldritch village. The real question was why he chose to live here instead of among his own people.

It was none of her business, really, but she was curious. There was some saying about curiosity and cats, of course, but she'd forgotten how that went, and even if it was bad news, she had a history of ignoring well-meant, cautionary words.

Even now, years past those terrible times, the memory

could cut down to the bone, past the protective scar tissue, and leave her bleeding. She breathed in. Out. Looking at the stranger, but not really seeing him, until she realized her blank regard had drawn his gaze.

With a grace impressive for his size, Titus uncoiled from the rug, took a few steps closer, and asked softly, "Do you need help, glorious queen? I see these wicked villagers have stolen your clothes."

Oh shit.

Suddenly, she realized she was still wrapped in her camp blanket, not a stitch beneath it either. Since she was meeting this man for the first time, maybe she ought to be embarrassed. Mags threw back her head and laughed.

"It's true, they got them while I was sleeping, and they badly needed washing. I appreciate the offer, but I'm fine."

"You look as if you can fight your own battles," Titus admitted with a tilt of his head, eyes sparkling. "But never let it be said that I left someone so lovely in the lurch. Let me know if there's anything I can do, anything at all."

He flicked a look at the Noxblade that indicated he could smell Gavriel on her skin, and he wanted to cause trouble. *This is probably why he lives alone.* Amused and willing to see how far the tiger male would go, she didn't snap Titus's wrist when he touched her shoulder and ran a hand down her arm. Mags stared at that point of contact until Titus pulled away, his mouth twisting into a self-satisfied smirk.

Then he leaned in to whisper, "As I'm sure you've gathered, lovely, I prefer to walk alone, but I'd be more than happy to leave you something to remember me by."

The sheer devil's nerve of this cat. "Are you offering sex or stud service?"

"Both, if you like. I'm vain enough to want to see my line go on, lazy enough that I'd rather not raise them myself. And you look like the responsible sort."

Ma would be over the moon. For a few seconds, she was even tempted. But while Arran had been perfectly clear about her never having a mate, he hadn't mentioned children. It would kill her if she lost a cub. *I can't take the risk.*

"No thanks," she said politely.

A sharp bark of laughter escaped the tiger male. "You'd think I offered you tea instead of a night you'd never forget."

Just then, Gavriel made a disgusted noise and stalked into the kitchen. Before Mags could do more than spare a look in that direction, he was back with an untidy bundle of cloth. The Noxblade thrust the fabric at her with a ferocious scowl. "These are a bit stiff but ready to wear. Get dressed."

That sounded perilously like an order, and he half-stepped between her and the Animari, like the sight of her bare shoulder might drive the man into a fit of uncontrollable lust. *Then again, he did just proposition me.* She considered taking issue with Gavriel's attitude, but since angry and grumpy were his default settings, this was business as usual.

"Thanks," she said to Gavriel, then she added to Titus, "Isolation may have clouded your judgment a bit, but I'll take the compliment. And for the record, *you'd* be the one who couldn't forget."

It felt good to flirt because apart from Raff, people didn't even try anymore. The reputation she'd built for being untouchable and unattainable protected her heart— and the safety of others—but it also left her lonely. She stepped lightly up the stairs, conscious of the flexing wood, and put on her clothes; the lighter set must have dried faster than her outdoor gear. Good enough, she wouldn't be going outside until the storm broke anyway.

In some ways, it felt as if that casual offer might have been her last chance. But no, her course was set. There could be no more mistakes, no more loss. The warmth of a mate and family were not for her.

Gathering that certainty like armor, she headed downstairs, only to find that Gavriel was gone.

THE WALLS WERE closing in on Gavriel and there was a ringing in his ears, so loud that it muffled the conversation swirling around him. And it was so damn hot, between the close quarters and the fire, that he might burst into flames.

"I'll check on Gray," he muttered.

His coat wasn't dry from his last excursion, but he put it on anyway and rushed into the swirling wall of white. He grabbed onto the line that led to the barn and held on with all his strength, fighting the wind as he wanted to fight the fucking Animari asshole who—well, Gavriel had no right to be angry. No right to want to smash the man's face for leering at Magda.

It wasn't jealousy. It was *not*.

How was he supposed to feel about that blatant disrespect, though? If the man had the usual Animari senses, he must know there was something between them, yet he'd chosen to act as if Gavriel didn't exist, not even worthy to be considered a rival. Not that he saw himself as such. They were expedient partners, who happened to be sexually compatible. That was all.

So why do I want to murder him?

He got inside the stable and with full strength, managed to close the door behind him. The animals seemed well enough, secure in their stalls, and the boy who lived in the loft had been tending the fire in the belly of the stove. The young Eldritch peered over the railing at him and Gavriel silently shook his head.

I don't need anything. I'm hiding.

That angered him even more.

But he couldn't have stayed in the common room to watch more of that revolting nonsense. Better for him to withdraw. If need be, he'd sleep in the loft with the stable boy, though he felt like chewing through a leather strap at the idea of yielding his place to that smug tiger bastard.

There was nothing to do out here except tend to Gray, so he tried to calm himself by grooming the vedda beast, who preened beneath the attention and let out happy chuffs. Sighing, Gavriel leaned his head against the animal's side. Gray was warm and smelled of summer, likely the fodder he'd been eating.

The stable doors blew open, then slammed shut. He didn't look up.

"Feeling antisocial?" Magda's voice, breathless from the wind and cold, from wrestling the door. She'd put on her outdoor gear even though it wasn't even dry. Wearing it couldn't be doing her any good.

She risked her well-being to follow me?

Stunned, he turned, and it was like seeing her for the first time: dark hair, light brown skin, angular features, those precious dimples, and her wide, full mouth. And oh, those eyes, golden and gorgeous, and his heart fluttered, an all-over quiver, that he felt in his thighs, in his belly, and he didn't know what to do with his hands. The brush dropped to the hay-covered floor with a thunk.

"What do you think?" he muttered.

"That you want to get away from everyone, especially Titus."

"Then you realize he was rude…and you did nothing to stop it."

"He's an ass. And you're angry." Her tone rose, as if sudden realization.

Before he could reply, the boy scampered down the loft. He was young for an Eldritch, twenty or so, still thin and fragile. "Will you be here a while?"

Gavriel nodded without looking at Magda. She could do whatever the hell she liked; he didn't care at all.

"Then I'm off to the public house for a hot meal. Do you think Leena will play darts with me?"

"I'm sure," Magda answered. "We'll stay until you get back."

"Much appreciated." Eyes shining, the boy bundled up and hurried out into the weather, leaving them alone.

Once the doors shut, Magda moved fast, so quick that Gavriel almost flinched, but then he recognized the gleam in her eyes. Hungry, impatient.

"You're angry," she said again. "But you have no right to be. Nothing happened, but even if it did, you can't say shit. You belong to me, not the other way around. If I wanted you to watch me with someone else, you'd take it or say the word."

Gavriel hated himself for the instant surge of arousal. Voyeurism had never interested him, but the idea of being pushed to it? Yes, that was pure heat, pooling in his cock. She got him all the way there when she put her hand on his throat and squeezed. "Nod if you accept what I'm saying."

Gavriel shuddered. Nodded. Now he was both furious and hard. He clenched his jaw and said nothing.

She smiled. "Now then, that's settled. I don't know how much time we have, so let's make this quick."

Grabbing his wrist, she dragged him behind the stove, where the tools were stored. There were a couple of wooden chairs as well, probably left for the stable lad's use. She nudged Gavriel toward one of them, and he sat without thinking, his mind fogged with the luscious possibility of what she might do.

"I'm going to use you. I won't let you move or touch me with your hands. You exist to please me. Understood? I'm going to take what I want, and if you're satisfactory, I'll let you come. Now extend your arms."

Ah, she knew him so well. It would start as slight discomfort, but in time, his arms would get heavy, his shoulders would start to burn, and it would only make the rest better, more intense. His breath came in sharp little pants as she unfastened his trousers and pulled out his cock. Though she'd washed him with the cloth, this was the first time bare hands besides his own had ever touched it. His thighs quivered, tensed, as she gave a few experimental squeezes, just hard enough that a desperate whine escaped him.

"You're such a horny beast," she whispered.

He didn't know what was more acutely arousing, the heat of her hands or the thrill of knowing that with her, the accusation was true. Thankfully she didn't torment him that way for long and skimmed out of her pants as if she'd been waiting for this moment.

"Ask me to take you." Her hot breath teased his ear. "Beg for it."

"Please." The only word he could get out, from somewhere dim and deep.

Then she sank onto his cock in a smooth sweep, grinding immediately with all her strength. She gave no quarter, no chance for him to get used to the feeling. This was all for her—her need, her pace, her desire—and it was just as she'd promised. He was a cock she was using. His arms burned as she fucked him, and it was just so hot and perfect that he went light-headed from the strain of holding back. His heart thundered and he couldn't get his breath. Gavriel gazed at her face in a wondering daze, in and out, light and shadow as she rode him, focused and relentless and magnificent.

God, this feels—

No, can't.

Hold on.

"I'm getting close, Gavriel. Move with me now."

Nearly mindless, he pushed up as she came down, marveling at the sleek heat, the slickness of her. She was panting too, head thrown back, and then she took his hand, and he knew what to do with his fingers because she'd taught him to do it with his mouth first. She gasped and clenched and he managed not to let go, though it was the toughest challenge he'd ever faced.

"There, that's good. You can come. Here, I'll help you." Then she brushed aside his shirt tenderly and bit down on his shoulder, hard enough to bruise, hidden where only a lover would see the mark.

He came so hard that he saw stars and she had to hold him to keep him from falling sideways off the chair. Magda wrapped her arms around him then, stroking his back, his shoulders. Her weight was hurting his legs a little, but he didn't move.

"Thank you," he said hoarsely.

"For what? The great sex?"

Slowly he lowered his arms to complete the hug, hardly daring to touch without permission even now, but she let it happen, and gratitude cascaded through him like fireworks. "For letting me feel this. I thought it would always be strange, dark, and awful, not something I could ever share with someone else, but this…"

It was sheer joy, the sweetest he'd ever known.

16.

THIS IS INTENSE.

Magda understood the importance of aftercare, so she held Gavriel for as long as he seemed to want. And while "You're welcome," seemed like too simple a response for what he was saying, she got that he was unraveling some personal stuff.

Later, he'd be grateful that she'd taught him enough for him to know what to look for when he went searching for a more appropriate partner. Odd, that gave her a twinge, though she should be used to this catch-and-release lifestyle by now.

"You good?" she asked eventually.

"Yes. We should—"

"Tidy up. It's fun to tease about the idea of being caught, but I suspect I'd find the reality more awkward than exciting," Mags said.

Gavriel's reply surprised her with its gentleness. "I agree wholeheartedly."

She didn't know how to handle that look in his eyes, all soft heat. Before, she had thought the color was strange and unsettling, but now, it made her think of lava that ran beneath volcanic rock, warming the world from the inside out.

It was a good thing they got their shit together fast because the stable boy breezed in two minutes after Gavriel buttoned his pants. Gray snorted an unnecessary warning, and Mags gave thanks that Titus hadn't come out, as he'd smell the sex, even amid the barnyard odors.

"Thanks for keeping watch," the boy said cheerfully.

"My pleasure," Gavriel answered, shooting a hooded look in her general direction.

Mags nearly choked. "Yeah. No problem at all. We're heading back now."

The curtain of night had lowered while they were fucking in the stable. Mags paused despite the freezing weather, caught by the unexpected beauty of the sky. There were no solar lights in Kelnora, and the snow had tapered to soft flurries, so visibility was better. *Beautiful.* The sky was midnight dressed in gossamer clouds with stars showing shy faces, and the moon was a silver coin ringed in frayed brightness. In Ash Valley, she never stopped to look up like this, and even if she did, it wouldn't look like this.

She reached out, grabbing Gavriel's shoulder, and he stopped without his usual impatience. Silently she pointed up and he inhaled, an expression of stunned wonder slowly softening his features.

"I don't even care that I'm up to my knees in snow," he said softly. "Have you ever seen anything so perfect?"

Maybe there had been a night like this, long ago. When I was twenty-three. When Brendan was alive. Or Tamara, when I was thirty-two. Other than that, her nights had been spent hunched over a screen in the security office or sparring with Slay. Sometimes she'd listened to him whine about his mother, who wouldn't let him marry his long-time lover, Pru. And she'd swallowed her bitterness, her outrage that his problems were so simple and easily resolved. *You only need a spine.*

I need a miracle.

She spoke none of that aloud. "I don't think I have. I'm glad the storm's over. With a sky this clear, we should be fine to travel tomorrow."

Gavriel shot her an unreadable look but he only nodded. "I hope it's quieted some. The constant noise is a bit wearing."

"That's because you're used to being alone," she guessed.

"True enough. You aren't?"

"Alone but surrounded by people." That encapsulated her situation pretty well.

After she'd fought with her mother, the elder Versai packed her shit and left, and like he always did, Mags's father followed his wife. Sometimes she wondered why they'd bothered having a kid when they wanted a pet, one that could be perfectly trained and taught to perform crowd-pleasing tricks.

Damn, this is really not like me.

She dropped her hand from Gavriel's shoulder and hastened to the public house, not glancing back to see if he was with her. The snow was no longer a threat; neither was the wind.

This interlude was over. Most likely, she should stop fucking him as well. This was the hardest part, quitting before a relationship went bad. All the signs pointed toward a burgeoning attachment, however, and she couldn't let that happen.

Whatever, I don't have to think about this tonight. He wouldn't make a move if she didn't. So that session in the stable could be the alpha and omega of their brief liaison.

Inside, the public house was quieter than it had been, at least. The children were lined up asleep in pallets on the floor, and Titus was sprawled beneath one of the tables, a choice surely, since it was hard for an Animari to get that drunk.

Silently Mags headed upstairs for their last night together. That thought birthed a tangled mess of regret, but she wouldn't change her mind.

Not now.

She'd underestimated how dangerous Gavriel could be. Before, she figured he was the last person who might develop feelings for her—and the reverse should have been true too—but he kept scraping up against her raw edges and finding the gaps in her protective armor. If she let him, he'd find a way inside her walls, like the sneaky bastard he was.

"You're quiet," he said, as she laid out the blankets.

"Yeah."

"Would you talk to me if I asked what's troubling you?"

You are. So much that I don't even know what I want anymore. I only know what I can't have.

Mags didn't answer until they settled under the covers. She didn't push him away when he came close enough to touch her because of course, he wouldn't. Not without permission. But she could feel the heat of him beside her in the blankets, and it was an aching warmth, one she couldn't share with anyone, night after night.

There might be a few days. A week. After that, it was *'good-bye, good-luck and thanks for all the orgasms'*. That used to be enough. It wasn't anymore, and she hated herself for the pointless wishing that filled her head.

"Do you ever wish your life was different?" she asked, instead of answering his question.

"I used to, when training was difficult. I'd imagine that Oriel and I had been mislaid, like lost parcels, and that our desperate parents would turn up, crying because they'd been searching ceaselessly all those years. That wasn't the case, of course. People don't return for what they've thrown away."

Part of her couldn't believe he was speaking to her so openly, and that made everything worse. While she was worrying about him getting too close, somehow, she'd turned into somebody he trusted, and she was probably going to hurt him when she put an end to…whatever this was. It had to be soon.

Just not tonight.

Still, she tried to be what he needed, if only for a moment. "There's nothing I can say. You don't want a hug, and we already had sex. That's pretty much the extent of my emotional range."

"The fact that you're listening is enough," he said, his voice all honey and whiskey, two of her favorite things. "You know, I've never been able to sleep with anyone else. Until you. Why is that, I wonder? Even when I hated you for sleeping on my rug uninvited, I felt…safe. Comforted even."

"What about your brother?" Questions were good. They kept him talking, so she didn't have to.

"Oriel was part of me. Not someone else. That probably sounds strange?"

"Not at all. I get the twin bond. I can't imagine how you deal with…" *Losing him. Losing half of yourself.*

Gavriel turned his face into his arm, hiding that ever-present grief. "You don't."

Oh gods, I want to comfort him. How did this happen? Mags touched his head lightly, stroking his hair, and he let her.

"Guild life must've sucked. You mentioned before that you're a light sleeper."

Gavriel exhaled in a rumbling sound that was almost a purr and nuzzled his head against her hand. "In some ways. We slept ten to a dorm hall, and there was always noise…I don't even know why I'm telling you this. I must be drunk."

Mags knew damn well he hadn't taken a sip, but she let the lie pass. "Probably. Good night, Gavriel."

IN THE MORNING, they said farewell to everyone in Kelnora. Gray was rested and ready to be ridden. Gavriel had mapped the route to Ancalen, though he was still unsure what they were supposed to do once they got there.

Fight a small war, he supposed. For Magda Versai, he'd do exactly that, even if there was no chance in hell of winning.

"You're riding with me?" he asked, just to confirm, because there was no reason for her to shift.

Yet she hesitated, sending a frisson of unease through him. She had been strange last night, and was more so this morning, remote as an untouched, snowy field. Leena ran out of the inn to hug Magda around the knees and the tiger woman bent to return the embrace with gentleness that was all the more amazing because he knew firsthand how strong she was.

"I'll be back," she promised the little girl, who smeared a wet kiss across her cheek.

"You swear?"

"Pinky swear." Magda completed a complicated finger lock and Leena seemed satisfied when she returned to her mother, who was crying to see them go.

Crying.

A buoyant feeling fizzed through him, akin to happiness, but he'd mostly seen that in other people. It was close to how he'd felt, the first time Mistress Alana praised him for completing a mission and taking out one of the princess's most dangerous enemies. Like that but not.

Finally, Magda turned to him. "Conserving my energy makes sense. I'll ride."

"Running in the snow isn't fun," Titus said. "Damned cold on the paws."

"We could get you some tiger shoes." Gavriel couldn't believe he was teasing someone. Teasing.

"I'll knit some," Keriel volunteered.

When Magda smiled and shook a fist at him, it didn't matter that he felt ridiculous. "I will *kill* you."

"Departure now, violence later."

Finally, he got her on Gray's back, and they were riding away. While he was grateful to these folks for offering shelter and glad they'd chosen to save the refugees, he wanted Magda to himself. Privately he admitted that he was tired of sharing her, tired of seeing her smile at other people. Acknowledging that, even in his own head, created a minor mental shockwave.

Ugh. It's like I've caught some terrible emotional disease.

Like before, she wasn't touching him. Instead, she was holding onto the back of the saddle, but now everything had changed, and it pissed him off that she was still giving him space, still acting as she had before she broke him open like a funeral urn and found more than ashes inside.

Reaching back, he took her arm and pulled it around his waist. "Hold on tight. The ground is rough."

"Are you sure?" she asked, in such a grave tone that it seemed like another question entirely.

Still Gavriel said, "Yes," and then she looped her arms around him, pressed her solid heat against his back, and it was so lovely that the top of his head tingled. Not a sex feeling, but the sweetness of it was both extraordinary and exquisite. Nobody ever clung to him. They didn't look to him for heroic gestures or physical comfort.

Gavriel would have ridden a thousand miles like this. Too bad they only needed to go a bit beyond the border.

They stopped a couple of times for food, hydration, and bio. Gray had plenty of vigor, thanks to a long rest in the stables. One night sleeping rough and they should reach the town before noon the next day.

As night approached, he realized that she'd barely spoken, more lost in her own head than he'd ever known her to be. That quiet withdrawal alarmed him. He didn't know for sure what it meant, but it couldn't be anything good. Plus, Gavriel didn't know how to handle a silent Magda; she was fire and agitation, not the frozen stillness of a winter pond.

"Are you feeling sick?" he asked, as they set up camp.

Tent. Heat stick. Freshly washed blankets that smelled of homey kitchen fires and dried herbs. She didn't answer as he tethered Gray beneath a stand of trees nearby. There was no forage for him in the deep snow, but Gavriel had enough left in the bags to get them to Ancalen. He'd refused to accept supplies from Kelnora when they couldn't afford to be more generous than they already had been.

Her voice sounded terse, so he turned to gauge her

expression. "I'm fine. Look, do you remember when you preferred not talking to me? Let's do that."

Perversely, she was giving him exactly what he'd wanted from her in the beginning, which was nothing—and to be left alone—but now it felt like punishment. Gavriel wanted to protest, but he cringed at the words taking shape in his head.

This isn't fair. Did I do something? I can't make it right, if you don't tell me what.

That was far too close to begging, and he wouldn't do that outside of sex. This was something else entirely, so he set his jaw and finished the campsite in angry silence.

It was an hour before she joined him in the tent, and as if she wanted to stress the chasm between them, she came in as a tiger, all dense fur, teeth, and claws.

See, she seemed to be saying. *We're fundamentally different, you and me.*

Once, he'd agreed with that. Could hardly stand to be in the same room with the Animari because when he saw them, he relived the nightmare of his brother's death.

It took him a long time to fall asleep, and when he did, he dreamed.

"You worry too much, brother." Oriel clapped him on the shoulder, all smiles.

He was golden in the twilight, as they waited to be sure they hadn't been followed. Lord Talfayen's men were everywhere, and the princess was desperate to secure this alliance. She'd tried to get her people inside Ash Valley to warn the pride second of the plot she'd uncovered, but that mission failed, leaving them no choice but to approach the exiled pride master at the old seer's retreat.

"And you don't worry enough," he shot back.

"There's three of us," Oriel pointed out, "and by all accounts,

Asher's damn near done in by grief. I'm more worried about whether we can get him out safely. If he's gone feral, he won't understand that this is a rescue mission and he'll fight us to the death for trespassing on his territory."

He nodded, watching the house from his perch on the rock nearby. "The princess feels it'd be best to drug him and take him without discussion. She believes in asking forgiveness instead of permission."

Oriel grinned. "Trust me, I know. We'll get it done. Let's wait until the lights go out. We'll go in quiet and extricate him, quick and clean."

The world blurred, and then it was all darkness. Screaming cats. Smell of blood. He saw it again. Again. The tear in his brother's throat, red everywhere, moonlight and death. The face of the woman who murdered his brother was burned into his brain. She was a human sometimes, sometimes an ocelot, sometimes a monstrous hybrid—a cat with a woman's head.

He wanted to kill them both.

His training won. He ran. To save his own life, he ran.

Gavriel woke with a scream frozen in his throat, sweating and shivering at the same time. For a moment, he recalled that moment when he'd held Pru Bristow at his mercy. *Could've killed her then.*

Sometimes he wished he'd chosen vengeance and family loyalty over the princess's agenda. And right now, he mostly wanted Magda to notice—to ask if he was all right. The tiger curled up in the corner of the tent gave no sign that she realized he was awake. Shivering, he ran a hand through his hair. Remembered how she'd soothed him only the night before, gentle hands, petting his head.

Why am I like this?

The small space smelled of fear sweat and quiet desperation. *It should have been me. Not Oriel.* Silently he used one edge of his blanket to mop his face, then he slipped out into the chill night to settle his nerves. Gray greeted him with a chuff and a stamp of hooves, nuzzling his face against Gavriel's shoulder.

I should be stronger.

It had been a while since he had the dream, not since before he started sleeping with Magda Versai. Maybe it meant something that he was having it again.

17.

IN THE MORNING, Gavriel was his customary self, and Magda regarded the change with both relief and regret. In tiger form, she watched while he packed the camp, then she took off on her own toward Ancalen. If he asked later—and he probably wouldn't—she'd say she was scouting.

Titus had been right, damn him. Tigers weren't meant to run in the snow, and the going was miserable. She was too heavy to run along the surface as a smaller cat might, and she didn't have the snow leopard's broad, fur-lined paws or fatty tail to improve cold resistance. Still, she accepted this misery as a fair price for causing this situation.

It'll probably melt soon, just not fast enough to do me any good.

She smelled the smoke before she saw the town itself, and when she tipped her head back, she spied dark plumes swirling into the sky. Keriel had mentioned that their houses burned before they fled; it seemed like the violence was still raging. If things went on like this, there might not be anything left to save.

Gavriel caught up to her as she paused on the rise overlooking Ancalen. Even from here, she could hear shouts and cries, fear and hysteria. A small war was raging here, and it was unlikely they'd find any allies.

While it was tempting to go in as a tiger, she would draw too much attention, and she had combat skill on two legs as well as four. Making up her mind, Mags shifted and reached for her pack. The Noxblade kept his gaze fixed on the town below, where fresh fires were still burning.

"This is hell, isn't it?" he said. "All along, I thought it was Oriel who died, but I'm starting to think it must've been me. Otherwise, Eldritch lands could never look like this."

She didn't reply until she finished getting dressed, harder than it sounded in the freezing wind and in fresh snow. Her feet were wet and cold, so her socks stuck to her skin and her boots didn't want to go on properly.

"That's not like you, waxing philosophical." She aimed for a light, casual tone, but he didn't respond in kind.

"Don't act as if you know me," he said icily.

From his current attitude, it looked like Mags didn't need to worry about Gavriel trying to take what she chose not to give. Why did that cause such a painful twinge?

"They say war is hell," she answered, refusing to be drawn. "Can't remember who, but it seems accurate. Your skills will come into play here. We need to neutralize as many hostiles as we can while staying under the radar. I'm usually the shock and awe so I'll follow your lead. You say jump, I ask how high."

For the first time since the night before, he met her gaze, a reluctant smile tugging at the edges of his mouth. "That means you're in my hands for a change? I do believe I might enjoy this, provided we survive it."

"Yeah, yeah. Live it up, boss man. What's our first

move?"

"First we surveil the town." He pulled a small drone from his saddlebags then and input a few parameters on the remote. "This will do the legwork for us, so try to be patient, though it's not your forte."

Mags ground her teeth against the urge to bicker with him. That route led to losing her temper, letting down her guard, and then they'd be right back to intimacy, exactly what she was trying to avoid. With great effort, she muttered an assent and rubbed a hand along Gray's flank, earning a pleased chuff from the vedda beast.

"It'll take about an hour for the drone to complete a circuit of the town," Gavriel said, as it buzzed off to do his bidding.

Mags watched until the unit disappeared from sight, then she asked, "You think anybody will notice? Maybe shoot it down?"

He shrugged. "It's a risk, but better it than us, and it's streaming data as we speak."

Moving closer, she saw the live feed on his screen. Buildings on fire, Eldritch against Eldritch fighting in the streets—as they watched, a woman dropped to her knees, maybe to beg for her life, and the man looming over her smashed her skull with a makeshift club. Every part of her itched to charge in and start kicking ass, but she'd promised not to be impetuous. It wouldn't help the people of Ancalen if she got herself killed, overwhelmed by sheer numbers. While Gavriel had his bad points, he knew how to kill quietly, and he always got away with it.

That's what we need right now. Stay calm.

"Understood," she forced herself to say. "How's your shoulder, by the way?"

"A bit sore, but it won't slow me down."

Mags waited in tense silence until the drone returned and Gavriel analyzed the number of targets it had detected. Finally, he glanced up with a grim expression. "There are more combatants than I'd hoped, at least fifty. Many of the townspeople have taken shelter in a stone building at the south edge of town. They don't seem to be letting anyone else in, either, so those caught outside are left to fend for themselves."

"There's no militia or police force?"

"It's up to the governor of the territory. In this case, that would be Ruark Gilbraith, and he follows Lord Talfayen's playbook in that regard."

"Not giving a shit, you mean?"

"Exactly so. He would certainly send a punitive force if their taxes went unpaid, but he has nothing to gain from saving lives or defending people from civil unrest."

Mags growled. "He's probably hoping this will make folks blame Thalia."

"That's one plausible outcome," Gavriel agreed. "This is our entry point. Most of the fighting is centered in the square. If we approach from here..." He indicated a spot on the screen. "There's good cover and the shadows will be with us as the sun sets. Night will grant us greater anonymity and allow us to pick them off without them realizing we've joined the fight."

"I like the way you think."

"This is what I was trained to do. Ordinarily, I'd have a specific target, someone important and well protected. Tonight, my goal will be to kill as many as I can."

"Should we make this more interesting?" Mags never could resist a good bet.

Gavriel raised a brow. "Life and death stakes aren't interesting enough for you?"

"Are you in or out?"

"I'm listening."

"The highest kill count wins a favor from the loser."

"Anything we want?" he asked.

Briefly, she considered tagging a self-protective caveat into the wording. *Nah.* Where was the fun in that? He wasn't going to win, and even if he did, he'd probably ask for something he hoped would embarrass her.

Yeah, good luck with that.

"Yep, anything at all. No whining, no refusal."

"Then I'm in. I'll attach my phone to my belt and start recording once we're in combat range."

"Good idea. I'll do the same. We can count kills together afterward, so there's no doubt who won."

Sighing, Gavriel shook his head with an expression Mags couldn't interpret. "I truly don't know what to make of you. This should be a nightmare for me because I must kill my own people yet now, I'm almost looking forward to it. I ought to find everything about you appalling, but…"

Don't finish that sentence.

"It's horrifying," she said quietly. "But you're helping your people too, doing awful things so they don't have to. And this is a defense mechanism, I guess. Turning the terrible thing into a game so I don't focus on how bad it is." She hesitated, weighing whether to say this and deciding to go for it. "Maybe this sounds callous, but you can't act if you think too much about your enemies. Why are they doing this? What made them take that drug? That doesn't matter anymore, really. Even if they did shitty things for good reasons, they're hurting people and they have to be stopped."

GAVRIEL LET OUT a long, slow breath. Somehow, she always knew what to say. He hadn't thought he had any conscience left, but the frayed tatters of it had been pulling at him. "Nobody will thank me. If Gilbraith prevails, I'll become a butcher who preyed on this town, used it as my private hunting ground to indulge my taste for blood sport."

"Then we make sure he doesn't win," Magda said firmly.

Nodding, he indicated the path before them. "Let's go."

He could've said thanks, but she'd made it clear that he ought to stay on his side of the line. While she hadn't said they were done playing sex games, he'd grasped that fact from her behavior. He should be glad that she wouldn't cling to him and demand emotional outpourings that would confound him and leave him feeling baffled and inadequate. This, this was perfect.

A bit of entertainment, no strings and no regrets. Exactly right.

Exactly over.

They had worked together well before they had sex, and there was no reason past coitus should inhibit their ability to cooperate. He fixed his mind on the mission and led the way around, staying on the other side of the slope. It was unlikely that the chaotic force pillaging Ancalen would have posted a watch, but it paid to be cautious.

If only I'd been careful at the retreat. Grimly, Gavriel banished the memory—the dream too—from his head. Superstitious, but he feared past failure might cloud his judgment and impact tonight's outcome. Part of him couldn't believe he was moving to pacify an entire town in enemy territory because Magda said it was the right thing to do.

While other reasons motivated his decision also, he wanted her to think well of him, even if their brief encounter was done. Of all the Animari in the world, her opinion was the only one that mattered.

He reached the point where they'd enter town and dismounted. After tethering Gray loosely, so he could pull free if they were gone too long, Gavriel patted the animal and turned to survey Ancalen. Magda came up behind him, hunched low and not particularly adept at it. Her awkward attempts to hide made him smile.

So many things about her did.

"Why have we stopped?" she whispered.

"I'm waiting for the sun to drop a little more. Though the days are a bit longer than they were in the heart of winter, it still gets dark relatively early."

"Understood. There's a little food left. We should eat before we move anyway."

"Help yourself." Gavriel preferred not to fight on a full stomach. Food made him sluggish, slowed his reaction times, and sometimes, if the conflict got bloody, it was better not to have anything to toss up.

"I'll wait if you're not having anything," she said.

A flash of annoyance made him glare at her. "Don't be foolish. Your metabolism is higher than mine, and you haven't eaten properly for days."

"I won't pass out," she muttered.

"No, but you will digest muscle and lose strength."

Magda blinked at him, seeming startled by his awareness. "Did you study up on Animari physiology or something?"

Not for all the gold in the world would Gavriel admit that he had, but probably not for reasons that would please her. He'd wanted to know how to make Pru Bristow suffer, how long she could go without food, and how much he could torment her without letting her die. He hadn't given up the idea either, though he had no doubt Dominic Asher would end him for it. Currently, the issue was tabled, until they dealt with Tycho Vega. Then he'd decide once and for all—life or death, forgiveness or revenge.

"Or something. Eat your food, dammit."

As expected, his bad temper didn't faze her, though she did consume the last of their provisions as the shadows lengthened. Finally, he gave a silent signal, leading the way down the hillside toward the dilapidated buildings on the south end of town.

Ancalen was a newer settlement than Kelnora with more wood buildings. Therefore, it was also more flammable. The fires were spreading, leaping from house to house, and soon there would be little left to save. If there ever had been an active fire brigade, they were either dead or fleeing, no help to be had there.

"If we can stop the fighting, maybe we can organize the citizens to put out the fires," Magda said at his shoulder.

Odd how closely her thoughts often paralleled his, though she usually went a step further, seeking a means to help rather than dismissing a cause as lost.

"One step at a time." Nearby, he spotted a fallen combatant, and nobody had the presence of mind to loot the body. After grabbing the rifle on the ground, he handed it to her. "Get to high ground, away from the blaze, and cover me. You'll be more useful if I don't have to worry about you."

She stared at him, fury and incredulity warring in her face. "Are you serious? Do you honestly think I'll hinder you on the ground? I could kick your ass."

"You could, but not silently. You can't disappear afterward, either. This is what I *do*, and you are not asking how high."

"When I said that, I didn't think you'd actually make me jump," she muttered.

"Climb, you mean." Gavriel scanned the terrain quickly and pointed. "The church tower looks sound enough. The chapel is stone and it has a view of the square. When I strike, take out as many as you can from up there and demolish anyone stupid enough to try to melee you."

Finally, she sighed. "Tactically, it's a good position. It will be hard for them to mass enough numbers to overwhelm me in the tower, even if I run out of ammo, and you're right. I can't vanish after a kill like you do. I won't be a liability." With a quick salute, she turned and hurried toward the cathedral.

Freeing Gavriel to head for the square, where the mayhem was taking place.

He was used to fighting alone; this was better. If he was constantly watching out for Magda, he'd make a mistake sooner rather than later, and under these circumstances, it might be fatal. He lacked her ability to heal grievous wounds, and he couldn't walk away from poison either.

What he could do was become a shadow. And he did.

First, he centered himself, slowing his heart and his breathing. This gift also let him fool technical equipment, but the brain sensed things in much the same way. Gavriel let go of everything for the first time in a long while and became what he was most famous for—Death's Shadow.

Even his blades were black, carved from obsidian and tipped with volcanic glass. The handles were wrapped in onyx leather, a final gift from Oriel. That day, there had been no last words, no inkling that things would go terribly wrong, and that Gavriel would be left with these knives instead of his brother.

Now he knew all too well how quickly an encounter could go bad, how unforeseen factors could change everything. That was precisely why he'd sent Magda to the tower. Some mistakes must never be repeated.

In the plaza, the Dead-Eyes were holding court, judging captives by some mysterious criteria. Either they were searching for something or playing a monstrous game because they let nobody live at the end of their diabolical interrogation. The one in charge couldn't be on the drug, however, because he was questioning the prisoners, and none of the Dead-Eyes Gavriel had met could speak.

I'll leave him for last. If he's asking questions, he can answer them as well.

Staying to the shadows, he stalked to the edge the group and struck. He wrapped his arm around a Dead-Eyes' neck and twisted. Sometimes this didn't work, and he had to follow with a silent cut, but the spine popped, and the body went limp in his arms. Perfect. Gavriel dragged the corpse back toward the rim of the frozen fountain. So far, so good.

He hoped Magda wouldn't open fire until he was spotted. If she let him, he could execute quite a few without anyone noticing. Though he'd always secretly hated the nickname his people had bestowed, they'd done it for good reason.

If murder was money, he'd be one of the richest men alive.

18.

THERE WERE TWO Dead-Eyes guarding the church, which suggested something important might be inside. Magda made a snap decision and went up the exterior wall, free-climbing as fast she could manage. The roof tiles were old, but they should hold her weight.

Only need to take five or six steps anyway.

Remembering their bet with a faint smile, she activated her camera and whispered, "It's on, Gavriel," then she clipped it to her belt.

Time to play.

After setting the rifle down carefully, she launched herself from directly above her targets and let her weight do the hard work. They both dropped, and she snapped the first one's neck before he could get up. The other one brought up a gun, but she kicked it away and then followed with an open palm slam to his temples. Normally that would be a stunning blow, not a kill shot, but she didn't pull the strike, and Eldritch bones couldn't survive Animari strength. His skull caved in with a sickening crunch, and viscous blood greased her palm.

Mags smeared that on the dead man's clothing, looking

for a likely place to hide the bodies. *There.* Twenty meters away, she spotted a trash receptacle, big enough to hold these two. She grabbed one, then the other, one on each shoulder, and race-walked to the bin. A couple of heaves, and she hid the evidence of her kills.

Good, Gavriel would be proud.

Why am I thinking about him anyway?

She hurried to the back of the church and collected the bag one of them had dropped, but it only contained a stash of the med that was making the Eldritch weird and violent. Her blood chilled when she recognized the trademark stamped on the vial, even as relief spilled through her.

That's from Burnt Amber's lab. Seems like the leak is a bear problem.

It didn't improve the situation in Ancalen, but she could contact Callum McRae about this; it wasn't an Ash Valley issue. They still had Slay at large, a fact she hadn't forgotten despite taking this detour.

I'll keep this as evidence in case the war priest doesn't believe me.

Mags slung the sack over her shoulder and went back up the wall to retrieve her rifle. There, she hesitated. Most likely she could access internal stairs if she went in the back of the chapel, but there might be more guards inside. Ascending outside didn't look impossible but scaling the tower itself might be a problem without equipment, and she risked being spotted.

Inside, it is.

She dropped from the roof a second time, wincing at the impact in her knees. Their bodies really had cushioned her fall. Then she crept up to the back of the church, listening for signs of life within. If anyone was talking, she'd be able to hear it, but the Dead-Eyes were silent as the grave. To her, it seemed like the longer they took the drug, the more their minds deteriorated, until they were only creatures of rage and violence. Mags suspected that they probably couldn't even follow orders after a while. Somebody had tried to create super soldiers and wound up with a bunch of unruly addicts instead. She'd probably have more sympathy for the Eldritch who got hooked on the stuff, if she didn't feel sure they'd started taking it out of fear of the 'brutal and bestial' Animari.

The door was locked, and she wasn't about to waste time searching their bodies for the key, so Mags used brute force to break off the door handle. That let her pull it open, and she slipped inside, paused to breathe in, searching for more sentries. The fires burning all around messed with her senses, filling her lungs with smoke.

Damn. I'll just go carefully.

Sneaking around like this felt weird. She was used to hunting as a tiger, not crouching on two legs while carrying a rifle, but she'd promised to follow Gavriel's orders, at least for this engagement. Funny thing was, he didn't even ask if she could shoot. That unquestioning confidence in her skills felt pretty good. In fact, Mags was better at unarmed combat, but she did weapons training too, especially after the conclave went boom.

There were no guards in the main worship area, and she debated silently whether she should search the place first, looking for enemies and maybe to find out what those Dead-Eyes were guarding. Finally, she shook her head and started looking for the stairs.

Anyone in here would find her the minute she started shooting and she'd told Gavriel she'd cover him. The longer she spent inside the church, the longer he was working on his own.

That wasn't the plan.

Behind the chancel, she found a narrow staircase that led to a loft overlooking the pulpit. Mags headed up, keeping her head on swivel. The rifle was a welcome and reassuring weight, but she only had so many rounds.

Got to make them count.

The stairs spiraled upward, until she came to a small door. She could feel the cold air coming from the cracks in the frame. This must be the entrance to the tower. She didn't have to break the knob this time, as it wasn't locked.

The door opened easily, and ancient steps led into darkness. She could see just fine with the ambient light, however, so she went up quickly, practically jogging. It had been too long since she split from Gavriel; he might need help.

Normally, she might've admired the view for a few seconds, but hell, everything was on fire, and she was scanning for a ghost. This would be an impossible job for someone without special abilities or advanced equipment, but only a bird shifter could've done better for hunting at night.

There he is.

Mags caught the barest flicker of movement as Gavriel took down a target, then she lost track of him. It was like he *could* fucking vanish at will. A little shiver ran through her, as reluctant admiration sprang to life.

No wonder they call him Death's Shadow.

She didn't make a move, biding her time while he worked, picking off targets with a quickness and precision that amazed her. What the hell was he doing with all the bodies?

Soon the square was visibly less crowded; she guessed he'd taken out ten potential combatants, at least. A few times, she tensed because someone would glance to the side, as if wondering where the person next to them went, but the Dead-Eyes weren't sharp thinkers, and the asshole in charge was too busy screaming at the hostages to notice what was happening beyond his immediate proximity.

Just to be safe, she got in position, checked her weapon, and peered down the scope, zooming in on various faces in the crowd. It was hard to pull back without taking action, especially when she saw the tears streaming down the face of the young Eldritch they had kneeling before the boss man. *Pop, I could take him out right now.*

That'd be instant chaos, easy pickings for Gavriel. Something told her there was a reason he was thinning the opposition first, however, so she refrained. *What the hell are they looking for, anyway?*

Mags leaned forward, straining her ears to the utmost, and she could just make out what the head guy was saying. "Swear fealty. Swear it and swallow this blessed gray tar, the elixir of life. Follow me to glory. To greatness!"

Oh shit. This is a recruitment drive.

That made more sense, as these people couldn't know anything that the houses would find useful. These bastards were just trying to drag civilians into their sick power games. Gavriel had probably gathered as much already.

That's why he's leaving the leader alive. To find out what the endgame is.

At that moment, the Noxblade finally slipped—or maybe he was tiring. Either way, she saw him clearly as he struck his next victim and the man in the center of the square did as well, saving the Eldritch on his knees from being forcibly fed the drug.

"Intruders!" he shouted. "Slaughter them and bring me their heads!"

Mags opened fire.

STILL TOO MANY, Gavriel thought. Too much chaos to predict how this would end.

But Magda was shooting from the tower, as he'd asked, providing cover. When they tried to pursue him, she dropped two running the hardest, and that gave him the chance to slip into the shadows. Not invisible, that was impossible, and they were still hunting him. His heart hammered in his ears, and it sickened him, how thrilling this was.

The guild had trained him too well. Some part of him came alive only when he was stalking a target, pitting himself against life and death odds. The adrenaline pumping through his veins streamed like the most irresistible drug, brutal and euphoric at once.

Now, it was a game of hide and seek. To live, he had to win. Briefly, he spared a moment to worry for Magda in the tower, as there was no doubt where the shots were coming from, but the approach was narrow, exactly why he'd sent her to hold that ground. She should be able to kill them as they came while he picked them off on the ground.

As he decided to trust Magda to carry her half of the plan, a lone Dead-Eyes came around the corner of the building he was using for cover. Gavriel struck and sliced him a crimson smile, then booted him into the shadows. There was no need to hide the bodies so well anymore.

Keep moving. Don't let them corner you.

The leader was barking orders, but his henchmen didn't listen, running with weapons out and murder in their eyes. Too much movement for him to tell how many were left. At least twenty, though the tiger woman was shooting like there was a trophy in it for her. *Wait, I forgot about the bet.*

She'd allowed him a head start, but she was catching up quick. *Can't let her win; it's the principle.*

Still, he was more vulnerable than she was, so he had to pick targets carefully, a spider, not a dragon, as Leena had suggested. In truth, it was flattering that Magda called him a shadow warrior when he was a killer, plain and simple. If he did his job properly, there was no battle, no resistance, only a dead enemy at his feet.

Distracted by these thoughts, Gavriel missed his next strike, his knives glancing off bone instead of the clean slice over pliant flesh. The Dead-Eyes flung him off, nearly strong as an Animari, and Gavriel slammed into the wall. His back popped, not enough to break his spine, but if he tussled with this one too long, it would sap his endurance. He was pulling hard on his gift tonight, and the memory of what happened to Zan haunted him.

This Dead-Eyes was fast too. He barely got his arm up to counter a killing strike, and the blade still sliced across his forearm. An immediate burn told him the knife must be poisoned. Hopefully, it was a toxin he'd trained on, as the guild insisted on a regimen of poison resistance training. That burn traveled up his arm, weakening his grip on the blade, and then the enemy jerked once, twice, and dropped.

Thanks, tiger woman.

Gavriel scrambled, taking the opportunity she'd given him. The square was nearly empty now, just the leader and two bodyguards. Even the boy they'd been tormenting had fled. As he gauged the distance, Mags iced one of the guards, so Gavriel rushed the other. Before the leader could react, she shot him in the knee.

Clever woman.

He shrieked and fell over while Gavriel went toe to toe with the last Dead-Eyes standing. Well, the last in the square anyway. Any moment he expected her to end the fight, but perhaps she was out of ammunition. That, or she respected his kill.

His opponent had no finesse, only fury, and he charged like an enraged beast. Gavriel slid aside smoothly and aimed a kicked at the back of his knees. Not quite strong enough to drop him, though he did stagger. Gavriel slid into a crouch, making himself a smaller target, then he dove and rolled, coming up with his knives in a strike that should have finished the fight. Only this fiend had no sense of pain, no hesitation, and he put his hands in front of the blades, readily impaling his own palms. He didn't react, didn't cry out.

These Dead-Eyes truly are lost.

With all his strength—and his wounded right arm was flagging—he hauled on the knives and tried again, only to fail to dodge a brutal kick to the face. He tumbled backward, tasting blood.

This is why I don't fight.

Fortunately, the toxin on his own blades was working. Not even an Animari drug could counteract the quick impact of Nightbane, a powerful poison that took five days to make properly. Gavriel had brewed this batch personally.

The enemy slowed, stumbled, and then Gavriel finished him with a jab and twist of the knife. Breathing hard, he turned to make sure the leader wasn't hiding a gun, but no, he was rolling around on the ground, leaking blood, and it smelled as if he'd pissed himself.

First things first.

He wrapped the gunshot wound so this disgusting creature wouldn't bleed out, then he knelt, staring into the man's face. At this distance, he recognized him. "You serve House Manwaring," he said in astonishment. "What the hell are you doing in Gilbraith lands?"

The only reply was the sound of hysterical laughter. No matter what Gavriel did or how he pushed, the man refused to speak, though he had been before. His eyes rolled in his head, and he eventually passed out. Gavriel kicked him in the side, but he still didn't rouse.

Magda joined him then. "Any luck?"

"None. There's no getting any sense out of him. I suspect I could torture him to death, and it would only waste our time."

"I'm not a huge fan of torture anyway," she said. "Finish him, then we can clean up any resistance and organize the survivors. There might be something valuable in the church also, but since you're in charge of this op, you should call our next move."

Warmth spread through him, so sharp it left him dizzy. Her respect felt like the finest reward he'd ever received—no, wait, that...might be the poison, making him lightheaded. At the moment, Gavriel could barely rub two thoughts together.

When she stepped closer, her eyes widened. "You're injured."

Just a flesh wound, he tried to say, but his tongue was swollen, and it came out, "Jub a fled wud."

"Shit, do you have an antidote? Will this kill you?"

Probably not. Maybe so.

Currently, Gavriel couldn't muster much concern one way or another. His whole body hurt, and he was tasting colors. Purple was magically delicious, just like crab and seaweed soup. Her eyes smelled like cinnamon fry bread; he'd eaten some in Hallowell, right before everything exploded.

"Wonder if there's any fucking medics left in this town," she muttered, sounding as close to frantic as he'd ever heard. "Come here, I've got you. No, do *not* sit down. Gavriel, open your eyes."

It was nice that she kept saying his name in that worried tone, less nice when she shook him. Feebly he tried to swat her hands away, and then she lifted him. *I'm flying!* Then she was moving fast, wind streaming on his skin, and it felt good because his head had somehow gotten filled with bees, which wasn't the way heads were supposed to feel at all. As far as he remembered.

"Stay with me, all right? I'll figure something out. We're partners, and I promised I had your back. Do you remember me saying I might eventually manage to be your friend? Congratulations, that day is today. We're battle buddies, no take backs, and I don't care who won the bet. Just…stay with me."

That was the last thing he heard, and as final moments went, he figured this one was pretty good.

19.

MAGS RAN IN wild panic, desperate to find some help for Gavriel when she realized it was damn unlikely that there were any doctors left in Ancalen. There was a faint chance somebody with medical skill might be sheltering with the rest of the terrified citizens, but she couldn't risk Gavriel's life on that.

Pausing, she took stock of his condition. He was always pale, but his skin had taken on an ashen, lifeless tone, and his breathing was strained, whistling in his chest. That couldn't be good.

Making a quick decision, she headed for a deserted building marked with a symbol that she recognized, even if she couldn't read Eldritch fluently. *This is a pharmacy.* The windows and doors were smashed, and the place had been looted, but maybe she could find something useful in here. She went in over broken glass, crunching it beneath her feet.

No lights, of course, so she got out her phone and turned on the torch. Shining it around did no good, and time was running out. Gavriel was wheezing, clawing at his throat and trying to fight her, but he had no strength left.

Beyond the counter, there was an open door, leading to

a small exam room. Possibly they'd kept a GP on staff to do a brief checkup before prescribing medication. Hands trembling, Mags laid Gavriel on the bed, wishing Sheyla was here. That would be—

Before the idea even formed fully, she was dialing up her pride mate. *Come on, answer the damn phone. I don't care what time it is.*

"Sheyla Halek." The doc sounded cranky, but then, she always did.

"Mags here. I've got an urgent situation, just listen and advise. Eldritch male, severe case of poisoning. I have no idea what the enemy used and he's dying. Ideas?"

"You don't make social calls, do you?" Sheyla sounded wide awake now and interested. "Does he have any antidotes on him?"

"Not that I've seen and we're nowhere near his pack. Come on, Sheyla. I need a miracle here."

"Then there's only one play. I saved a Golgoth warrior with an Animari transfusion back in Hallowell. Don't know if it'll work the same on the Eldritch, but it's your only shot. You'll need…" As Sheyla listed supplies, Mags raced through the pharmacy, like she was in a competitive shopping contest.

In the end, she had everything ready and she put the call on speaker with Sheyla giving step by step instructions. She wasn't a doctor, so this might kill Gavriel, but he was dying anyway. Mags hissed in discomfort as she tied off her arm. Supplies were primitive and basic, lucky she'd even managed to find needles and tubing.

"This is all guesswork and it may kill him if you're an incompatible donor, but if you don't do this, he'll definitely die, considering the conditions you've described. What's your blood type?"

Mags closed her eyes, momentarily so relieved that she could barely speak to reply. "Universal donor, thank the fates. I'm going for it."

By this point, Gavriel was so far gone that he didn't even flinch when she sank the shunt and started piping her red blood into him. Sheyla was still talking, telling her about how long to permit the donation. The doc paused. "Still with me, Mags? You didn't pass out at the sight of your own blood, did you?"

She let out a shaky laugh. "Screw you, Halek. I'm trying to measure how much I've given him."

"Based on typical arterial pressure, I've been timing you and… stop now."

"On it."

Her hands were none too steady when she cut the flow and sealed the two sites with gauze and tape. *That's probably lack of food combined with excess adrenaline. There's no way I'm this scared.*

Sheyla went on, "Normally I'd recommend getting him on an IV drip, but I doubt you have the supplies, plus if you screw up the intubation, it'll be more trouble than it's worth."

"What else can I do then?"

"Try to get some fluids in him orally. Unless the place has been completely ransacked, there should be some electrolyte drinks somewhere. Keep him warm and massage the affected area. Even if you manage to save his life, if the poison is virulent enough, he might lose functionality—"

"It's his arm. I'll take care of it. Thanks, Sheyla."

"You seem pretty invested. Who is this Eldritch you're trying so hard to save anyway?"

"What? I can't hear you. Must be losing signal." Mags cut the call without a gram of remorse and went to rummage for the drink Sheyla had mentioned.

There were none left on the shelves, but she found a box in the back room. Cracking it open, she grabbed six bottles and hurried back to Gavriel. The lights didn't work, but she unearthed some solar lamps that had been stashed, probably for an emergency less dire than this one, and they still had enough of a charge to brighten the room from utter darkness. While Mags could function well enough using her night vision, Gavriel might be scared if he woke and couldn't see shit.

In the faint light, his color didn't look much better, but his breathing had eased. Sheyla hadn't explained why Mags's blood would help, but she guessed their accelerated healing would give him a fighting chance against the toxin. *Okay, keep him warm.* There was a rough brown blanket folded at the bottom of the cot, so she drew it over him.

What else?

Massage the area.

The wound itself wasn't deep at all, but the dark streaks radiating from it had to be poison-related. She'd given him blood in this arm, reasoning that it was better to get the Animari healing as close to the problem as possible. Mags cleaned the gash, decided it didn't need stitches, and wrapped the wound in gauze, then she kneaded the muscle above and below, hoping Sheyla knew what the hell she was talking about.

At some point in the night, Gavriel roused and she got half a bottle of Vitamil in him before he passed out again. Her eyes felt like sandpaper, but she couldn't let herself sleep. First time she'd ever played nurse, and just her luck, she had to be the guard on watch, too.

It was cold as hell in here, even with the door shut, because there was no fireplace, no functional heat, and all the glass was smashed out front. When Gavriel started shivering, she sighed and got on the cot with him, drawing him close to share her body heat.

He's still alive. Good job.

Mags tried her best not to sleep, but she felt like twice-baked shit. At dawn, Gavriel was breathing much easier, and by the time the sky brightened fully, his face even looked normal, no longer like a fish slowly gasping to death.

She peeked beneath the bandage and found that the scarlet rays had faded to gentle pink, a sure sign that the transfusion was doing its job. Mags didn't know that much about blood work, but she did understand that if their Rh factors had been incompatible, he would've died despite her best efforts. *Hell, if it becomes common knowledge that Animari healing can work like this, the Eldritch and the Golgoth might start kidnapping us—oh shit.* Mags froze, wondering if that was why the Golgoth had been known to kidnap the Animari, even when the Pax Protocols were still in place.

They took Eamon, tortured him. He barely made it back alive. But was there a method to that madness? Medical experiments...?

Alarmed, she considered calling Sheyla to check but then she remembered that the doc was on deck to become the next Golgoth queen, or so she'd heard. Most probably she shouldn't ask Sheyla to pose awkward questions to her mate. Mags didn't trust Prince Alastor even a little, but the former Ash Valley physician did and meddling in somebody else's relationship wasn't her style. Sighing, she cracked open a fresh bottle of Vitamil and grimaced. This shit was terrible; good thing it offered nourishment or there would be no reason to drink it.

When she set her hand on Gavriel's forehead to see if he was feverish, his eyes opened. At first, he looked dazed, but his gaze rapidly focused on her face.

"I'm...alive?"

THROUGH A TERRIBLE throbbing in his right arm, Gavriel struggled to put the pieces together. All he could see was Magda's face, streaked with dirt and blood, puffy eyes, and hair standing on end. *She looks like hell.*

Her gaze skittered away from his. "You owe me, shadow warrior. I've never had to doctor anybody before, and I'd rather not repeat this."

"I apologize for the inconvenience. This is..." He glanced around, unable to identify his surroundings.

"An abandoned pharmacy in Ancalen. You probably want a pain reliever, but I wasn't sure if you had any allergies." She hesitated, then went on with a shrug. "I also can't read Eldritch too well, so I thought it would be better if you told me what to get."

"I'll have a look." But when he tried to sit up, the room spun, and she steadied him with sturdy, capable arms.

That...feels familiar. He fought the impulse to lean into her and rest his head on her shoulder. *It's just a fucking scratch, Noxblade. Tough it out.*

"The blade was poisoned. It must've been something I've developed a resistance to or I wouldn't have made it." He tried that theory and watched her face for a reaction.

Magda's expression told him nothing. "Sure, it could've happened that way."

Belatedly, Gavriel noticed all the medical supplies scattered around: gauze and tape and used IV tubing. He had two bandages on his arm, one for the knife wound, another unknown puncture, tender but not severe.

"You gave me your blood," he said. Not a question.

"So help me, if you say a word about purity," she started.

He kissed her.

Or he tried, rather, but he was weak, and his aim was off. His mouth glanced off her sharp cheekbone and grazed a path to her ear. Still, that was enough to quiet her.

"Many thanks. I can't believe you cared enough to do that for me," he whispered.

"It's not a declaration of love," she snapped. "I'd have done the same for anyone I partnered up with."

"And how many partners have you had in the last ten years?" he asked.

"Shut up."

"I think you mean to say 'you're welcome'." Suddenly, despite his overall exhaustion and intermittent throbs of pain, Gavriel felt as if his whole body was filled with sunlight. He had an inexplicable, illogical urge to tease her. "You know, among the Eldritch, it's said that if you save someone's life, you must take responsibility for them until they repay the favor. Are you prepared for that, Magda Versai?"

She stared at him, eyes wide. Her mouth opened but for long moments, no sound came out. Then she took a step back. "What?"

"It was a joke."

"Are you really Gavriel d'Alana or did some spirit take possession of this body?" she demanded.

He smiled, and it didn't feel strange or unnatural at all.

Perhaps there was some merit in the question because he did feel...changed. By her gift of blood? By the near-death experience? Whatever the reason, he'd awakened feeling lighter, less burdened by things he couldn't change.

Rather than try to explain, he changed the subject. "Get the prescription pad and a pen. I'll write down the name of the pain medication that works best for me."

She tilted her head, visibly confused, and that look was rather...adorable. Oh gods, the emotional disease was worsening. Gavriel feared there was no cure.

"Okay." She did as he asked, then took the sheet. "I'll see if I can find it. Have some more Vitamil, then I'll massage your arm again. Doctor's orders."

Magda bolted before he could ask 'what doctor', but she was back in a flash, offering a battered box. "Found it half-beneath the shelves. I think somebody must've dropped it during the riots that drove the refugees out."

"This is the one." He popped open the carton, unsealed the bottle, then downed a couple of pills, washing them down with the energy drink she'd mentioned.

Foul stuff.

"Finish it," she ordered.

For once in his life, Gavriel obeyed someone besides Princess Thalia without a word of protest. "You mentioned a doctor. Did you find one here?"

She shook her head, as she started massaging his arm. "I called our pride physician. She helped me save you, using an experimental treatment that worked in Hallowell."

"So that's how you knew what to do. I truly do owe you my life."

"Anyone would have—"

"Don't do that," he cut in. "Hasn't anyone ever taught

you to accept gratitude graciously?"

"I don't do anything graciously," she mumbled.

Recognizing her deep discomfort, he decided to let it go. For now. "What's the status in Ancalen?"

"Not sure. I didn't have a chance to clean up any resistance and I haven't spoken to any of the citizens. Last night I was a bit busy."

"Understood. If you're willing to help me a little, I should be able to move. We can take stock together."

She seemed relieved to have a concrete goal again, leaning down so he could grab onto her shoulder. It took a few tries for Gavriel to stand, but once he got upright, his legs were sound enough. The room swam a little and he closed his eyes until everything steadied. When he opened them Magda's face was too close, giving him the perfect opportunity to gaze into her eyes.

She jerked back. "You… you're not passing out, are you?"

"Have a little faith in your medical treatment. I'm doing well for someone who was on the verge of death last night." He moved past her with slow but steady steps. "Let's see how Ancalen looks this morning."

Outside, the fires had mostly burned down. Even without intervention, the buildings that were too close together had been consumed, but the fires couldn't spread farther and some of the stone structures were charred but salvageable.

"We didn't manage that fire brigade," she said with a sigh.

"One can only do what's possible. Last night you made a choice and I'm thankful that you chose me." Before, he'd thought he had nothing left to live for, but in what he'd believed would be his last moment, he realized he wasn't quite ready to quit.

In fact, he'd never lived at all.

They didn't find any sign of the Dead-Eyes. With their leader eliminated, they must have scattered. They'd be attacking travelers at random now, plaguing the forests and the roads, but that threat was less than an organized horde of unquenchable violence. House Manwaring had gambled and lost.

Mags mumbled something, cleared her throat, and added, "Anyway, enough about that. I did what I had to. Today we need to reassure the civilians and destroy any drugs we find in town."

"Agreed. Let's head for the town hall, where they'd taken shelter."

By the time they got there, however, the doors were open, and people were slowly, tentatively creeping out. Not many, Gavriel counted forty-eight, a low number of survivors for the whole town. So many died here, and for no reason at all.

The terrified Eldritch townsfolk whispered amongst themselves before finally nudging a venerable male out as the spokesman. Gavriel could tell his great age in the thinning of his hair and the faint lines on his face. For an Eldritch to show visible signs of aging, he must be ancient indeed. The old man managed a bow.

"We heard the battle last night but didn't dare hope it was anyone who meant us well," he said. "Lord Gilbraith has already ignored so many of our messages."

"Some of your people made it to freedom in Talfayen lands," Gavriel said. "We came in response to their request."

A gasp and a murmur of shock ran through the crowd,

then the old man said, "You mean the lady sent aid, though we're not even her people?"

"The princess believes that *all* Eldritch are her people," Gavriel said firmly. Even if he didn't idolize Thalia as he once had, he still trusted that to be true. She was the best person to lead the Eldritch away from the old ways, into tolerance and prosperity. She would halt damaging, outdated customs and perhaps their people could thrive once more.

"What does she want from us?" a young Eldritch asked, fearful.

"Just remember she helped you when there was no gain in it for her," he replied.

20.

MAGS COULD HAVE barfed.

Even now, Gavriel was serving as Thalia's mouthpiece and it made her want to punch through a wall. She must have revealed some sign of her scorn because suddenly, the townsfolk were staring at her wide-eyed and a few had backed off like she might attack them. Now she was waiting for the 'beast' talk to begin; that would round out the shit storm the last day had been.

Not enough food or sleep and now this—just fucking perfect. I'm tired of this crap.

"This is Magda Versai," Gavriel said. "My partner and the goodwill ambassador from the Animari. She's here to help."

That pronouncement sent whispers of shock through the group—and Mags herself. She mouthed 'goodwill ambassador' at him while he gestured her to silence. That was such a crock of crap that her anger faded to amusement. If Ash Valley had chosen someone for diplomatic work, she'd be the second to last choice, coming in only ahead of Slay, whose temper was even worse than hers.

"A thousand thanks." The feeble Eldritch tried to dip a

bow to her but his knees popped, and Mags caught him with a quickness that impressed all the onlookers. "We had no idea that the Animari cared so much about us," he continued in a humble tone. "I only wish we had more to give you in appreciation than these poor words."

"Eh, I don't need anything," she started, then a sudden thought struck her. "You don't happen to know about another Animari passing through? He would've been with a party of Eldritch." A long shot, but she pulled up a picture of Slay and showed it around.

The Eldritch all shook their heads, until the phone came to a young girl. She stared at it long and hard, then she glanced at her father as if for permission to speak and received a slight nod. "I...think I saw him. Some travelers came to our store just before the Dead-Eyes attacked, and he might have been in the Rover outside."

"Are you sure?" Mags demanded.

"Not completely. It was getting dark by then and I was rushing to fill their order."

"Did they say anything while they were waiting?" Gavriel asked.

"Uhm. Something about Golgerra?"

Mags closed her eyes. *Gavriel was right; I did choose the path that would make it impossible for me to catch up to Slay.* In a Rover, the party they'd been tracking was probably already underground by now and she still didn't know if he was a collaborator or a hostage. As if he could read her mind, Gavriel rested his fingers on her shoulder, a butterfly touch but it settled her down.

Can't scare these nice folks. They've been through enough.

With effort, she calmed her expression and managed a smile. "Thank you. That was very helpful."

"It was?" The Eldritch girl didn't seem too sure, but she smiled back anyway.

The old man took a step toward Gavriel, reaching out for a handshake. "You truly don't want anything from us? Not that we have aught left to give, but—"

"Princess Thalia will send aid workers and supplies when she can. Until then, try your best to rebuild."

"We shall."

"If you'll excuse us, we need to investigate a little more, then we must be on our way," Gavriel added.

Feeling like a jackass, Mags bowed to the group, then they bowed back, and she returned the courtesy. Since she didn't know etiquette from a hole in the ground, that might have gone on all day if Gavriel hadn't intervened. She'd never been so grateful to be dragged away.

"That's enough, my lady ambassador."

Oh gods, he was teasing her again. This day was a twisted nightmare that simply wouldn't end. If she had to hear him sing Thalia's praises one more time, she might bite him. No, dammit, he'd enjoy that, and for once she didn't want him to.

How am I supposed to punish a man who gets off on pain?

Muttering to herself, she increased her pace. "We need to check out the church. It was the only building under guard."

"Good idea. Lead the way."

She cut a sharp look over one shoulder. "Is everything okay? You hate following people, especially me."

He smiled at her, and the look was so warm and inviting, even the teasing crinkle of his eyes, that her heart quickened. *Oh no you don't. Stop that.*

And then he said, "That's true, but I do love to watch

you leave."

"You mean that you want to be rid of me or...did you just compliment my ass?" She nearly tripped on a crack in the pavement because she was staring in shock.

"Take it as you will," he said, still smiling.

"We have to get you to a doctor. There is something deeply wrong with your brain." She shook her head in disbelief, wishing that her pulse would stop reacting to his weirdness. "Maybe a Seer. An exorcist even."

"Stop prattling and pay attention. There could still be hostiles about." Now that sounded like the Gavriel she knew and...

Nope. No reasonable way to finish that sentence. Mags was wickedly good at closing off roads she couldn't travel down, so she hurried into the church, only to realize that Gavriel wasn't quite keeping up. Gritting her teeth, she offered her arm so he could lean on her, and it was totally fine when he linked his with hers as if they were lovers out for a stroll, not work partners who sometimes had sex.

"If you hid drugs in a church, where would you put them?" she asked.

"Below the nave."

"You mean the basement? Just say that."

"Cranky. I didn't let you rest enough last night."

Dammit, why did everything he said today sound flirtatious and suggestive? Maybe he really was possessed. With effort, she ignored the provocation and started looking for the stairs down.

They were on the opposite side as the ones that led to the tower, and the door was locked. Mags was about to break it down when Gavriel said, "Allow me." He fiddled with the lock until it clicked open, then he put away some small tools that had been concealed in an inner pocket. "Part of my training. You should probably go first, just in case."

To anyone else, that might sound like he didn't care about her safety, but for Mags, it registered as an endorsement of her skills. Since Gavriel didn't trust anyone, it mattered that he believed she could handle whatever might be waiting down in the dark.

The minute she opened the door, she smelled blood. And Slay. Holy shit, his scent was all over this fucking stairwell. She flicked the torch from her phone on, not much juice left, just to make sure the walls leading down weren't smeared with blood.

So far, so good.

Until now, she hadn't been sure about the girl's testimony, but now Mags was positive. *Slay definitely passed through Ancalen.*

"What's the matter?" Gavriel asked, touching her shoulder.

"Slay." Not much of an explanation, but clearly he got it when he didn't ask for clarification. "Let's keep moving."

Maybe he never made it out of here. Her heart was banging like an angry neighbor on a shared wall as she shined the light around, picking a path down the steps, which were old and cracked in spots, yielding under her solid weight. Eventually, she hit bottom, a packed earth floor, and the smell of blood intensified.

"Someone may have died here," Gavriel said softly. "Was it...?"

There was no body. That much, she could be grateful for, and the soil had soaked up so much blood that she couldn't be sure. It took a lot to kill an Animari.

"There's a chance he made it out alive." She whispered

the words like a prayer, hopeful yet aching.

Sorry, mate. I chose to help strangers instead of you.

"He was here, though?" Gavriel asked.

"Yeah. Held for several days, by the smell of the room. And they hurt him a lot."

"Then he's a captive, most likely. If he was a valued ally, they would treat him better and you wouldn't have found those bloody bandages along the trail, either."

She swallowed hard, trying not to cry. "Does it make me a terrible person?"

"What?"

"The fact that I'm glad."

THERE WERE EMOTIONAL devils in Gavriel's head, and he listened to them. They whispered that he should put his arms around Magda, and he was mildly surprised when she didn't shove him away. Instead, she leaned on him, just a bit, enough that he could feel her trust, her warmth, her weight, and revel in the sweetness of that trifecta.

"Mags…" He tried out of that diminutive form of her name for the first time, relishing it too, as if it was an endearment known only to him, instead of the name she offered everyone. "Of course not. I understand why you'd ask, but it means you haven't lost your friend."

She trembled a little in his arms. "Yeah, but it also means he's suffering and I'm happy about it. That's—"

"Enough," he interrupted. "You've learned some important facts today, possibly enough to save him. Take satisfaction in that and don't regret what can't be changed. Someone extremely wise taught me that."

"That person sounds like an ass," she muttered.

"I thought so at first, but the more I listened to her lectures, the more sense she made."

"You got brainwashed."

"If you keep arguing with me, I may have to kiss you."

"What?"

Her face jerked up, and though she was trying not to cry, a single tear worked loose and slid down her cheek. Gavriel leaned forward and took it with his mouth. Salt. Sorrow. Not things he wanted to share with her, but he would. Because it was her.

"See what you made me do."

"I thought you didn't like kissing," she whispered. "That it doesn't—"

"Do anything for me? Not in that way, but… because of you, I realized that's all right. I can enjoy it for its own sake, and it doesn't matter that my wires don't connect like everyone else's."

He cupped her cheek in his hand and touched his mouth to hers. This was novel to him, delicate and new, and it wasn't thrilling like being taken. Her lips didn't make him hard, but they made him want to be closer to her, to feel more, and to hold her. Mags deepened the kiss, hands delving into his hair, and then down to his shoulders, his arms, and finally his waist. She pulled him closer, and his heart ached with the wonder of it. Not sex, he wasn't built that way, but it was sweet and good.

Another tear slipped down her cheek and he caught that one with his mouth too. "Why are you doing this to me?" she asked.

"Kissing is its own reward. It's not a dead-end road." That wasn't an answer, and he knew it.

Gavriel didn't have one, except that her anguish over

Slay might do him in faster than some unidentified toxin. He'd liberated Ancalen because she asked. With that look on her face, he might well storm Golgerra, even if she didn't.

"Fine, don't tell me." She stepped away and scrubbed a hand through her hair, making it stand on end.

It was visibly longer than it had been when they first started traveling together. Kitten fluff, he thought, knowing she'd be horrified by the comparison.

"Let's look around." He made his tone brisk. "They can't have been guarding an empty cellar."

"Agreed." Relief in her tone, she headed away from him into the darkness.

Gavriel switched his own torch on and scanned the space in the far corner. "Got some boxes here. I'm opening them."

"Same," she called back.

He swore. "This must be their stockpile, the meds they planned to use to turn the town, if most hadn't panicked, hidden. or run away."

"We can't leave this intact," Mags said.

"My thoughts exactly. Let's move the crates out of the church and have a bonfire."

"I'll do the heavy lifting. You keep watch for me."

She's still protecting me.

Since Oriel died, nobody had his back like this. When Mags stacked two crates and set off with them, past Gavriel would have thought she was showing off. Now he understood that was her work ethic and the fact that she knew her own strength. As they came out of the church, a few Eldritch were waiting, eyes trained on the drug cartons.

"What do you plan to do with those?" the spokesman

asked.

"Burn everything in the square," Mags answered. "It's a waste of good Animari medicine, but I can't let it sit here until my people can reclaim it."

"Then we'll help you. Klem! Dalal! Go with them. Follow orders and stay out of the way, please."

Two young Eldritch fell in behind Mags while Gavriel stayed with the crates in the square. It was unlikely anyone would try to tamper with them, but just in case, he drew his knives. He would have preferred to escort her to and from the church himself, but the survivors wanted to help, and they were hale enough to haul boxes.

Still, every moment she was out of his sight, his skin itched and he paced like a captive animal, back and forth, the sun beaming down as if to mock his unease. At least the snow was melting, and Gray should be eating well.

The old man smirked at him. "Impatient, lad? She must be quite dear to you. I imagine that's a story."

He narrowed his eyes, staring hard at the other Eldritch. A touch of his old ice emerged. "Pardon?"

"You'd rather not talk about your lady. I understand."

Gavriel couldn't bring himself to disclaim Mags, though the old man's statement wasn't true. Part of him wished that it was—that it could be—but she had been crystal clear about the terms. Things were already a fucking mess, and he wouldn't make them worse.

He even knew the names of the loves she'd lost, though he didn't know how. Asking for more details would be the ultimate self-flagellation, so he'd probably never indulge his secret, silent curiosity, not least because he couldn't bear to see her heartbroken over someone else. For him, there had only ever been Oriel, a brotherly bond, and Thalia, whom he'd worshiped more than loved.

Even more townsfolk pitched in, so they got the boxes piled quickly, then someone fetched a bottle of cheap liquor to prime the contents for burning. Mags handled the enkindling—just as well because when the burn got hot and bright—the vials began to pop, tiny little blue bursts in the yellow-orange conflagration. Everyone backed off to watch the stockpile go up in smoke, a testament to the fall of House Manwaring.

When Mags stepped up beside him, he sensed her closeness and reached for her without thinking. When did touching her become second nature? He used to hate casual contact, and even now, he couldn't imagine letting anyone else put their hands on him. But Mags, he'd trust her to tend wounds that were killing him.

"All the boxes bore Burnt Amber's mark?" he asked.

"Yeah. I'll let Callum know once I charge my phone."

"Yours died? Mine's almost gone, and there's no power here." Since most towns had a public charging station available for use, he didn't carry his personal unit, and they'd been using them less since he realized there was a chance that Ruark Gilbraith had hacked their network.

"We're working on that," the spokesman said. "Not sure how long it will be, though, if you've an urgent need to contact someone."

One of the Eldritch who'd helped haul the crates asked, "What should we do if we find more of this stuff in town?"

"Burn it," Mags said flatly, and Gavriel nodded his agreement.

Just then, his phone lit up with an incoming call, and he was astonished to see Madam Isoline's desperate face appear on screen. Mags leaned in to listen and Gavriel let her.

There was damn little he'd deny the tiger woman at this point.

"I'm sorry to bother you, sire, but I've got nowhere else to turn. You see, Tirael turned traitor when the princess was presumed dead. She made her move, Tirael, that is. Quite a brutal coup, it was, blood everywhere.

"The princess and wolf lord *did* take care of that, and I thought things had settled, even though we are on rations, but now I fear the princess has dashed off to her death—something about assassinating Lord Gilbraith—while leaving the wolf lord in charge. Maybe that would've been all right, except he bolted during a meeting with Commander Olwyn, and I don't know what else to do. Please, can't you come back?"

21.

"Holy shit," Mags said.

Gavriel motioned her to silence with an impatient expression. "We're some distance away, but if we travel hard, we should be there by nightfall."

That sounded brutal. Mags could handle it, but she felt bad for Gray. Before she could speak, Gavriel made his excuses to the townsfolk and was already headed to where they'd left the vedda beast. The mount was still waiting patiently, grazing on bits of dry grass and leaves he could reach, though he did chuff a welcome when he spotted them.

The Noxblade untied the vedda beast and mounted up as Mags undressed; he caught her belongings and stowed them, then she shifted, and he set off without another word. This mindless urgency seriously pissed her off when she considered the matter properly. Earlier in the day, he was kissing Mags, but now that he'd heard that Thalia was in trouble, he was acting like his pants were on fire. She grumbled in tiger form, not that he understood or cared.

Thankfully, some of the snow had melted or she might not have been able to keep up. Gavriel didn't pause once or even look back to check on her; he just kept nudging the animal to greater speed, whispering pleas or threats as the situation required. They ran without pausing, not for food or drink, and eventually, Mags hunted her own meal and ate it raw, then she caught up with Gavriel, who hadn't even noticed. If she could speak, she'd cuss him out for mistreating his mount that way, but as night fell, she recognized that they were getting close. Without the detour to Kelnora, it wasn't that far from Daruvar to the border in a straight line.

Even so, she was fucking exhausted, muscles burning, when they finally got back to the fortress. Everything seemed quiet—sentries on the walls as usual—but from what Madam Isoline had said, the situation was shitty. The guards stopped them at the gate and Gavriel shot them an imperious glare.

"You cannot fail to recognize me. Open the portal at once."

"Apologies, S-shadow Hand," the man stammered.

Soon, the heavy metal apparatus clanked and groaned, letting them inside. Gavriel paused in the bailey to deliver her clothes, then he raced off to do gods knew what. Thoroughly pissed, Mags shifted and groaned at the exhaustion that left her head spinning. *Every part of me hurts. What a brutal run.* The worst part was, she had no idea what they could even *do* here. They couldn't magically retrieve Raff or teleport to wherever the princess was. Gavriel couldn't keep calm where Thalia was concerned, and that made Mags want to punch through a wall.

She's married to someone else, dumbass. Enough of this already.

At this point, she might kill someone for a hot shower, even with the crappy water pressure, but she wasn't sure what room to use. One of the wolf women was still in residence, and Mags didn't want to make small talk or explain the situation to one of Raff's people. *Hell with it.* She knew where Gavriel's room was, and he probably wouldn't be in it. With that in mind, she headed for his quarters, but the sound of male voices in the strategy room made her pause. Once, she would have spied without hesitation, but things felt different now, even if she was mad at Gavriel.

The Noxblade's voice rose, sharpened. "Lileth is dead?"

"I regret to inform you that this is so. The wedding…had its complications."

"Tell me everything," Gavriel demanded.

Mags listened in as the other man summarized the events: a poisoning attempt on everyone at the head table, instigated by Tirael, who was secretly allied to Ruark Gilbraith. "Thanks to Prince Raff's sharp senses, Lileth was the only casualty. A tragedy, but things could have been much worse. She left a letter for you."

"Who did?" Gavriel asked, sounding furious and distracted.

"Lileth. She entrusted the missive to me some time ago, to be opened only in the event of her death."

"Thank you, Olwyn. Give it to me when things settle a bit. I need to see Madam Isoline about the supplies and find out how things have been managed in my absence."

"Understood, sire. I'll listen to the reports of returning patrols and check the status of the minefield. You were lucky you didn't set off any—"

"Not luck," Gavriel cut in. "Gray is trained to avoid them."

"That's a fine beast. I'm going then."

Mags slipped away, contemplating what she'd learned.

What the hell was Raff doing, anyway? It sounded like things were absolute crap and he'd piked off at the worst possible moment. Oh, she'd heard gossip when she was visiting Pine Ridge, unkind rumors that he contributed nothing to pack management, and that Korin held all the real power, but she'd thought better of him. Sighing, she slipped away and found Gavriel's room, heading straight into the shower.

Normally, she was efficient about such things, but she lingered for half an hour, scrubbing until her skin was red. There was only one towel hanging in the bathroom, and it was clean. She took a petty satisfaction in rubbing her smell all over it. Mags wouldn't let herself think too long about why she was so irate over Gavriel's concern for Thalia. It wasn't like he'd made any secret of his adoration.

Between Pine Ridge, Daruvar, and roaming around with that damn Noxblade, her hair was longer than it ever had been, so she got it out of her face in a neat halo braid; it was long enough for that. There was no fire in the hearth, and the room was cold. Mags got dressed in her other set of clothes, thinking about Keriel and Leena in Kelnora. They had washed her gear, and the shirt still smelled faintly of whatever herbs they'd used, along with the smoke from the kitchen fire.

Mags slipped out then, as she didn't want Gavriel to find her skulking around his room. A pair of workers were gossiping some distance down the hall. They thought they were being quiet, but she fell into step behind them, senses pitched to catch every word.

"You really saw Death's Shadow hit the wolf prince?" Such an excited tone.

"Right in the face! Then he came after the wolf again,

but he got slapped in the back of the head. That wolf's a slippery one. I was scared I'd get caught spying, so I scampered then, but I imagine it'll get messy."

"Are they fighting over the princess?"

"Who knows?"

Now that she knew Raff was back, Mags only had to scan for his scent. It galled her to play peacemaker when they were fighting because of Thalia, who ought to damn well clean up her own messes, but Mags couldn't let those two boneheads hurt each other. She picked up the trail and ran for the strategy room, startling the two staffers who'd alerted her to trouble a few minutes prior.

They'll be whispering about me next.

As Mags raced into the room, she caught Gavriel going for round two, his hand on Raff's shoulder. Part of her wanted to comfort the Noxblade, but mostly, she was furious with him, so she defended the wolf lord without even knowing what the hell was up. With any luck, it would irk Gavriel to see her taking Raff's side.

See how it feels, asshole.

"Leave him alone, he's trying to help your princess." When Gavriel didn't let go, Mags grabbed his arm and twisted. "Do we have to fight…again?"

Gavriel glared at her and uncoiled his fingers. "Don't test me."

"Why, do you like it or something?" She smirked, knowing damn well that he did, and he'd hate her for messing with him like this.

"Get out of my way or get a fucking room," Raff snapped, rushing out.

When Gavriel followed, of course, Mags did too. She had no idea what Raff was doing, but she wouldn't let

Gavriel go at him, much as the Noxblade wanted to. He caught her gaze as they stepped into the hall, and she baited him with what she hoped was a sweet smile. That look should put anyone on guard.

WHAT THE HELL is this woman's problem? Gavriel's pride stung.

He hadn't realized how much he had come to depend upon her support, but now that they were back, she was taking the wolf's side without even asking why Gavriel was angry. That... well, he could scarcely stop gritting his teeth over the injustice of it. He clenched a fist, wanting to hit Raff Pineda even more, and for once, it had nothing to do with the wolf's lack of qualifications to rule alongside Princess Thalia.

In the hallway, they ran into Commander Olwyn on the way to...wherever they were going. He had a small contingent of guards with him, and Raff asked the group, "Do you know how to arm and load the drones?"

Mags nodded, but the Eldritch men offered blank looks. Raff sighed. "I'll teach Olwyn. Mags, you show Gavriel the ropes. We need these in the air as soon as possible."

Gavriel half-expected her to refuse, but she only nodded. "You're striking at Braithwaite," she guessed.

Certainly, accept his *orders without question.*

"Damn right I am. I'll drop payloads on the fences. I don't know exactly where Thalia is, but if she's already inside, the distraction will draw forces away, and if she's trying to get in, a breach in their defenses can only help her."

"You're planning to bombard a location where—" Gavriel couldn't finish the sentence. This was typical of the wolf lord, all impulse and no logic. These weren't his people, so why would Raff care about potential civilian casualties? "What an idiotic idea!"

"It's the best I can do from here," Raff said. "She left Daruvar in my care, but I'll be damned if I leave her without backup. I can program the drones to scan for her, and if she's nearby, I'll abort the strike."

"Do it," Mags urged. "I agree with your assessment, and it seems unlikely that she can take out Ruark Gilbraith with only one Noxblade at her side."

She's agreeing with him again.

Gavriel caught Mags's gaze, incredulous, wondering if she truly didn't see how risky this notion was. After her kindness in Kelnora and Ancalen, he'd thought that she was starting to care about his people. This course of action could end in blood and tears. The tiger woman held his look, and while he still couldn't read her that well, he did have the impression that she was angry.

Fair enough, so was he. Silently, he turned away.

The wolf lord seemed oblivious to the tension, focused on his work on the screen. "All right, new flight pattern laid in. I'll monitor remotely from the strategy room. Payloads will deploy in five and a half hours."

That was their cue to return to the strategy room, though Gavriel could imagine nothing he wanted to do less. Endless waiting? No concrete solutions. That was hell.

Hours passed while he paced, wishing he hadn't asked to be excused from Princess Thalia's service. If he had gone with her, the success of the mission would be more certain. That was no judgment on Ferith; Gavriel simply had more faith in his own skills.

At some point, Madam Isoline brought tea. He accepted

the drink and leaned in when she whispered, "I'm sorry, it seems I called you back for nothing. He'd only gone hunting, I gather." She indicated Raff with a tilt of her head.

"No, it's better that I'm here," Gavriel said softly.

That earned him another glare from Mags. Hell if he knew why.

It irked him profoundly when Mags caught Raff's eye and made a face over the tea. Gavriel understood she didn't much care for it—his personal blend being the exception—but he clenched his teeth over the comradery she shared with the wolf lord. If he could build a wall around her, he might damn well do it.

I'm losing it. There was no explanation for his attitude when he should concentrate on Thalia's situation, but he couldn't take his eyes off Mags, couldn't stop watching, reacting, and wanting to punch Raff Pineda.

I shouldn't get involved. He did anyway.

"You don't like it?" Gavriel asked Mags.

"It tastes like wet weeds." Her candor was refreshing. Among his people, most chose to swallow their feelings and play games with one another.

For some reason, the wolf lord glared at her. "Tact can be charming. You should read up on it," Raff said.

She chuckled. "Fuck that. Honesty is the best policy. That way nobody can ever claim they didn't know what I'm about."

"I'm sorry," Madam Isoline said quietly. "Will there be anything else?"

"No, thank you," Raff spoke in a gentle tone.

Did you not see that? He cares more about the chatelaine than you, his supposed friend. And yet she'd defended Pineda. Threatened Gavriel over this asshole. While he did value

Isoline's service, there was no insult in not liking a drink. What was wrong with the wolf lord anyway?

Commander Olwyn cleared his throat, fidgeting as if the tension was getting to him. "Are the drones on target?"

Before Gavriel could respond, Raff stood, heading over to the screen to check. "ETA ten minutes now. Too soon to scan for the princess specifically, but I'm not showing any humanoid life signs to the west."

"That will be perfect as a distraction," the commander said.

Mags nodded. "Let's hope she's found a way inside."

With a sibilant curse, Gavriel lunged to his feet and started to pace. He wished Mags would look at him like she used to, but she was busy pretending he didn't exist, and he had no idea why things had changed. To distract himself from that puzzle, he focused on Thalia. "I tried calling her, but her phone is off."

Raff smirked. "If that surprises you, then you're dumber than you look."

"She's smart to run silent. There's always a way to pick up on electronic chatter. Coming in quick and quiet offers the best chance for success," Mags noted.

Waiting was the worst. Gavriel didn't know what he might've done, but just then, the symbols on the screen reached their target, one by one, and flared red, indicating multiple successful strikes.

Raff let out a breath, visibly relieved. "It's done. Only time will tell if we made a difference."

Gavriel grabbed the wolf lord by the shirt front, struggling to keep his temper in check. "If she falls to Gilbraith, if you let her die, I'll kill you. I hope you know that."

Raff only nodded. "My life is in your hands."

As the hours rolled on, nobody could sustain the razor-sharp tension, and people curled up or dozed off. Others joined them in the strategy room, waiting for news. Part of Gavriel wished he'd remained ignorant—that Isoline had left him to go about his business and to learn of this secondhand, much later—but that seemed disloyal. Even so, he couldn't quell his regret over losing the rapport he'd built with the tiger woman.

Who still wasn't speaking to him.

Gavriel nodded off in a chair and woke sharply at Commander Olwyn's words. "You need to hear this."

He bolted to his feet, realizing what he was listening to a few seconds later. "This is Thalia Talfayen. House Gilbraith has fallen to me, and their lands are mine. I claim, by right of conquest, the Silver Throne. You have three days to send emissaries to Daruvar to pledge fealty, or you will share this traitor's fate. That is all."

"She did it," Raff crowed.

She's fine without me. He shouldn't be so relieved by that, but now there could be no question. He was free to live as he wished. The princess did not require any further service or sacrifice. Gavriel relaxed, closing his eyes to savor that realization. Then he grinned at the wolf lord, offering a small joke for the occasion.

"Looks like you get to live, beast."

"I'm grateful," Raff said, smiling.

For the first time all evening, Mags came up to him. When she set her hand on his shoulder, his whole body eased. Without knowing it, he'd been waiting for that touch. It was too much power for one person to possess over him yet she had it and he couldn't bring himself to mind.

"Be careful with that word," she cautioned softly. "I know you were kidding, but others might not. They speak it with hate, and—"

"I won't use it again, even in jest," he promised.

"It's not enough that you see *me* as different. You have to be better to my people as well, you know? It's hard for me to overcome certain prejudices too, but…" She shrugged and let the rest go without saying.

He got the gist.

From all around the keep, revelry echoed in the night. Music and exultant shouts suggested that the rest of Daruvar had heard the message as well, and while food might be scarce, they were tapping the wine casks. Commander Olwyn opened a decanter of good whiskey, pouring shots for everyone.

Gavriel took his and handed one to Mags. "I'm sorry. I won't make that mistake again. To new beginnings?"

She hesitated only a second before clinking her glass against his. "I'll drink to that."

22.

MAGS DOWNED THE drink and decided she'd had enough of being social.

Raff and Gavriel weren't going to end each other now that they knew the ice princess was fine. And that was her cue to bail. All over Daruvar, people were losing their minds, singing and cavorting because Thalia had finally realized her dream of becoming queen. Privately Mags thought the woman could stand to care a little more about her people and less about claiming antiquated titles.

Whatever, it's none of my business.

Her promise to return to Kelnora to see Keriel and Leena held more allure than these celebrations. Not since her arrival had she felt like such an outsider, and she didn't much care for the sensation. The Eldritch second in command signaled to the Noxblade. "Could I have a word?"

Gavriel did give her an apologetic look as he went to join Commander Olwyn, but it didn't change anything. He'd still half-killed poor Gray to get here fast enough, only to find there was nothing for them to do. The whole endeavor was pointless and... no. *Not* hurtful. Just annoying, that was all.

She slipped out while Gavriel was talking to Olwyn and she wandered the halls, avoiding the merriment. Despite everyone else's euphoria, Mags was in no mood to party. Slay was likely a prisoner in Golgerra by now, and she still hadn't managed to call Callum to give him the bad news about the drug trafficking. Plus, she'd heard the workers mention a resurgence in Golgoth activity in wolf and bear lands. Things might be looking up for the Eldritch, but for the Animari, there was trouble to spare.

Her steps carried her to the stable first, where she checked on Gray, who blustered his lips and shook his mane at her in greeting. "Hey, there. Who's a good boy? You all right after that terrible run?"

In response, the vedda beast nuzzled her shoulder and she indulged him with a good rub down, checking his hooves, just in case. He seemed sound enough and someone had scattered fodder for him. The other mounts reacted uneasily to her presence, shifting and stomping in their stalls, unaccustomed to predators. She ignored them and moved on, steering clear of the festivities.

Need to charge my phone.

She headed for the quietest corner of the fortress. Nobody was in the medical center, not even Dr. Wyeth, but he did have a charging station. Mags dropped her phone on the pad and glanced around the room. There was a cot...maybe she'd crash here for the night, as it was unlikely there would be any emergencies unless someone got super drunk and cracked his head falling down the steps.

In the morning, she'd call Callum, keep her promise to Leena and Keriel, then she had to get back to Ash Valley. Dom would be waiting for her report, crappy as it was. Still, she figured he might be relieved too—that Slay hadn't rolled on them over breaking up with Pru. With a weary sigh, she sank down on the cot and tried to sleep.

Of course it wouldn't be that easy. Not because of the noise, though that was bad enough. Her own mind wouldn't leave her alone, then an annoying Noxblade found her, hovering in the doorway like he expected an engraved invitation.

"What?" she demanded.

"I've been looking for you." His tone was off, ragged and broken.

"Did something happen?" She sat up then, all senses sharpening. Mags noticed that he wasn't hesitating in the doorway. Rather, Gavriel was holding onto it, like he couldn't walk without support.

But she didn't smell booze on him, at least not so much that he'd be incapacitated, and he was too careful for that anyway. Reflexively, she bounded to her feet and reached him in a few steps. When he let her put an arm around his waist, no, more than that, he wrapped an arm about her shoulders and leaned, his breath coming in sharp bursts.

"I can't—"

"Okay, calm down. Sit with me for a minute. When you feel up to it, tell me."

He collapsed on the cot where she had been trying to sleep, falling against the wall with a thud that highlighted his weakness. With shaking hands, he offered her a letter, lips compressed so tightly that she feared he might never speak again. Her confusion mounting, Mags took the page, unfolded it, and started reading:

My Dearest Gavriel,

If you're reading this, I must be gone. Please forgive my cowardice. I looked at you a thousand times and consid-

ered telling you the truth, especially after Oriel died. If Thalia had ever shown signs of returning your affections, I would have, I swear to you. I watched and measured the situation and judged my own pain to be graver than yours. I wish I had been a better woman, but I couldn't raise you. It wasn't for the reasons people thought, not because your coloring was a curse, but because I wasn't strong enough.

Now you will learn the secret of your birth, for good or ill. Lord Talfayen was not a man to be denied when he wanted something. At one point, he wanted me. You and Oriel came of that much-despised union. It is no surprise that you have always loved Thalia; she is your half-sister. I let you serve her, just as I did, believing it to be the best for both of us.

I don't know if that was the right choice, but now you know the truth. I could not take this secret to the afterworld. You have a right to know. And I am deeply sorry that I could not live as your mother. I hated Lord Talfayen too much and when I saw you and Oriel, I saw him. None of it is your fault. I don't dare hope for your forgiveness, but I wish for it nonetheless. Please be happy and find your own path, just as your sister has hers.

Perhaps one day, you won't hate me for giving both my sons to the guild.

Lileth

Somehow Mags bit back her startled exclamation, not wanting to make it worse for him. If she was shocked, he must be mentally wrecked. Going with her gut, she dropped the letter and put her arms around him. *Hugs or sex, that's what I've got.* Hopefully, he'd want one if not the other. Slowly, he leaned in, and soon he was huddled in her arms, shivering, face tucked against her neck.

She tried to imagine what it would be like, wondering about your family and then finding out this way. Silently, she stroked his back, marveling that he'd come looking for her when he was falling to pieces. That meant something, but she wouldn't reflect on what, not right now. He needed her too much.

"I did wonder. You said the birthrate was low, yet you were sent to the guild as orphans. I figured there must have been a dramatic reason why, but I never expected this."

"Neither did I. Oriel and I used to invent stories about who they were and why they left us. It was best when I made myself believe they must be dead—that they had no choice in the matter."

"I'm so sorry," she whispered.

Because he was right. It was so much worse that he'd seen his mother every day—his father too for that matter—and neither of them ever acknowledged him. Talfayen probably hadn't known or he would've tried to use Gavriel as he had Tirael, pitting him against Thalia. But Lileth, she'd chosen to ignore Gavriel and let him nurse an impossible love for his damned half-sister. He must feel sick and awful, considering that devotion.

"It's not your fault," she said.

His laugh had a bitter edge, breathed against her skin. "This doesn't feel real, but she wouldn't leave such a thing in jest. It must be true, and…"

"And…?"

"I'm *so* fucking angry." He spoke through clenched teeth, and Mags realized the tremors came from rage, not sorrow. "I'm the asshole who had no idea, all this time. Hell, if we're judging by blasted Talfayen blood, I have as much right to be king, don't I?"

"Do you want to be?"

"That's not the point! Lileth stole my family from me, and what's worse..." He got up then and paced like a caged animal. "You were right, you know. When you said Thalia was to blame as much as anyone else. We went in following *her* orders. My sister sent my brother off to die! How am I supposed to live with that?"

"I don't know," she said honestly. "Do you plan to tell Thalia the truth?"

AN URGE TO violence thrummed inside Gavriel like an electric current.

When he'd first read the message, he'd only known that he might crawl out of his skin if he didn't find Mags. Now the shock had given way to rage, and he couldn't keep still, lurching from one side of the infirmary to the other. She watched him with concerned eyes, but he couldn't bring himself under control. No, she'd just have to bear witness to him unraveling; it was unthinkable that it would be anyone else.

"No," he said finally. "She's not my sister. She never will be. The truth is, she took Oriel from me and I'll be damned if I acknowledge her as family because of a letter Lileth wrote in a moment of remorse. I've lived as an outcast. I'll die as one."

"Are you sure?" Mags asked.

"There is no doubt. I'm afraid of what I may do when I see her. None of this is her fault, but I feel as if she's betrayed me as well, treating me like a tool when she should have known—ah, never mind. That's not fair."

"Your feelings don't have to be. Your mother discarded you for reasons beyond your control and your half-sister used you, unknowingly. You've been *wronged*, Gavriel. Nobody ever gave you the chance to make your own choices."

This, this was why it had to be her. Only Mags gave him the freedom to say such things. She had no loyalty to the Eldritch or to Thalia. Some of the turmoil in his head steadied, leaving him trembling again, shock or reaction, or hell if he knew what.

"I could hate her," he whispered. "As much as I used to love her. Now I'm just grateful that I revered her so much that I never—"

"Yeah, I got it," Mags cut in. "Take comfort in small mercies, I guess."

He ran an unsteady hand through his hair, dropping down beside her on the cot. "Turns out, Tirael was my sister too, and I never knew that either. I had *two* sisters, Mags, not just a brother. One sister is dead, the other is queen, and… I don't know how to feel."

"No shit, low birth rates, my ass. Seems like old Lord Talfayen was quite a stallion." She waggled her eyebrows while making an obscene gesture.

That shouldn't have been funny; he was such a mess, and it was so disrespectful, but suddenly he was laughing, astonished at her ability to disarm him like a ticking bomb. Some of his bleak moods, even Oriel had been unable to banish, but she was like sunshine to his storm cloud—hot, powerful, and impossible to resist.

She gave him a tentative smile and put a hand on his head. "It's better if you can laugh. Sometimes life is just so fucked up that it's all you can do."

"You didn't, though."

"What?"

"Laugh. At the idea of your curse." Maybe he shouldn't bring that up, but her support made him brave, daring, even.

"Not about what happened," she agreed in a somber tone, glancing away.

"Would you tell me?"

"You want some mutual commiseration, is that it? Or you just can't handle me knowing some shit about you without demanding equal access?"

Gavriel had no idea how to respond but he didn't have to. She sighed and added, "Fine, it's not a secret, so I'll give you the short version. A week to the day after I told Brendan I loved him, he died. In the shower."

"That doesn't even make sense," he said.

"Tell me about it. The Animari don't die of freak accidents. Even if we fall and get hurt, we heal. It's almost unheard of for anyone to fall at precisely the right angle, crack their skull in a way that results in an aneurysm that causes instant death."

"But it happened to the person you loved."

"It broke my heart," she said softly. "I blamed myself and wished I had taken Arran's warning seriously. Then time wore on and I forgot a little of that feeling. As years passed, I wondered if it could have been an awful coincidence. So when Tamara came into my life, I was reluctant, but I let her persuade me."

Her aching tone twisted at his heart, almost to the point that he couldn't ask, "Something happened again?"

"A week after I told her I loved her, she was struck by lightning."

"To borrow your favorite phrase, holy shit."

She smiled, though her expression still held more sorrow than he could stand. "You can see why I don't say that to people anymore."

Gavriel didn't consider himself superstitious, but the timing of the tragic instances were damned convincing. "I didn't think it was possible, but you're making my problems seem less dire."

"Guess a fatal curse is good for something," she said with a lopsided smile. "Are we done talking about this? It's not fun for me."

"Yes. Sorry. Perhaps I shouldn't have—"

"Nah, it's fine. In a way, it's nice to tell someone. Except for Arran, nobody at home knows. I did some traveling when I was younger, and everything happened away from Ash Valley. Maybe it's misplaced pride, I'd rather be famous as a bad-ass than as the loneliest person alive."

"I'm honored that you trusted me."

She nudged him. "Seriously? You really said that."

Gavriel leaned against her, savoring the warmth of her body against his side. "I don't know about you, but I'm done in. Shall we go to bed?"

Mags blinked at him, one brow lifting in apparent astonishment. "I was planning to crash here. You can go wherever you want."

Why had he assumed they'd retire together? The idea of going alone...no, it was all wrong. If she wouldn't sleep in his bed, he wanted her on the rug in tiger form. Gavriel cleared his throat. "It will be warmer in my room. You like that spot by the fireplace."

That's not what I want.

Mustering his courage, he added, "Honestly, I'd rather

have you in my bed. I'm...used to you now. I sleep better when you're there."

For a long moment, he feared she'd refuse. She seemed to be thinking over the suggestion. At last she said, "What's on offer here? Your rug, your bed, or is it sex? Because we should be precise about these things."

"If you prefer the rug, that's fine," he said. "I've already stated my preference on sleeping arrangements. As to sex, I'm tired tonight, as it's been a hell of a day, but tomorrow…" He wasn't used to saying such things, and heat filled his cheeks until they felt hot enough to fry a fish. Clearing his throat, he tried again. "When we're both rested, I want more of that."

Her lips twitched. "More sex, that is? Not sleep."

"You live to plague me, don't you? I can't believe you mentioned my...proclivities in front of Raff Pineda." Dammit, he didn't mean to say that.

Her eyes narrowed and she folded her arms, all bristling cat. "Yeah, well, *I* can't believe you made Gray and me run like demons were chasing us because you were worried about an old flame who turned out to be your half-sister."

Sudden realization dawned, and he had a hard time suppressing the smile. *Was she...jealous?* He knew better than to inquire; he liked his fingers where they were. "Is that why you've been pissy? Mags, this wasn't about Thalia. I was worried about everyone at Daruvar, especially when I found out Raff was in charge, and they were on rations."

"I am *never* pissy," she growled.

"Certainly not. Can we please go to bed?" He rose and offered his hand, keeping his expression neutral. Somehow she'd changed his mood from wild disorder to soft amusement, though if he told her that, she'd just disavow all credit.

"Fine, but if you hog the covers, I'll kick you onto the floor."

He didn't say that was music to his ears. When he considered the matter deeply, he still wasn't sure when or how she'd become so...necessary, or why her threats brought him so much joy. She took his hand tentatively, as if she wasn't sure she had the right. A pox on all Animari nonsense anyway. He didn't doubt that her lovers had died, but she didn't deserve to spend her life alone.

She'll leave me soon.

Gavriel knew better than to suggest otherwise; he'd take whatever she gave and be glad of it, hoarding memories in anticipation of loneliness to come.

23.

Mags shut her conscience up by reminding it what Gavriel had discovered.

If she could offer comfort during a rough patch, she ought to do that. As a friend. The pangs quieted then. Things still hadn't settled down in the fortress and probably wouldn't until dawn or later. Thalia had won a decisive victory and claimed her crown; she also had no idea of what she'd lost.

In the hall, she pulled her hand from his. "You take a shower. I'll stop by the kitchen to find us something to eat."

Gavriel searched her gaze with serious eyes. "This isn't an excuse to disappear?"

"I can remember a time when that was all you wanted from me."

"Times change," he said.

Mags sighed, wondering why she found his persistence so endearing. "I'm not bailing. I really am hungry, aren't you?"

"Starving," he admitted.

"Then I'll see you in fifteen minutes. Go on." She nudged him toward his room while she headed for the kitchen.

Like the med center, the kitchen was empty, so she rummaged to her heart's content. There wasn't much, which proved Gavriel had been right to worry about the workers starving. Supplies should start arriving soon, though. She did find some roast venison and guessed Raff must have done well when he was hunting. Mags claimed some for herself and got fruit and bread for Gavriel. Since they were supposed to be celebrating, she added a bottle of wine to her haul.

The shower was still running when she got in. Naturally, Gavriel hadn't built the fire, as that was a creature comfort, and he tended to live like an ascetic. She knelt, taking care of that task so the room would be warmer when he emerged. Then she set the food on a low table, arranging it in a way that felt both alien and domestic. She didn't *do* these things for people. It was just as well she was leaving. Otherwise, she might start to fool herself that they had a future.

Every instinct insisted she should go now, before he joined her, but she ignored that demanding voice and stayed. *It's one night. What difference can it make after everything we've been through?* She stayed on the rug, which was as warm and soft as she'd remembered. Funny, his lovely carpet was the main reason she'd slept here the first time—well, that and a desire to annoy Gavriel. Now everything was much more complex.

He emerged in a dark robe, his hair standing up, a towel in one hand. She must be the only person who'd ever seen him like this: messy, wet, and completely undone. When he saw her, he smiled, such an innocent expression, and her heart throbbed over the impossibility of it.

"Dinner," she said.

He had said he was too tired to play bed games, and Mags respected that, but looking at him, she wished she could have him one last time. She was quiet while they ate and polished off most of the wine. Gavriel had only a glass and even that was enough to make him seem loopy, as he seldom indulged.

Wearing a silly smile, he slid an arm across her shoulder. "Let's sleep."

The bed was chilly, the sheets so cool as to feel damp, but with both their bodies beneath the covers, it soon warmed. Gavriel settled in against her and winked out with a quickness that she envied. In secret, she touched him gently, stroking his damp hair, smoothing her hands down his back. He stirred in his sleep and pressed closer, his face completely open and trusting.

I'm sorry. If I say good-bye in the morning, I'm not sure if I can leave.

Mags didn't sleep much, and she roused fully just before dawn. He had an arm around her, his cheek against her back, and she tried to detach slowly enough that he wouldn't notice, but Gavriel snapped awake, grabbing her wrist in a steely hold.

"Trying to sneak away like a thief?" he asked in a low, silky voice.

"I haven't stolen anything."

His tone turned musing. "Haven't you?"

She rolled over to glare at him. "I don't know what this is about, but—"

"Did you forget? We're partners. Together, we vowed to return to Kelnora, and you said you'd help me hunt down the loyalist stronghold if I helped you find Slay. You know where he is now, even if you didn't rescue him, while *my* work remains undone. Are you planning to renege on our agreement because you got what you wanted?"

Dammit, he had her there. Part of her was relieved to have an excuse to stay, if only for a week or two longer, but she couldn't let that show. She donned angry emotional armor like it was second-nature. "Go to hell, Gavriel."

"What's that supposed to mean?"

"I didn't know the hunt was still on. After what you learned about Thalia, I figured you wouldn't want to work for her anymore."

He sighed. "It's not for her. The loyalists have no compunction about killing their own, and if they're allowed to—"

"I get it. For the good of the people and all that."

"Why does it feel like you don't believe me? What did I do to deserve this?" Lifting his face, he appealed to the ceiling like Mags couldn't see reason.

"You're pissing me off," she growled.

At the hint of her anger, answering sparks snapped in his eyes, and he bit his lip, inhaling sharply through his nose. It was simple for her to recognize the visual signals of his arousal now, especially when coupled with his warming scent, cloves and cinnamon with a hint of copper. Mags didn't hesitate; she pounced and pressed his hands flat against the mattress. He was already fighting, eyes bright with anticipation. Gavriel didn't make it easy. He resisted with all his strength, until he was quivering and breathless when she tied him with cords she found in a drawer, doubtless meant for more murderous enterprises. His ironhard cock revealed the depth of his excitement and by the time she bound his ankles, he was bucking at the air, soft moans escaping him.

Sitting back on her heels, Mags surveyed her handiwork. "You look gorgeous like this," she whispered. "Spread and helpless."

His body jerked, reacting to the words, to her husky voice. "What are you planning to do to me?"

"That would spoil the surprise."

With no preamble, Mags feasted on him. She bit him all over, light on his stomach, painful on his thighs. She claimed him from head to toe, alternating soft strokes with harsh slaps, and Gavriel went wild, panting, straining against his bonds. For at least an hour, she tormented him until his cock was leaking nonstop. Then she paused to finish her leftovers from the night before, smirking as she ate.

"You can't…" he gasped. "Please."

She shut him up by feeding him a slice of fruit. "I can do anything I want with you. Haven't we been over this?"

He chewed, swallowed, still trembling. His whole body was flushed, marked from her hands and mouth, and it was hard for Mags to keep her craving leashed, but she knew it would be better when she finally let go. She returned to the bed and stroked a gentle fingertip down his aching cock, knowing that wasn't how he wanted to be touched.

"Please," he said again. "I don't know how much more I can take."

Those were the magic words, as they melted the last of her self-control. She took him then, hard and fast, and she put her hand on his throat, just enough to give the feeling an edge as she rode him. This time, he didn't wait for her order, moving helplessly on his own. She didn't reprimand him. The depth of that desire was delicious, and she leaned down for a fierce, open-mouthed kiss.

The orgasm surprised her. She hadn't realized she was

quite there, but suddenly, she was coming, gasping into his mouth, and trying her best not to say anything that would reveal how deeply he'd gotten to her. Odd to think that way with his cock jerking and spurting inside her, but that was sex. This feeling... she couldn't let it grow. Quietly panicked, she rolled off him and untied his arms and legs, massaging them to make sure he had good circulation.

Then Mags flopped backward on the bed, and she didn't even have the energy to resist when Gavriel pulled her close.

GAVRIEL BREATHED IN Mags's scent and put his face in her hair while his breathing steadied.

His whole body stung—in a good way—and he felt used in the best possible sense. There was no doubt that she desired him, strange and miraculous as it seemed. Such a marvel seemed almost transcendental—that he could be wanted and not feared. She was so capable that she had no need of his protection, but the realization roused a flutter of unease. That meant she might well have no use for him beyond the bedroom.

Outside, he could hear the staff stirring, hurrying through the halls. He barely caught the tail end of an excited cry. "The queen has returned!"

Beside him, Mags stiffened, and he felt her gaze focused on his face. "You don't want to greet Thalia?" she asked.

"To hell with Thalia." Once, he couldn't have imagined saying such a thing, especially referring to her without a title, but it felt liberating. "Our paths have diverged, as you well know. I'm spending the entire day in bed with you."

"What if I have other plans?" Her tone was a challenge.

"I can't force you. But what else do you have to do?"

She made a sound that could've been a laugh. "Not me, you. I thought you were in a hurry to root out the loyalists. Isn't work your life?"

"Not anymore." Because Gavriel didn't think she'd want to hear how she'd already changed him, he chose to say no more.

That day, they stayed in his room like fugitives and had more sex than he could have imagined in his wildest dreams. He surfaced only long enough to get more food from the kitchen, then he went back for more of her wildly inventive games.

His entire body hurt, and she was such a smug cat, gloating over his complete and utter ruin. Somehow, he was smiling too, wishing this interlude would never end. As he gazed into her golden eyes and stroked her dark hair, he finally put a name to the feeling. *I love you, Mags.*

Gods help me, but I do.

She wouldn't want to hear that either, so he kept the feeling quiet, caught in his heart like a fossilized insect in amber.

"This was a good day," she said in a dreamy tone. "I should shower."

Maybe he was starting to become a little more Animari in spirit because he loathed the idea of her washing off his scent. Gavriel sat up. "We could bathe together."

"Your bath isn't very luxurious," she said dubiously.

"If you prefer not to try…"

"Let's give it a shot. Is there a way to increase the water pressure?"

He fiddled with the shower head and got a slightly better flow, but the equipment was ancient. Though he had mostly bad memories of his time in Ash Valley, he did picture the bathhouse with a wistful sigh, then he called to her. "I did the best I could. Come in!"

She padded into the bathroom naked, comfortable with her body. He was learning not to mind either because her eyes smiled when they lit on the marks she'd left on his skin. His people took longer to heal, so he'd carry them for a while—secret souvenirs of what they did to each other.

He had only one cloth, one towel, but they crowded into the narrow stall and washed each other. She was gentle now, as she never was in bed, and this felt good in ways he couldn't have envisioned. Not arousing, but sweet and tender, all the care he'd never received from anyone else. Gavriel closed his eyes and tipped his head back while she washed his hair, not realizing that he was humming until she pointed it out.

"What's that song?"

"Ah, it's my favorite. I could play it for you, if you like." How absurd, feeling shy about his taste in music when she was lathering his bare ass.

Turning, he rinsed and took his time washing her, trying to convey without words how precious and vital she'd become. Mags never showed much of what she was feeling, so he couldn't tell if his sentiments reached her. In time, they stepped out, clean and shivering.

"We should change the sheets," she said. "If you have any spares."

"I don't know where they're kept. The workers handle such matters here."

"Do you have someplace where you'd be in charge of that?" she asked unexpectedly. "Like a flat or a retreat that belongs only to you?"

Startled, he shook his head. "Until now, I followed Thalia's orders and stayed wherever she assigned me."

"That's—"

"Sad," he finished, mostly so she wouldn't. "I'm aware."

"Well, you can do something about it now."

"I plan to."

"Another round?" she asked.

Hard to say if she was joking, but before he could reply, she tackled him. Gavriel hit the bed hard and twisted in defiance. At any point, he could have said the stopping word, but with her, he probably never would.

In the morning, Daruvar crackled like a live wire with guests arriving nonstop. He ventured out because the food was gone, and when he returned, Mags was nowhere to be found. His heart nearly stopped as he raced through the keep in search of her. The workers drew back against the wall, staring as he ran past, but he didn't care what they thought, or what they whispered about him.

She wouldn't have left. Not yet.

They'd talked about finishing the job. He staggered when he spotted her in the corridor by the med center, deep in conversation with Callum McRae. The bear clan leader was standing too close to her, and Gavriel didn't give a damn if he was a monk. A woman like Mags could make a man break a lifetime habit of celibacy; he ought to know.

"I was just going to call you," Mags was saying. "You're here to congratulate the new queen, I reckon?"

"Bunch of damned nonsense," McRae muttered. "I should be at Burnt Amber, but no, here I am doing diplomatic bullshit with the enemy marching on my lands."

"I heard you're taking the brunt," Mags said. "Sorry to hear it."

McRae dismissed her sympathy with a curt gesture, and Gavriel didn't know if he should slip away or keep listening. Now that he knew she hadn't left like she'd tried to before, he could relax a little. With Animari senses, he realized, they probably already knew of his arrival, so he rounded the corner and joined them. He inclined his head in greeting, but remained silent, making it clear he wouldn't interrupt. Mags touched his arm in welcome, but she was clearly trying to figure out how to break the bad news.

The war priest sighed. "Spit it out already. I'm heading back to Burnt Amber as soon as I do the bare minimum here."

"You mean the bear minimum?" Mags was grinning as if she'd cracked the best joke in the world.

At first, Gavriel didn't get it, but he laughed at the other man's expression more than anything else. McRae half-turned like he was done, but Mags grabbed his arm.

"Sorry, couldn't resist. There's no good way to tell you this, but…"

Gavriel admired the succinct way she summed up the drug issue. He spoke for the first time to support her. "We kept a few vials as proof, if you need to see them."

Until now, he hadn't known that monks cursed, but this one did, explicitly and in colorful detail. When McRae finally wound down, Mags was gazing at him in open admiration. "That was a thing of beauty."

"Whatever. Dead-Eyes and gray tar, my day just keeps getting worse." Sighing, McRae added, "Send pictures of what you found, and I'll take care of it. There aren't many people with the power and opportunity to do this."

"Then I'll consider the matter resolved," Mags said. "By the way, I heard Joss was looking for you earlier. You better run, war priest. That woman is relentless."

McRae made an obscene gesture as he stomped away; he'd be loads of fun at Thalia's coronation. It was petty but imagining the bear's endless glower on that auspicious occasion put a smile on Gavriel's face.

With a graceful stretch that caught his eye and held it, Mags tucked her phone in her pocket. Right, she left it in the med center the other night.

"I'm ready to go," she said. "That was the last thing on my to-do list. Do you want to say bye to…anyone?"

"Not at all. Let me get my things."

24.

SINCE GAVRIEL WAS avoiding Thalia, Mags figured they should wait until the reception moved from the courtyard to the great hall.

Once everyone went inside, she headed out and he met her beyond the walls, leading Gray. "Ready?" Gavriel asked.

She nodded. "I looted some provisions for the road from the wedding gifts. Should I feel guilty?"

"They'll never miss whatever you took," he said.

With a bright sun overhead and a soft breeze blowing in from the sea, the weather was better than it had been since they started traveling together. She lifted her face toward the sky and smiled. "Feels good to be on the move again."

He hesitated. "We could borrow a Rover, if you prefer, but—"

"No, I'd rather travel like this, with you and Gray. I don't mind if it takes longer."

That was an understatement. Mags knew damn well this was a terrible idea, but she was clutching at straws and making excuses to stick around. *I must be out of my mind.* Yet when he mounted and offered his hand, she took it and pulled herself up behind him without hesitation.

"Hold on," he called.

Mags wrapped her arms around his waist and leaned against his back, listening to the beat of his heart, peculiarly in tempo with the thud of Gray's hooves. The trip to Kelnora went faster this time since they didn't roam for hours in the opposite direction looking for an elusive scent trail. They rode away from Daruvar, then angled toward the sea. By nightfall, they reached the outskirts of town, much prettier wreathed in purple twilight instead of an ice storm.

Most of the snow had melted, leaving patches of bare mud. In the center of town, there was a farmer's market winding down with crates of wrinkly vegetables, barrels of fresh fish, and rounds of white cheese the merchant was selling by the slice. Farther along, there was a stall with hot savory pies and sugared fry bread. Everything smelled delicious, reminding Mags that they'd only paused once today.

The boy from the stable appeared, crooning to Gray, then he spoke to Gavriel in a pleading tone. "I'll take him. Can I?"

Normally, Gavriel didn't let anyone look after his mount, but this time, he nodded.

"Let's get dinner," she started to say, just as Gavriel asked, "Should we…?"

He leapt down from Gray's back, smiling, and turned the reins over to the lad. "Seems we're in agreement."

Thankfully he had Eldritch coin to spend, as she doubted Animari currency would be any good here. They strolled together, buying enough food—whatever looked good—to create a meal. She ate mushroom pie and grilled fish with lemon, a slice of cheese and then Gavriel bought some cinnamon fry bread, breaking off a piece.

He offered her a bite, an echo of how she'd fed him when he was tied to the bed. She parted her lips and ate the pastry, conscious of the way he was watching her. Hungry, attentive. Mags knew exactly what she was doing when she licked her lips.

"Good?" he asked.

"I like it."

"Want more?"

Why did I teach him these things? Before, he had no idea how to flirt, but he was a damned fast learner. "Yes, please."

The role reversal tantalized them both, especially since they were out in public where nothing could happen. He fed her another tidbit, alternating between them, until the bread was gone. A devil came over her then, and she licked his fingers clean, then she bit the tips, one by one. The sudden blaze in his eyes said she'd gotten the reaction she desired.

"Temptress," he whispered.

"Thank you," she said demurely.

Away from their various roles and responsibilities, this felt like a…date. Such an innocent word, one she had no reason to use any longer. Gavriel took her hand and carried it to his mouth, eyes on hers. And dammit, her heart fluttered. No, more than that, it was trying to turn over for him. *This shouldn't be happening.*

"Unless you stop me, I'm going to kiss you."

Her pulse went wild when he pulled her into the shadows of a nearby building. Gavriel kissed just as she'd taught him, open-mouthed and hungry. His tongue was hot, and he tasted of sugar. It was new to feel him hard against her already as she bit down on his lower lip. He moaned, breaking the kiss to angle his neck for her mouth, and she marked him there, eagerly, gladly.

"There's no end to this want," he said in a raw, aching tone.

"Rein it in. I'm not yanking you off right now, though if you're good, I'll do you with my mouth later."

He groaned and stepped away, so they weren't touching anymore. When he finally spoke, his voice was composed, no sign of his recent excitement. "Do you think Keriel and Leena are still at the public house?"

"It's as good a place to start as any."

He didn't let go of her hand as they walked, and she didn't insist, but she was oddly conscious of that single point of contact. His fingers were slender and callused, likely from long years of combat training, and his palms were hard. She remembered how gently he'd touched her in the bath and—

Enough of that. Live in the moment.

She had her emotions under control by the time they reached the inn. Even in good weather, the place was lively. She spotted Keriel right away; she seemed to be carrying drinks and wiping tables. *Did Haryk give her a job?* Leena was playing by the hearth and she glanced up as the door opened.

The little girl beamed when she spied Mags and Gavriel, rushing to them with such exuberance that Mags caught her, swung her around, and then tossed her to the Noxblade, who didn't miss a step. He snatched the child firmly and twirled her as well, until Leena was clinging to his neck and giggling.

The unfettered joy of his expression—that was how he should look. He wasn't meant for poison and shadows, being used as a weapon in someone else's war. If life had been kind, he would've grown up with a mother who loved him with all her heart and a father who could teach him the things a man should know. Suddenly, her eyes stung, and her throat was thick with tears.

What the hell.

Gently, Gavriel set Leena down, kneeling so she could still reach him. The little girl patted his cheek. "You came! You kept your promise. Did you bring me anything?"

Mags hadn't even thought of that, but to her surprise, he nodded, reaching into his pack. First, he produced two metal soldiers, next a softly worn cloth doll. He held up the first toy. "Play with these if you're feeling fierce."

Leena took them with a rapt smile and promptly banged their heads together. "Take that! No, you take this." Another headbutt.

"She has a future in combat," Mags said, grinning.

Gavriel gave her the doll next. "She'll keep you company if you're lonely. Play with her when you're feeling gentle."

"I won't let her fight the men," Leena declared.

"Why not?" Gavriel asked before Mags could.

"She's bigger. And maybe it seems like she's weak because she's soft, but they can't hurt her because she bends, see?" The girl demonstrated by folding the doll in half.

She can't be broken because she bends.

Why did that seem like such an astonishing piece of wisdom? She caught Gavriel's eye and thought he looked equally shocked by that insight. Mags smiled a little, and he smiled a lot, and *oh gods, we're doing that again*.

"You are unbearably clever," Gavriel said.

"Thank you." Leena kissed him on the cheek, and it wasn't clear if she meant for the toys or the compliment.

Either way, the sweetness left him motionless, watching Leena with a wistful expression. Mags found herself wishing he could meet someone who would understand him, cherish him, and give him a place to belong. *Someone who isn't me.*

Damn, that stings.

She masked that pain as best she could, asking brightly, "When did you prepare those gifts anyway? There are no shops in Daruvar."

He met her look, eyes sparkling. "I stole them. They belonged to Thalia at one point, but she won't miss them. She's not the sentimental sort."

"I love…that." The words almost came without her volition, and she barely swallowed the last one.

Your love's a curse. Never speak of it.

Bad enough that the feeling had fought past her locks and gates, despite all her efforts at self-preservation. It was too late now; she'd just have to ride it out and wait until the feeling faded. Six months should do it, maybe a year. For now, though, she devoured his face with her gaze, tracing his austere features with mental fingertips.

There's no stopping. I'm too far gone.

GAVRIEL NEARLY STOPPED breathing at the warmth of Mags's look. For long moments, he stared at her, wondering how it was possible that she got more beautiful every time he blinked. To test the theory, he opened and closed his eyes several times, and each time, she became more luminous, more enchanting, more…everything.

"Drinks are on me," Keriel said, cheerfully interrupting. Bending to set them on the table, she lowered her voice. "I have some information if you want it."

Gavriel glanced up, instantly alert. "Please tell us."

"Soon after you left, a party came through, bought up a suspicious amount of supplies, and when Haryk tried to be sociable, they shut him down. They were definitely citizens, but something about them set my teeth on edge."

"Why are you telling us this?"

"Well, it was plain you were hunting for something or someone when you found us. I thought maybe this would help."

"Do you have any idea which way they went?" Mags asked. She seemed to suspect the same as Gavriel, that those men could've been sent from the loyalist stronghold.

Keriel shrugged. "They said something about the finger islands if that means anything to you?"

Gavriel bit back a curse. "Well, that's good news, bad news territory," he said, as Keriel hurried to tend another table.

"Good first?" Mags suggested.

"I know exactly where they're hiding."

"Bad?"

"It'll be hard as hell to root them out…and we'll need to find someone who can loan us a boat."

She raised a brow. "Do you know how to sail?"

"Hell no. You?"

Laughing, she shook her head. "So we're both stumped. I guess tomorrow we ask at the docks. This is a fishing town, right? If you have some coin left, we can hire help."

Haryk came over then, shaking hands with Gavriel and Mags in turn. "You couldn't stay away, huh? Your room in the attic is available again if you want it. I won't even charge you for old times' sake."

"Come on, you couldn't anyway!" Mags protested. "There's no bed."

"I'm unclear why you're offering us special treatment," Gavriel said.

Perhaps it was his nature to be suspicious, but he wasn't taking favors, only to be dunned for them later. He fixed a skeptical stare on the innkeeper who bent to whisper, "I'm courting Keriel. Don't tell her, I'm not sure she's figured it out yet. If you hadn't brought them to town, we wouldn't have met. I'd still be a lonely old crust instead of the vibrant swain you behold today."

"Why is she working as a barmaid?" Mags asked. "Irina said she's a seamstress."

"I offered to build her a shop, but my lady love insists on paying her own way. She'll earn the money to open her own business, she says. I wish she'd just marry me and let me spoil her, but…" Haryk let out a gusty sigh.

"Then…felicitations," Gavriel said.

"Too soon! Do you want the room or not?"

"We'll take it," Mags answered.

Though he didn't normally drink the stuff, he finished the beer and watched Haryk chase Keriel, who didn't seem to know what to make of her employer's attention. He nudged Mags.

"What odds do you give them?"

Canting her head, she considered. "He's going about it wrong. If he wants to win Keriel, he needs to earn Leena's heart first, and she seems fairly indifferent."

The little girl was still playing in front of the fireplace, acting out dramatic scenes with her metal soldiers. Gavriel nodded. "You might be right. Shall we go up?"

Before, she'd asked if he had a place that belonged only to him, and the answer was no. But wherever she was felt like home. He didn't know when it had become that way, but it was truth now, so when they went upstairs to that cramped attic space with the round porthole window and boxes piled around, a sense of homecoming washed over him.

"Is it weird that I feel…nostalgic?" she asked. "Though it hasn't been that long."

"A lot has happened in a short time. So no, not at all."

As they talked, they laid the blankets together, and such a simple chore filled him with incredible joy. She took it for granted that they'd share the same covers now. He settled in first, waiting for her with a heart that wouldn't stop singing. It was all he could do to hide this absurd delight, biting his lower lip to smother the smile.

"They need so many things here," she went on, oblivious to his mood. "I wish there was something we could do."

"Perhaps we can, once we resolve our unfinished business."

"Yours, more than mine. But I did promise," she added, likely responding to Gavriel's sharp look.

I won't give you any excuse to slip away. Once we finish this, I'll come up with another reason why you must stay.

If he was lucky, this tactic would work for forty years or so, and they'd never speak of love. He didn't need to say the words or hear them; he only needed for Mags to stay beside him. As in response to his unspoken wish, she crawled under the covers.

"Let's play a game," he said then.

"Does this end with one of us tied up and—"

He set a finger against her lips, stopping the flow of tantalizing words. "Listen until I'm finished, please."

"Fine, go ahead."

"Sometimes in the guild, at night, after lessons were

done, they played 'Would You Rather'."

"They?" she asked softly.

"I was never invited." He didn't even care anymore. Those memories didn't have the power to gnaw at him. She'd granted him that shield with her warmth and her desire. "They thought I was silent and strange and ill-starred. Oriel sometimes joined their games, but he felt guilty about leaving me alone, and it was almost worse when he stayed."

"I get it. And I think I know this game. 'Would you rather eat a beetle or shave your head?' That sort of thing."

"I'd shave my head," Gavriel answered.

"That was only an example, but I guess we're playing for real now. Your turn."

Really, this was a chance to learn more about her without giving away his intentions, so he thought hard about the question. "Would you rather live without touching anyone or without being touched?"

"That's an easy one. Without being touched. That way I can still…"

His imagination filled in the blank in all manner of interesting ways. "I predicted that one. Go ahead."

"Hm, I don't like being predictable. Would you rather drink nothing but beer or eat nothing but cheese?"

"Cheese," he answered promptly. "It's embarrassing how much I love it."

"And you hate beer."

"You noticed?" he asked in surprise.

"Obviously. Your mouth curls ever so slightly to the left when you're not enjoying something."

He tried to look away, but he couldn't, even though she was like the sun burning away at his shadows, until his eyes stung. Nobody had ever observed him so closely. *What does that mean...?* He could barely stand the flicker of hope, blooming like some fragile flower inside him.

"It's a trifle alarming how well you seem to know me."

"Relax, I'm not cataloguing your weaknesses to use against you."

"I'm not concerned about that. Should we continue the game?"

"In all honesty, I'd rather get naked. I've been thinking about it ever since we kissed in the market." She leaned in, staring into his eyes, until he was dizzy with her scent, her touch, her warmth. "But I don't want you to feel like I'm disinterested in the talking, like I'm using you as a sex object."

"Use me," he said at once. "I'll be any object you wish. A desk, a table. Even a lamp, though the wiring might prove troublesome—" Then she kissed him, laughing and kissing at the same time.

It was the softest, silkiest kiss, and silly as well, and it filled his chest with helium. That he could make her smile, her eyes warm as melted honey. She broke away, touched her brow to his.

"I've never had anyone offer to be my sex lamp before."

"Rub me and make a wish," he blurted. Where was this nonsense coming from?

But her smile widened, and she giggled. Then she pinned him, whispered what she intended to do to him, and his whole body went up in flames.

25.

Morning came too quickly.

For Mags, it seemed like she'd barely fallen asleep and suddenly there were birds chirping, light streaming in the porthole window, and people bustling around downstairs. She rolled over and found Gavriel right there, eyes open, as if he'd been watching her for a while. When he saw that she was awake, he smiled.

"Ready to start the day?"

"Do I have a choice?" she grumbled.

"Of course. You could stay here instead of venturing to the islands with me."

"That's not happening," she said firmly.

Gavriel took that as his cue; he rolled out of the blankets and started getting dressed. With a groan, she did the same. They packed quickly, collected their gear, and went downstairs, where Haryk had breakfast waiting—fresh pastries, juice, hot tea, and sliced fruit. She would've been grateful for some fish, regretting her complaints about the food at Daruvar. In fair weather, there weren't many guests, just Mags, Gavriel, and another couple, who didn't seem sociable.

"You're on the way out, I see," Haryk observed.

Leena glanced up from shredding the pastry on her plate. "You're going already?"

"We can't ask them to stay forever." Keriel knelt beside her daughter's chair and put a gentle hand on her head. "I'm sure they'll visit again if they can."

"Definitely," Gavriel said.

He disappeared into the kitchen while Mags tried to be enthusiastic about another day without sufficient protein. As she filled a plate, Gavriel returned with a plate piled with dried fish. There was no controlling her smile when he offered it to her.

"Were you charming this out of the cook just now?" she asked.

"I don't know about that, but I did request it for you."

"Thanks. Our meals are typically heavier and more savory."

"I should do what I can to look after my partner properly," he said.

And he probably didn't mean that how it sounded. In some settlements, they used that word instead of 'mate' because it sounded more modern. Rather than wishing for impossible things before breakfast, she wolfed down the food, focusing on fish and bread, finishing with a bit of fruit and tea.

"Thanks."

"We should get to the docks, though I don't know anything about the tide situation. Perhaps we've already missed our opportunity."

Mags didn't think he sounded all that broken up at the prospect. "Then we'd have to spend the day wandering around together, seeing the sights."

"That would be a pity," he said, smiling.

"Let's stop by the stable to make sure Gray is all right. We also need to mention that we'll be gone for a bit."

"Sometimes I think you treasure that vedda beast more than I do." He cocked a brow, eyes gentle and amused.

"He's a very good boy." Mags knew she sounded defensive.

"But he's not a pet."

"Says you," she muttered.

Gavriel stood. "After you, then."

With a wave for everyone in the common room, he escorted her from the public house with a light touch on her back. In perfect sync, their steps turned toward the stable, across the road on a diagonal. Though it was early, she could hear the boy singing to the animals inside, which was all kinds of adorable.

A sudden thought occurred to her. "You never did play me your favorite song, the one you were humming in the shower."

"Since you didn't pursue it, I thought you weren't interested."

"There are levels of interest," she pointed out. "You were naked at the time, so I was a little distracted."

"I've never been called a distraction before, at least not in that way."

She nudged him with an elbow. "Don't let it go to your head."

"Too late. 'Very distracting when naked', I may have business cards printed up bearing that slogan."

"I hate you," she said mildly.

Instead of responding, he pushed open the stable doors. Half the stalls were occupied and Gray blustered when he saw them, lifting his head in excitement. The boy turned, brush in hand.

"Are you taking him already?"

Gavriel shook his head. "I'm here to compensate you and to ask that you look after him until we return. As yet, I'm not sure how long that will be."

Mags went to rub the sweet spot between Gray's horns while Gavriel completed the transaction. She heard the clink of coins being counted, but she didn't check on the details. The vedda beast bumped his head against her shoulder when she paused in the scratching. "Demanding, aren't you? Just like a certain someone."

"I heard that," Gavriel said.

The boy let out a muffled snicker. "I'll take good care of him, I promise."

"Then our business here is done. Mags?"

He held out a hand, and she took it, like they were vacationing instead of heading off on what might be a suicide mission. Sometimes she thought maybe she'd lost her mind because nobody in the pride knew what she was doing. This wasn't Ash Valley business, which was why Dom had let her go in the first place. Now that she had an answer about Slay, she should've headed back and resumed her normal life.

She forced these disquieting thoughts down, keeping them at bay with silent justification. *I'm keeping a promise; that's all. The pride can function without me for a bit.*

In silence, they headed for the docks, an ambitious name for a small cluster of boats. A few fishermen were tending to their nets on the pier, and one man was headed for his sloop with determined strides. Gavriel quickened his step, towing Mags with him. Unless she wanted to let go, she had to keep up.

"Are you open to hire?" Gavriel called, instead of a more traditional greeting.

The man paused with his hands on the ropes that tethered his small craft to the dock. "I suppose that depends on what you want and how much you're paying."

"Do you know the way to the finger islands?" Mags asked.

"Of course, it's not far. The approach is a bit risky, though. Are you looking to book an excursion?" He glanced between them, but whatever he thought about their linked hands didn't show in his face.

"You could say that. I've heard there's a large group sheltering there, and they come periodically to buy supplies. Do you know anything about that?"

The sailor spat, over the side of his boat and into the sea. "Bastards, the lot of them. They claim to be revolutionaries, but they're just a bunch of raiders and thieves."

"Raiders?" She glanced at Gavriel, wondering what he made of this.

"They only buy what they can't steal. They've been taking produce and livestock from farmers all along the coast. Oh, they call it expropriation, claiming there will be reimbursement for loyalists after they take Talfayen lands from the pretender, but I heard the radio message. They're outlaws now, plain and simple."

Mags decided to cut to the chase. "Sounds like they need to be dealt with. We'll take care of the problem if you get us there. How much for transport?"

"The two of you against a small army?" The sailor laughed and shook his head. "Still, it's your funeral." He named a price and Gavriel paid it without hesitation. "Come aboard, then. I'll drop you off but I'm not staying. I know how dangerous those men are. They butchered a family who tried to resist."

"Consider us warned," Mags said, hopping from the pier to the deck of the boat.

Even tied to the dock, she could feel the roll of the water beneath her. *This is not optimum for a tiger.* She turned to Gavriel as he joined her. "Do we need to arrange for our pickup beforehand?"

As the sailor set off, Gavriel said, "Return in five days. If we're not waiting where you left us, you're free to go."

"Whatever you say, mate. They've got a boat you could steal, provided you survive whatever you have planned, but I don't suppose you'd know what to do with it."

Mags was starting to like how plain-spoken this man was. "That's true. I'm Magda, by the way, and this is Gavriel."

"Ceras, pleasure and what-not. There's a bench in the prow if you care to park it for a while. It's about two hours, give or take."

THE DAY BRIGHTENED as the sun rose, but it never warmed Gavriel completely.

His chill was more of the spirit anyway, contemplating all the harm that had been wrought in his father's name. Just thinking that sent a low-grade wave of nausea through him, though that could also be the unaccustomed rocking of the ship. Mags had been standing in the front of the boat, looking out over the water, but she suddenly came to perch beside him, taking his hand in hers.

He expected her to thread their fingers together but

instead she flattened his palm and pressed two fingers firmly to a spot on his wrist. "What are you doing?" he asked.

"This is supposed to help with nausea."

Once again, she'd discerned the tiniest shift in his demeanor. Maybe the pressure really was helping, but he suspected it might also be her care. The queasy roll of his stomach faded as he gazed at the top of her head, deep brown burnished with gold from the spring sun. Those braids had been pretty and fresh a few days before. Now they were messy and half-unraveled, and she had never looked more beautiful.

"It's better," he said.

"Just let me finish. Hold still for another minute."

That was no hardship, though her words filled his head with illicit images. Gavriel knew damn well she didn't mean for her words to make him think of sex, but now, she was inextricably linked to certain urges. "Thanks," he managed to say, feeling the heat rising in his neck, cheeks, ears.

Oh gods.

She peered at him. "Are you feeling better?"

"Physically, yes."

"Do you want to talk about it?"

"This is my father's legacy," he said softly. "Violence. Hate. I wish Lileth had taken that secret to her grave. Before, I was ashamed of what he represented, but now I know that *his* blood runs in my veins."

"We don't get to choose our families. I know a lot of people who would've picked otherwise if they could. The only thing you can control is where you go from here." She offered a tentative smile and added, "You want a hug? I got hugs."

Gavriel could scarcely have imagined finding that awkward offer so endearing or so irresistible. "At the moment I can't think of anything I want more."

She wrapped her arms around him tightly, and he let his head rest on her shoulder. Her incredible strength surrounded him, as did her scent, and he raised his face to rub his cheek against hers because he'd seen the cats doing that in Ash Valley. While he didn't know what it meant, her soft intake of breath pleased him.

The time passed quicker than he wanted. Soon, Ceras was calling, "This is as far as I can take you. There's no proper dock here, so you'll have to swim for it."

"Oh gods," Mags whimpered.

Gavriel stared at her, suddenly worried. "You can swim?"

"It's not my favorite sport, but I can manage. I think."

It was strange to see her so uncertain, peering over the side with a troubled look. Ceras burst out laughing. "Can't believe how gullible you two are. For hell's sake, borrow my life raft." He chucked a yellow, inflatable boat in their general direction.

Gavriel caught it easily. "Thanks."

It took a good ten minutes to put air in the thing, even taking turns with Mags, then they went down a rope ladder and managed to get into the raft without flipping it. Ceras tossed them a paddle. "Be waiting here in the raft in five days. If you're not, our deal is done, and you're on your own."

"Understood," Mags said. "One quick question, are there any settlements on this island? Other than the raiders."

Ceras shook his head. "That's a hell no."

After some experimentation, Gavriel got the hang of nudging them toward shore. This would be hell in heavy weather but for now, the sea was calm. Hopefully, it would be in five days as well. Near the shore, the water was clear enough to show the sandy bottom, along with startled fish and rocky outcroppings. He hopped over the side into calf-deep water and towed the raft until Mags could get out without drenching her pants.

"Chivalrous," she noted.

"I'm already wet. There's no need for you to be also."

She nodded. "We should deflate this thing and find a place to stash it, where it won't wash away or be spotted by our enemies."

Our enemies. Odd, how much he loved the easy way she said that. Gavriel tried to control his delight, as this was not the time to be dwelling on emotional issues. They were deep in enemy territory with limited supplies and no help coming. On impulse, he set the raft down and checked his phone.

"No signal," he said.

Mags shrugged, seeming less alarmed than he might have anticipated. "We already knew that we're on our own. Even if we could call for help, it would take too long for anyone to get here as backup. Whatever happens, it's on us."

"And you're all right with that?"

"I made you a promise," she said softly. "No take backs."

He searched her face intently. "Is that the only reason?"

Her golden gaze skittered away, a fact he found fascinating. "Are we going to stand here all day? I'm sure they have eyes on the coast. We need to keep moving and find a good spot to do some recon."

"Point taken."

Gavriel scanned the narrow, rocky beach where they'd come ashore, a small break between the sheer cliffs that dominated this side of the island. Seabirds nested in the crags and hollows of the rock, so the stone was liberally drizzled in white, and that wasn't sea salt. There didn't appear to be much in the way of shelter—*aha*.

"We can bury it over there." Mags had followed his line of sight and found the hollow just as he did. "Near the rock shaped like a heart."

"That is not anatomically correct."

She laughed and opened the nozzle, already stepping on the raft to deflate it. "Why are you like this? You know damn well what I mean." Then she curved her hands together, making a romantic heart with them. "Tell me that rock doesn't look—"

"You're right. I'm teasing," he cut in.

"I don't hate it."

The warmth of her smile carried him through the camouflage of their exit strategy. They also removed a few necessary items to carry with them in shoulder bags, then they stashed their larger packs as well. Once they finished, Gavriel dusted off his hands and turned inland. Depending on how big the island was, it could take a while to track down the hideout, despite being this close.

Only he'd forgotten that he was traveling with the brilliant, relentless Magda Versai. There was nobody better suited to finishing what they'd started.

She was already stripping off her clothes. "Here, hold my stuff."

"You can track someone without a particular scent?" he asked, putting her pants in his bag. "Sorry if that's an ignorant or offensive question."

"It's not. Basically, I'll be looking for traces of anyone who's not us. From what Ceras said, I won't run across scent markers left by civilians or settlers. If they've gone hunting, I might follow the trail at random for a while, but eventually, it will lead us where we need to go."

"Unless they died alone in the wild," Gavriel said.

"In which case, we'll find the body and I'll look for another trail to follow. Do you have a better plan?"

"Certainly not. I do have a request, however."

"What's that?"

"Before you shift, I'd like a kiss for luck."

"That's practically science," she said.

"We can't omit science," he agreed.

Mags smirked. Somehow she was completely in her element, even standing in her underwear on a beach deep in enemy territory. She closed the distance between them, and Gavriel wrapped her up in his arms, loving how substantial she felt there. Hard to say if that was the best part or when she put her mouth to his, soft as a butterfly wing.

Closing his eyes, he deepened the kiss, tasting her, sipping at her tongue. Her nipping at his lower lip made him shiver, not the brisk sea breeze. It was dangerous here—he knew it was—but he couldn't muster even a trace of fear.

Dying held little terror for him, far less than the prospect of a life without her.

26.

AFTER A KISS that straight up curled her toes, Mags stepped back, trying not to smile. It was a losing battle. "You feeling lucky yet?"

"You have no idea."

She finished taking off her clothes and shifted, relishing the pull on her muscles. Prowling in a circle, she butted her head against his leg and Gavriel stilled. He looked comically unprepared to have a tiger circling him this way.

"Do you… that is, should I…pet you? May I?"

Mags dipped her head once to indicate assent, and he set a hand on her head with such delicacy that she could barely feel it, until he tickled the backs of her ears. They flickered in response, but she didn't swipe at him as she would anyone else.

Soon, he knelt and ran a confident palm down her back. "Your fur is thicker than I thought it would be." Then he cupped her face and rubbed her cheeks, like she was a house cat, and… she didn't hate it.

Tigers couldn't purr, but she rumbled her approval, followed by a happy chuff. When she padded away, it was her signal that she was done. He straightened at once.

"Apologies, I got carried away. Lead on."

Hurriedly he stuffed her panties and bra in his bag and shouldered it, and Mags wished she could laugh, but tiger vocalization didn't permit it. She settled into tracking mode, but this might prove difficult, as there were only wildlife odors on the beach. It stood to reason that the settlement wouldn't be too far inland, though, maybe closer to a more hospitable port. She headed up the rocky slope toward the top of the cliffs, hoping to find a better vantage point. That gave her an incredible sea view, but nothing more.

The birds scattered on their approach, circling and screeching overhead. Gavriel shaded his eyes. "You're not finding anything?"

She stared at him.

"Never mind, it was rhetorical. You'd already be racing in the right direction if you had a lead." He knelt, examining faint signs of wear on the stone. "This is a path, if a little used one. Should we see where it goes?"

In answer, she set off along the rocky trail, following it down the hill away from the sea. It veered north after a while. So far, she'd only smelled small animals and the fresh salt tang of the air. A pile of rocks stood directly ahead. Old Animari ruins featured balanced stacks like this as grave markers; she couldn't ask if that was the case with the Eldritch, but she stopped to sniff around the base, circling it in curiosity.

Beyond the earthy rock smell and the green of the surrounding plant life, she caught a faint whiff of carrion. *Something or someone is buried here.* On the far side of the memorial, there was the faintest hint of Eldritch, old enough that the elements had nearly erased all signs of passage.

She moved in widening circles, aggravated over all the

competing odors. Gavriel watched her work; he probably knew what she was doing. Finally, she locked onto the scent trail and heaved a mental sigh of relief. This sort of thing was better left to Pine Ridge, but there was no wolf handy, so she had to make it work.

Mags ran a few steps, then glanced back to make sure Gavriel was with her. On foot, she could easily outpace him, except that she was moving at less than half speed, constantly checking to make sure she hadn't lost the scent. In that way, they edged along, heading back toward the sea, though farther down the coast.

The land was craggy and rough, covered in yellow and purple flowers. Someone more botanically inclined might know their names. Mags passed through the flower field with a few sneezes and paused in astonishment when she saw the ruined keep rising in the distance, all crumbling stone that made Daruvar look modern.

Beyond, the sea glittered blue-gray in the spring sun, the perfect buffer against incursion. The inlet didn't look any kinder to ships, so the loyalists didn't need to fear an armada sailing in under the cover of darkness, not that anyone had a navy these days. The Pax Protocols had let the Numina relax, content with the accords as they were drawn hundreds of years ago.

"This is what's left of Perlsea," Gavriel breathed.

She cocked her head and tapped her paw twice, hoping he'd read it as a cue to elaborate.

"How much do you know of Eldritch history?" he asked.

Mags shook her head. That would be essentially nothing.

"Then I'll give you the short version. Perlsea was the

final bastion of the Silver Queen, the queen who last reigned over a unified Eldritch empire. When her vassals turned on her, she retreated here for her last stand. I suppose these bastards think this is a fitting place to do the same."

Mags studied the ruins, noting all the breaches in the walls. It wouldn't be hard to get in there. Hunting all the men down might prove problematic, but she had an expert in silent kills standing beside her, and she wasn't bad at stealth strikes either, especially in tiger form.

A sudden thought occurred to her. That grave marker, would it have been the fabled Eldritch queen? If so, then she'd probably caught the scent trail of one of the loyalists paying homage to her memory, a pilgrimage to ask for her blessing on their endeavor. Yeah, they were shit out of luck in that regard.

A sudden sigh drew her eyes to Gavriel, still crouched and staring down at the keep. The Seer's retreat was the oldest structure in the Ash Valley holdings, and it didn't compare to either Daruvar or Perlsea. She tried to guess what was troubling him, came up empty. Mags bumped his leg with her head and asked silently, though maybe that was pointless. He hadn't proven particularly adept at reading feline expressions.

This time, though, he said, "You're wondering what's the matter?"

Mags nodded.

"It's... probably I shouldn't tell you, as it's one of our darkest secrets, but...there are stories. Have you heard them? That my people created the Golgoth to fight for us, our brutish foot soldiers."

That was the gossip, but Mags hadn't put any stock in it. She tilted her head, waiting for him to go on.

"That's true. I ran across an account in the guild's forbidden archives. I wasn't supposed to be there, of course, but I'd just come into my gift, and there was nowhere I wouldn't go, confident in my ability to evade detection."

Damn.

Part of her wanted to shift so she could ask questions properly. The other half figured he'd tell her whatever he wanted, and her own words were extraneous. So she tapped the ground twice.

He smiled slightly. "I'm not sure exactly what that means, but I hear you saying 'go on' when you do it."

She growled her agreement.

"Anyway, after the Silver Queen's fall, this place fell into disuse for a long time. Until House Talfayen began its...experiments, crossing Eldritch and Animari lines through unethical science. Do you take my meaning?"

The Golgoth were created here? She wondered if there was a secret lab, if there would be failed versions of the Golgoth roaming the ruins, monstrous, mindless, and brutal. To get clarification, she'd have to shift, and that would burn energy she couldn't spare. Plus, Gavriel probably didn't know those answers either.

He went on, "I'm telling you this because I don't know what's down there. It may be more dangerous than we anticipated."

This was all kinds of fucked up. The Eldritch made the Golgoth, and now they were following the path of their progenitors, kidnapping Animari to do gods knew what with them. She bared her teeth and snarled.

Gavriel misread her response. "Yes, you can look after yourself, but you should know this much at least. As before, we should wait until dark to make our move. We'll watch from here until then and note their movements."

To show that she had no quarrel with that plan, Mags settled on the rock, staring down at the ruins with laser focus.

Don't get comfortable. We're coming for you, assholes.

GAVRIEL MISSED TALKING with Mags instead of at her, but he understood why she was sticking to tiger form.

He'd packed bottles of water, adding to the supplies she'd pilfered from Daruvar, so they had a strange, makeshift picnic while keeping watch. There was a boat moored at the base of the cliff, so the loyalists must know the safe way to traverse the treacherous rocks. That was also how they stayed clear of Talfayen patrols on the mainland.

If not for the intel from Keriel and Ceras, he never would have suspected they'd claimed one of Thalia's holdings, even if Perlsea was remote and abandoned. Actually, that made it perfect for loyalist purposes. There was historic gravitas on this soil, for multiple reasons, and as the saying went, it was always darkest beneath the lamppost.

The waiting part of surveillance was the worst, and he envied Mags's ability to curl up anywhere and go to sleep, leaving the actual observation to him. He had long-range binocs in his bag as part of his toolkit, and at first, there was no movement at all.

In time, however, a few people emerged and moved across what would be the bailey, if the walls were intact. It looked like there had to be a substructure, an underground level. His stomach roiled at the prospect of confronting the dreadful deeds his people had done in the name of progress. No, not even that—from the desire to kill and maim without risking their own bodies. Even to Gavriel, that was despicable.

Just as well Mags couldn't ask questions right now or demand he speak in Eldritch defense, because he had no words to give to that cause.

Silently, Gavriel watched and waited. He recorded movements and numbers, calculating their odds, though it was impossible to be sure how many enemies the sublevel concealed. There could be hundreds hidden below.

In time, the sun dropped in the west, painting the sky orange and scarlet with ribbons of pink that faded to silver and then deepest blue. Mags roused when it cooled and glanced around with sleepy golden eyes. She looked at the starry sky and cocked her head at Gavriel as if to ask, *Are we ready?*

"I know as much as I'm going to," he answered. "I've seen at least thirty over the course of the day. Though I hate to suggest this, we should split up. You'll have an easier time picking them off in the ruins. Inside what I'm guessing is a lab, it will be better lit with less cover. My gift should keep me safe, but…"

She nodded her agreement; it seemed that she saw his point about a tiger roving the corridors inside. That would be too dangerous and fearing for her might distract him so much that he made a fatal mistake. While he didn't fear death, he wasn't quite ready to make his final bow yet, especially when it was preventable.

"Whatever happens tonight, keep yourself safe. We'll meet back here at dawn. If we haven't finished them, we'll find a place to lay low and make another run tomorrow night."

Depending on the numbers in play, they might need to deploy guerilla warfare tactics. He had no compunction about whittling away at the opposition and vanishing like a ghost. That was his wheelhouse, after all.

Mags nodded once, rubbed her head against his leg, then she dragged her claws across the loose dirt and bounded off. Possibly he should have said something else, but it was too late. He lost sight of her swiftly, as she used rocks and scrub to her advantage.

Kneeling, he saw that she'd drawn a heart, like the one she'd made with her hands earlier that day. He wished he could scoop up that dirt and take it with him because nobody had ever done anything like this for him before. It was absurd and adorable, and he did take a pinch of soil from the center.

For luck, he told himself, trying not to feel like ten kinds of fool for having loose dirt in his pocket.

Now it was his turn to move. No need to use his gift yet—ever since Zan died, he'd been painfully conscious that he was burning life energy when it kicked in. Sometimes Gavriel did wonder how much time he had left, as he'd once ghosted like a child gleefully tossing bits of colored paper on a fire. It wasn't time to worry about that, either. Once he finished this last job, he could retire as Death's Shadow and find some other purpose, something that didn't leave him feeling bitter and bedeviled.

The shadows cradled him as he crept toward Perlsea. Ancient stones, ancient mortar and broken bits of stained glass, tributes to a fallen monarch. Drawing closer, he heard the rumble of voices, male and female. Gavriel paused to listen in case their words should prove useful.

"I'm telling you, we should go while the getting is good," a woman said. "Vayne's lost it. The houses are all swearing to that Talfayen whelp, and once she's crowned, we don't have a chance in hell of success."

"He'll cut your tongue out if he hears you talking that way," a male voice responded.

"I'm with Vera," someone else said.

A chorus of general agreement rippled through the group. He identified five or six different voices from the talk. If there was dissent in the ranks, that might help, if only he could figure some way to use it.

"I'll run away with you, Vera m'love," a new voice said cheerfully. "I wanted a place in the old lord's glorious new empire, but there's not gonna be anything like that and I'm sick of squatting in this pile of stones."

"Then die here," said an immeasurably cold voice.

Someone gasped, whimpered, and Gavriel heard the wet sound of a blade leaving a bloody wound. The woman was breathing hard, barely restraining her sobs. The dead man must have been important to her or maybe she feared taking a knife in the gut.

"Anyone else care to defy me?"

That must be Vayne.

A rumble of negatives in response, most tinged in fear. The lot of them must stink of terror sweat, easy targets for Mags when he moved off. Making a snap decision, Gavriel followed him, hoping to learn the way inside the base. He skirted the rest of the group, who were whispering as the leader stalked away.

Focusing, he activated his gift, and it whined in his ear, annoying as a bee, but now his footsteps felt light as air. He was a shadow, slipping after the one they called Vayne.

There were no lights posted outside, and in the starlight, he evaded rocks that would trip him up, avoiding dry sticks and the odd tripwire, laid by a paranoid and possibly insane commander.

He was deep inside the ruins now. So far, he hadn't noticed any hint of Magda, who must be killing with remarkable stealth and efficiency. Gavriel spared a brief wish for her safety, then centered his whole being on tracking this monster to his lair. Someone who didn't hesitate to dispose of his own men was exactly the sort of devil Lord Talfayen—*my father*—would choose to do his bidding.

That was another reason he had to finish this, one he couldn't bear to speak aloud, even to Mags. *I must finish what my father started.* But not in the way Lord Talfayen would have wanted. Gavriel would nail shut the coffin of that new Eldritch empire, where they ruled with an iron fist and treated the other Numina as chattel, and then bury it so deep that no other power-mad nationalist could exhume it.

At the heart of the keep, which was more like a labyrinth from olden times, there was a set of heavy metal doors, set into the earth like steel teeth. There were no locks or chains; nobody would imagine that they were needed out here. He waited in the shadows as Vayne threw them open and stormed into the darkness below.

Gavriel counted to a hundred and followed. Time for the killing to commence.

27.

M<small>AGS WAS OUTNUMBERED</small>, beyond backup, and completely content with her situation, even if she was ass-deep in enemy territory.

She waited for Gavriel to slip past those wandering the ruins, as her strike might put the facility on alert. Once his scent faded from the wind, she figured it was safe to start the carnage. Blood lingered in the air from the recent killing, though they seemed to be leaving the body where it was. It could be fear of their unhinged leader or disregard for a fallen comrade. Either way, they'd be joining him soon enough.

There were ten loyalists moving around the ruins, solo, and in small groups. Most didn't seem to be formally patrolling, and two were noisily having sex. They must have no fear whatsoever of being found. Tigers couldn't smile, per se, but Mags showed her teeth as she crept up behind the man standing by himself, gazing out to sea. She leapt on him and snapped his neck with a powerful crunch of her jaws, then she hauled the body toward the cliff and let it fall. The birds would feast tonight.

She lacked Gavriel's ability to disappear in plain sight,

and the night was bright with a waxing gibbous moon bright as a sky lantern, and the stars boosted its brilliance, leaving her fewer shadows to hide in. Using the half-fallen walls as cover, she moved on silent paws through the wreckage of Perlsea. Every second she recalled his warning that there could be monsters, though if they roamed the surface freely, it seemed like the nine Eldritch nearby might show a bit more wariness.

The two finished hooking up, and one of them ambled away to smoke. *Didn't anyone teach you how bad this is for you?* He lit up, the tip of the cigarette glowing orange as he inhaled, and Mags rushed, slamming him face-first into the wall. She bit through his spinal cord and then clamped down, dashing his head against the wall for good measure. There was a thump, but the quick kill prevented any outcry. It was a risk to drag the body all the way to the cliff, so she left him there, mostly hidden by a fall of stones.

To her acute senses, the night reeked of blood, but the Eldritch probably wouldn't notice. She had the taste in her mouth now, too sweet, but not viscous or tainted like those who used gray tar. Plus, these Eldritch were talking just fine, proving the Talfayen loyalists weren't involved in House Manwaring's plot.

Eight more.

She listened, creating a mental map of her targets, based on what she heard. The woman was looking for the smoking man. If she knew where her lover liked to light up, she'd be here soon. Mags crouched, waiting for the opportunity to attack. Steps crunched over loose rock, getting closer. When she glimpsed the woman's profile, she struck, blindsiding her with a flank attack, and tore out her throat with her teeth. This was a wet, messy kill and she silenced the gurgles with two large paws, then she dragged the body to conceal it beside the other one.

Mags spat, trying to get the taste out of her mouth. She'd been lucky so far, but it would be a mistake to count on that good fortune holding. And sure enough, as she turned, there came the sound of someone moving toward her quickly, steps more purposeful than anyone she'd encountered so far, and he was shining a light around too.

"Where the hell is everyone?"

She tried to get behind him, but his senses were sharp, and he whirled before she hit his back. *Dammit, he has a weapon too.* He was fast enough to get a round off, firing point-blank across her side. The thickness of her hide and fur prevented the bullet from penetrating, but the pain…damn. Even a graze stung like a bitch. She hit him with her full strength, knocking him down. As the gun clattered out of his hand, she swiped with both claws and slashed open his stomach, finishing with a clamp of her powerful jaws.

But this wasn't a quiet, tidy kill. Now there was a lot of noise heading in her direction, and she had six more to take out. Leaving the body where it was, she bounded toward the hill leading away from the ruins. If they were foolish enough to give chase, she'd do better drawing them away from Perlsea.

"What the hell," a male voice exclaimed. "We've got multiple people down! Looks like a wild animal attack."

"What could've done this?" A woman asked, maybe the one whose love got murdered by their leader.

"Maybe a bear?" the first person guessed. "If it woke up from hibernation hungry and there was no food…?"

Dumbasses. The wounds she'd inflicted looked nothing

like a bear attack, but better if they didn't think this was a calculated invasion. That meant if she waited, they'd let down their guard. Nobody seemed to want to go out into the dark hills, despite the brightness of the night. Her side burned, but it was healing; that would cost her in terms of energy. With all the tracking beforehand, she'd already been a tiger for a while. Mags didn't know how much longer she could hold on.

When her wound sealed fully, she crept back toward Perlsea, pausing every few steps to listen. There were only four left here. Two had probably gone inside to report on the situation up top. Gavriel hadn't said what he wanted her to do once she whittled their numbers down, so she'd make that call when the time came. The idea of leaving him on his own chafed at her, worry bubbling up around the seal she'd set on her emotions. Attachments only got in the way at a time like this, but when she imagined something happening to him, losing him like she had Brendan and Tamara—*no, stop thinking about it.*

You have four targets left. Figure it out after they're dead.

Listening revealed their locations; they were searching in teams of two, which would make her task more difficult, but she'd killed way more at once. The main issue here was trying to avoid setting off a high-alert alarm, so loyalists all came flooding out at once. That rush might screw up whatever Gavriel was doing inside.

Luckily, she had the strength to overpower two at once, even if they were ready. She just had to abandon caution and go for it. Mags chose the closest pair and stalked them, listening to their fearful conversation with a touch of amusement.

"You think it'll come back? It didn't get a chance to…eat

anything."

"Probably. It must still be hungry, though it's strange that it didn't try to take one of the kills when it ran."

"We haven't found Darrel's body. Maybe…"

"Oh, that's a good point. Maybe it's eating him and won't bother us again."

Darrel must be the one she'd pushed off the cliff. It was funny, the stories people made up to comfort themselves. They were a bit casual about the prospect of their former comrade being devoured by a fictional bear, though.

Maybe nobody liked Darrel.

When they passed close enough to her, she pounced from behind, taking them down in a powerful leap. A slash and a bite left them both gargling red, and she finished them quickly with two more bites. Ugh, the sweetness of Eldritch blood must stem from their diet, and she wished she could cleanse her palate.

No time for that. Two left.

These Eldritch had weapons out and ready; they were taking no chances. From the smell, they were armed with knives and guns. Safest to assume the blades were poisoned. Mags hoped they weren't using Animari killing rounds; she could shake off almost anything else. Hell, a graze had almost ended her on the mainland; a full shot out here would do the job.

She'd bet her life that they weren't. They still hadn't figured out that someone smarter and more strategic than a wild animal was hunting them. Once they were dead, she'd go in to provide backup to Gavriel.

Her mind made up, she leapt. And took two bullets and a burning, poisoned slash before they died in agony.

Yeah, this…could be a problem.

The facility had seen better days.

Fifty years ago, this technology might have been cutting edge, but now, this place looked like a villainous cliché, where evil retreated to lick its wounds. The place was a warren, and Gavriel did recon first, counting heads and evading security cameras with a proficiency befitting Death's Shadow. There were more forces quartered here than he'd reckoned on, closer to one hundred than fifty, and picking them off would take forever. Though it was certainly possible, he preferred a quicker solution.

For now, he'd start at the top. If he eliminated Vayne, the hierarchy might collapse, and the rest would scatter, no longer willing to fight for a lost cause. It wasn't an ideal solution because the sudden vacuum might result in a power struggle, giving some other fanatic the opportunity to step up. Without knowing more about their organization, it was impossible for him to predict what would happen.

Either way, I'm killing Vayne.

From his observations, the leader moved with at least three men, even inside the stronghold. That explained why nobody had attempted to stop the execution earlier. There had been enough followers gathered to overwhelm Vayne if they had mutiny in mind, but the presence of multiple bodyguards changed the scenario. It might be best to bide his time and wait until they settled in for the night, then he could execute Vayne in his sleep.

Amused, Gavriel watched them scurry in and out; Mags must be wreaking havoc above. He was hidden in an old research room, and judging by the thick coating of dust, this place hadn't been used in years. The observation window offered the perfect vantage for him to note their routines, time their patrols, and even track their indiscretions.

Already, he'd noticed that one guard had a drug habit, and another seemed to be drinking on duty.

Isolation did take its toll. They'd followed Lord Talfayen this far—funny how he shied from calling the bastard anything else—and it must be difficult to admit that their road to glory led to a dead end. Well, that and the fact that Vayne murdered anyone who considered abandoning the cause.

The time passed slowly, but Gavriel was used to long periods of inaction. Above all else, he was a patient hunter. When the lights dropped into low for the night and patrols lessened, the time between them expanding to half an hour, he made his move. Stepping lightly, he wondered in passing how he might appear to others, a ghost slipping in and out of existence with each flicker of the lights. *There, not there.*

Near Vayne's room, he mistimed a step and wound up squaring off against two surprised sentries. On a burst of inspiration, he whipped the dirt from his pocket and flung it into their eyes. While they scratched at their faces, fearing poison dust that would dissolve their corneas, Gavriel dispatched them with two precise strikes.

Well-played, Mags. You saved me again.

Quickly he hid the bodies and continued to Vayne's quarters. The door was locked, but technology this old proved no challenge for his skills. He cracked the panel, sliced two wires with his dagger, then crossed them, and the short popped the door open.

Keeping his blade out, he glided inside. The lights were out, and heavy breathing sounded nearby. Gavriel waited for his eyes to acclimate, identifying the furniture as part of a sitting room. A quick scan confirmed no concealed heat signatures, just the one he expected in the bedchamber.

Seems like Vayne sleeps alone.

That was good news. Light as a feather, he edged toward the bedroom and nearly, nearly, got caught by the tripwire strung across the doorway. Gavriel smiled. While he could disarm it, why bother? Stepping over the trap, he padded the last few meters to the bed. Luck stayed with him, as Vayne was sprawled on his stomach, face turned away. Gavriel struck with clinical precision, blade to the kidney, turn and twist, then a slash to the neck. The first blow was to disable; the second finished him off. He put a pillow over Vayne's head, pressing his face into the mattress, to muffle his death cries and catch some of the blood, and he didn't budge until the man stopped moving.

Perfect, quiet, and relatively clean.

Since this bastard was the only one who had his own room, the rest might be complicated. It was harder to kill without detection with others in the room. If someone roused at the wrong time, he might have a fight on his hands, and that wasn't his preferred setup. Before leaving the room, he washed his face and hands, then wiped down his shoes. Though the floors were old and worn, bloody traces would give him away even if his gift let him avoid notice. The tingle at the back of his head reminded Gavriel how much life he was burning, and he let the gift go.

Most probably, his own natural stealth would allow him to avoid detection, and he didn't intend to leave anyone alive to check security footage. He just hadn't decided how to go about it yet. In his usual kit, he had various poisons, maybe enough to take out everyone if he laced their food. That was a risky move, however. If one guard ate before everyone else and showed symptoms, they'd be put on alert.

I'll set that idea on the back burner.

He'd never needed to take out so many in one strike before; as swan songs went, this was a hit for the history books. Thinking that prompted a bitter smile as he slipped out of the dead man's quarters. *Hope Mags is all right.* With no signal on their phones, there was no way to check in with her. Better to stay focused and trust she'd keep safe until their scheduled rendezvous at first light.

There were eight barracks-style rooms, and each slept ten—grunts, he guessed. The officers were quartered together in another part of the facility, two to a room. It was probably best to continue his bloody work there, working his way down the hierarchy, reducing the probability that there would be anyone left to lead. On his way to his next target, he passed the armory, then backed up in silent interest.

Maybe they had something in here to make his job easier. Since nobody knew he was inside, they weren't hunting him, and with plenty of time before daybreak, he could check out their offensive capabilities. This door was sealed, but he repeated the workaround that got him inside Vayne's room, and soon he had full access to their stockpile.

Gavriel found the usual stash of ammo and poison, nothing too exciting, but on the bottom shelf…he dropped to his knees, verifying the find. *This is what they used to blow up half of Ash Valley.* They must be planning another bombing, but he wouldn't give them the opportunity. Quickly, he stuffed all the charges, detonator, and related supplies into a canvas bag. His vicious inner voice insisted that this was the perfect end for these loyalist bastards. They'd die in terror and anguish, just like the innocent cats.

Instead of taking them out one by one, he'd end them with an enormous fireball, and their stronghold would become a mass grave. Delighted with the poetic justice of it, he planted charges while these assholes slept. Though it took hours, Gavriel reckoned it was well worth the time and patience when he slipped out, detonator in hand.

He put plenty of space between him and the facility as the sky began to lighten. Mags should be out of the ruins, well on her way to the meeting point, so he whispered, "Good night, Lord Talfayen's loyal men." And hit the button.

Even at this distance, the ground rumbled beneath his feet, trembling with the series of explosions that would collapse the lab, incinerate the loyalists, or bury them alive. No matter what became of them, no help was coming, so they'd die as they'd lived, isolated from the rest of the world and wallowing in senseless hatred.

In the end, it wouldn't take five days to finish this. He and Mags could rest up here and take a break from the endless violence. They had the supplies from Daruvar, and if that wasn't enough, he'd fish and she could hunt. Gavriel had no doubt they could survive until Ceras collected them.

Except…she didn't come. He waited until the sun was high in the sky before fear sank sharp claws into him. And he searched. Everywhere.

No sign of Mags, his beloved tiger woman.

When he realized what might have happened, Gavriel's knees buckled and he screamed until his voice gave, eyes too dry for tears, heart too broken for him to survive it.

28.

MAGS HAD TWO massive problems.

One was the pair of bullets lodged in her body, inhibiting her ability to heal. Though they weren't Animari killers, they *were* treated black iron, which thinned her blood and kept it from coagulating, so the wounds were still trickling hours later. The second problem—and this one was even more serious—she was trapped in a fucking hole.

Before the explosion, she'd crept into the lab in tiger form, only to realize she had no way to contact Gavriel without alerting the other Eldritch. Since it was clear he was fine, not overrun in some loud and messy battle, she backed out with a quickness, not wanting to bleed all over his assassination protocol.

After shifting back, she'd retrieved her shoulder bag from its hiding spot and had been digging at her own wounds for hours, failing to perform a successful surgery when the whole world rocked, and a sinkhole opened beneath her. Now, she was in a sea cave that was slowly filling up with water. The gap above her was too small for her to get out that way, even if the water raised her high enough, and there were too many rocks piled for her strength to budge them.

Going for a long swim didn't seem like a good idea either, especially when she was bleeding. Her knowledge of the local sea life was nil, but she figured attracting predators when she was already out of her element qualified as a horrendous plan.

Which left her treading water while trying to get those damned bullets out. If she could dig them out—one in her upper arm, the other lodged against her ribs—then her wounds would seal, allowing her to risk the long swim to the surface. Well, assuming this cave opened to the sea.

She might have been in worse predicaments, but right now, she'd lost enough blood not to be able to name the occasion. *Okay, settle down. You're not dying like this. That would be pathetic.* The strongest member of the Ash Valley security team, taken out by two random shots and the indifferent ocean.

That mental pep talk helped slightly. Her phone had enough charge left that she could use the torch, and she scrambled over slick rocks to higher ground, trying to get out of the water to have another go at bullet extraction. *If one of these was stuck in my back, I'd be so screwed. Count your blessings, Versai.*

First, she went after the one under her left breast but there was muscle and fat to pierce through, and she had only a small knife she kept strapped to her ankle for emergencies. Cussing through the pain, she pressed with full strength and dug, hoping she didn't maim herself beyond recovery. This was damn near impossible without being able to see what she was doing, then she got the bright idea to use her phone as a mirror. Not perfect, but better, though she was shivering and nauseous by the time she got the twisted metal scrap out, scraped from atop her rib cage. If there were bone fragments or other problems in there, she couldn't handle that.

Please clot, wound. This is all I can do.

Mags flung the deformed bullet away, into the dark and swirling water. It was up to her ankles now, despite how she'd clambered to higher ground.

In pure frustration, she shouted, "Fuck this, fuck all of it."

The cave echoed her words back as if in mockery, and Mags wished she could fight a bunch of rocks. Glaring into the darkness, she breathed hard through her mouth, until she calmed enough to tackle the next issue. The outburst rallied her, though, so she didn't feel quite so sick and weak. If sheer temper could carry her through, she might make it after all.

"You can do this."

Compared to the rib one, this extrication should be easier. The bullet wasn't as deep, but she had to contort her body, using the wrong arm, to go at the entry point. *It's better that it's high on my arm.* Lower, there would be more tendons she might sever.

Taking a deep breath, she gouged her knife into the wound and rooted around until she heard a metallic ting. The pain froze her for a few seconds, then she marshaled her courage and forced it up through the raw meat of her biceps. Trembling, she flicked the mangled metal away and leaned her face against the dry stone like it was a lover who could comfort her.

Using the seawater, she washed away the blood as best she could, then set a timer on her phone. Fifteen minutes should be long enough to get a scab going, if she'd purged enough of the poison for accelerated healing to kick in.

Waiting might end her, because the water was rising, slowly but steadily, pushing her closer to the ceiling with every moment that ticked away. When the timer finally went off, she checked the sites and found them closed enough that she was willing to risk diving. There wouldn't be sea predators in the cave, but who knew what would be lurking when she hit the ocean?

Assuming she could find an outlet.

But that was a gamble she was willing to make, better than drowning for sure when the tide came in completely. There wouldn't be an air pocket when the water rose all the way. Mags could tell that much by the shine of the ceiling when she waved her light around. Otherwise, there would be marks on the walls indicating where the tides ended.

I'm really doing this? Hell yes, Gavriel must be wondering where the devil I am.

Trying to quiet her racing heart, she braced herself for the cold shock, then dove off the rocks and into the water. She had no experience in shit like this, so she let the current direct her, and after a while, it picked up speed, as if she was being carried. Mags swam with all her strength, lungs burning. Just when it felt like she had to let go—and she'd surely drown—the water shoved her with incredible force, and she exploded out the side of the cliff, then she was falling, screeching curses all the way.

She hit the water so hard it knocked the breath out of her, and it felt like she might've snapped a bone. Still, she struggled to the surface, grateful to be alive and not mangled on the sharp rocks to either side. She was close enough to shore not to worry about getting eaten by sharks; the cold was more of a concern.

Even with her innate resistance, she couldn't stop shivering as she swam, eyes locked on the rocky inlet that never seemed to get closer, no matter how she paddled.

I'm caught in the undertow.

It yanked her down once, and she fought the ocean like it was her greatest enemy, surfaced again, took a breath, and latched onto a rock to rest. *Don't quit now, dammit.* Mags pulled herself up onto it and saw that she might be able to leap from rock to rock to escape the dangerous current. If she miscalculated a single jump, she'd crack her head open and drown.

Still, this is my only shot.

She squatted to try to control her trembling, as that would affect her coordination, but she was too wet, too cold, for that to work. *I must be verging on hypothermia and I've lost a lot of blood. Hesitating won't save me.*

Whispering a prayer to the goddess of reckless souls, Mags launched herself and nearly slid off the next rock, clawed herself upright, and tore off two fingernails in the process. *Fucking hell, that smarts.*

Two more jumps, here we go.

From there, the water was clear and shallow. She dove and paddled weakly until she could touch bottom, dragging her exhausted ass out of the sea like her ankles were weighted with lead.

I did it. I'm alive.

Climbing to the meeting point seemed like a lot of work, and there was ice in her veins instead of blood. Mags took one step, still trying her best, but her legs wouldn't hold.

She didn't pass out, but there was no more fuel in the engine, no more anger for her to burn.

TIRELESSLY, GAVRIEL SEARCHED the ruins with terrified determination, but he found no trace of Mags.

There was no way to get inside the facility. *If she did what I'm afraid she did, if she followed me in…*

"I told her to wait outside," he said aloud. As if that changed anything.

He was trying to control the worst of his fear and despair, but there was no good reason for her to vanish on this island. Conscious of the passing time, he renewed the search, digging beneath tumbled stones. He lacked her ability to track by scent, and his high-tech equipment was relatively useless out here. Scanning for thermal signatures only located local wildlife, though sometimes the animal was large enough to let him hope.

Of course she wouldn't get lost. She had the capacity to find him by smell at any point; since she hadn't, Gavriel must conclude she couldn't. Panic howled in him, clawing his mind until he could barely think.

Where is she? What have I done?

For hours, he dug, until his hands bled. Gavriel staggered from the ruins to the hills, calling her name. Only silence answered, affirming his growing fear that he was the only person left alive. He didn't bother hiding his passage, running like a man chased by demons from one side of the island to the other.

No signs of life, apart from the birds and the small creatures that made their homes here. None of them were large enough to threaten him. They fled before his desperate calls.

Gavriel kept hoping to find her as he searched. Even a hint of what had become of her, that would be welcome. But it was as if the earth had swallowed her, and he was starting to believe it had.

"This can't be happening," he said aloud.

A vicious pinch to his inner arm didn't wake him up. He was still standing on a rocky hillside with a sticky sea breeze blowing over him. Behind, the ruins were still half-sunken into the wreckage of the hidden lab. There were no cries audible in the silence except for the calls of seabirds, irritated by his presence.

He tried to hold on, grasping at the fraying shreds of hope, and he spoke aloud, as if his own voice had ever offered him any comfort. "Calm down. If she's trapped, you're the only chance she has."

The words didn't offer solace, but sudden inspiration struck, and he sprinted back to the ruins to look for some scrap of metal he could use to signal. Eventually, he found a length of pipe jutting up from the collapse and he knocked on it, using a set pattern. If she was buried within reach of this, she could answer and let him know she was alive at least.

He wouldn't let himself entertain the other possibility. That she was gone, had been since the first explosion, and he'd never see her again, never touch her or breathe her in. Even the whisper of such an outcome nearly took his legs out from under him on a wash of anguish the like of which he hadn't known since Oriel died.

I ran then—to save my own life—and to fulfill Thalia's ambitions. I will never do that again.

Through pure will, Gavriel gathered the resolve to keep looking. He did find a sinkhole doubtless created by the blast, but when he called out, nobody responded. *Maybe she can't hear me.*

He tried again, shouting until he lost the last of his voice, already strained from his first breakdown. Then he dug through the loose earth and came up against a layer of tumbled stones that it would take heavy machinery to dislodge. *If she's down there, I can't save her.*

Despair went for the sucker punch, knocking all the wind out of him, because he couldn't stop the sudden onrush of dire mental images. Mags, trapped. Mags, suffocating slowly, clawing at the rock until her blood smeared the stone, and the light left her eyes.

Fuck, what do I have to live for anyway? When a beast bred for battle lost its will to fight, what did the owner do with it? *Somebody ought to put me down.*

When the sun dropped on the horizon, after hours of fruitless digging, he lost hope. If she could come, she would. For another hour, he sat in silent despair on a pile of stones. *This place is damned. It's where the Silver Queen fell, where the Golgoth were created for brutality and violence. And this place took her from me.*

It was fitting that this was where he'd end everything as well. Gavriel let his thoughts roam, taking a bleak satisfaction in considering all the ways he could do it. Falling from the cliffs? He might not die right away, and he *did* deserve to suffer.

A beautiful person who gave without asking anything in return...and I've killed her.

Yes, best not to allow it to be quick or clean. He'd heard drowning was fast, but terrifying and awful for those brief moments. No, he wouldn't let the water have him. It had to be something else, something suitably twisted and terrible. Today, Death's Shadow would take his place at his master's side.

Rising, he walked to the edge of the cliff and gazed at the rocks below, the sea spiking white around them.

Here. I'll jump from here.

Since he was so lost in bleak thoughts, at first, he thought he must have hallucinated the figure struggling in the surf. Then he took a second look, a third, his whole body hot with longing and relief. Gavriel got out his binocs to confirm, then he took off running, dashing along the cliffs like a mad mountain goat. From up here, he couldn't tell how badly she was hurt, but she was moving.

She's alive. She came back to me.

He didn't merit a miracle like this, and he had no fucking clue how she wound up in the water. None of that mattered. Gavriel leapt and landed hard on the rocks one level down, ignored the pain in his knees, and kept moving, scrambling, tumbling down the slope to get to her as fast as possible. He could hardly think for the excited primate banging rocks in his brain, all euphoria and exultation.

His customary grace deserted him, and he fell halfway down the hill, rolling like a drunken sailor, and he scraped all the skin off both knees, took a tree branch in the side that bruised him to the bone.

So worth it.

He got up without checking his wounds, gaze fixed on the bedraggled tiger woman crawling up the rocky hillside. The moment she lost the will to continue, he added speed, ignoring the blood trickling down his shins. When he finally reached her, she was sitting on a patch of stony ground, wearing a dazed look. She smiled when she saw him, and he dragged her into his arms, holding her so close that it must hurt, but she clung to him with the same desperation. The fact that she didn't break his ribs attested to her weakness.

Gavriel cupped her inexpressibly dear face in his hands, hardly daring to believe she wasn't a chimera conjured by his fractured hopes. No, he wouldn't have brought her to life with a healing scrape on her face. Her gorgeous mouth wouldn't be blue, nor would she be shivering with her hair in sea-drenched tangles about her face.

"You're here," he whispered, because he'd given most of his volume to the wind.

"Sorry I'm late. I..." Her words devolved into a coughing fit, and he held her through it, until she could get her breath. "Ran...into some complications."

"Tell me later. It's enough that you're here with me."

"You sound like hell," she managed to say.

"I know. It's been a...bad day." Such a comic understatement for how losing her had brought him to the brink of ruin.

Death would have to wait a while longer. Now that Mags had returned, Gavriel would fight all the way to the underworld and back again to keep her with him.

Now, he just had to convince her.

29.

Too tired to protest when Gavriel offered his shoulder, Mags leaned on him all the way to where they'd stashed their packs and the life raft. Her shoulder bag was sodden, and her phone was ruined, not that there was a signal. She hurt…everywhere. Now and then, she caught him staring, as if she was too good to be true.

Finally, they reached the stony beach where they'd hidden their belongings; thankfully, it was all still there. Gavriel immediately started setting up camp, far enough from the water that the tide couldn't touch them. She sank down, conscious that her body needed more energy to finish healing, but she didn't have the strength to shift. Too bad, because that would let her hunt.

Once he had the tent set up, she crawled inside. Sheltered from the wind, the sun was bright enough to warm it, but Gavriel didn't stop there. As she tried to go to sleep, he pulled at her clothes. "You can't rest like this. You'll get sick."

Mags never let anyone tend to her, but she was too tired to stop him—or that was what she told herself. Maybe it just felt good, knowing he cared enough about her to do it.

When she was naked, he took off his clothes too, using his own body heat and the thermal blanket to warm her. Her shivering didn't continued for long minutes, and he held her the whole time, stroking her back in long, languid strokes.

"Do you plan to explain what the hell happened?" she asked.

"I blew up the loyalists."

"Well, that's concise. A little more?"

"I had no idea you were close enough to be impacted by the blast. Per our timetable, I thought you'd left long since."

"It's not your fault. I went in looking for you, but I was wounded, so I came out and started trying to remove the bullets, lost track of time…" Sighing, she shook her head. "It wasn't my finest hour. It would've been better if you'd given me a heads up, though."

He ran his fingers through her damp hair, deftly working away the tangles. "I'm sorry. I should have looked for you and explained my plan first. It's—"

"Not worth rehashing. We're both alive, right? Our phones aren't working, and if you'd gone searching for me, maybe you wouldn't have taken out all the loyalists in one magnificent move." She closed her eyes on a blissful breath. His hands felt so damn good in her hair, gentle, applying pressure in just the right places.

When he stopped, Mags wasn't ready and she opened her eyes with a soft protest, especially when he moved away from her. If she had her head on straight, she'd probably put a stop to this, but what could it hurt to indulge herself? In three days, Ceras would return, and they'd go their separate ways once they reached the mainland.

Paper crinkled, then he passed her a lumpy rectangle. "Here, have a protein bar."

Even if it was plant protein, this would help. Mags took the food and devoured it in four bites. "Thanks."

As soon as she finished, Gavriel came back, wrapping her up in his arms. "We have time to rest. Get some sleep."

Good advice. That would conserve energy, maybe enough that her body could repair itself. She let him cuddle her because it was blessedly warm, and in no time at all, Mags winked out. The next thing she knew, it was dark, and Gavriel was touching her—nothing sexual—little compulsive strokes on her shoulders and back.

"Didn't you get any sleep?"

"A bit."

That smelled like a lie, but she didn't argue with him. Stretching, she slid out of the tent and tested her reserves. *Ah, I'm good now.*

"Time for me to cat up and go hunting. Should I bring anything back for you?" Mags suspected he'd decline, but it was polite to ask.

"No, I have enough protein bars to last until the boat returns."

"I'll be back."

Without waiting for his reply, she bounded off and found dinner quickly up in the hills. She ate in tiger form, feeling the last of her wounds seal, then she groomed, licking away the salt from her ordeal in the sea. Finally, she used the facilities, less lowering as a tiger, then Mags felt ready for anything, though it was the middle of the night. It was only a few hours, but Gavriel was pacing when she got back and he had been for a while, clearly, as he'd worn a shallow trench in front of the tent.

As she shifted back, he let out a slow, deep breath. "You're safe."

"Why wouldn't I be? There's nothing here that could hurt me now. You know I'm an apex predator, right?"

Ignoring that, he pulled her into his arms and kissed her. Mags tried to pull away, conscious that her mouth tasted like raw meat and blood, nothing any Eldritch would want, but he didn't let go, and she fell into the kiss, energized, if slightly confused by his urgency. Finally, she pulled away, panting.

"What's happening here? Some kind of life-affirming sex thing?"

"Yes. That," Gavriel said, so quickly that it made her suspicious but then he was pulling her toward the tent.

He didn't smell aroused, per se, and this didn't fit the usual parameters of his desire. Yet he was urging her down, covering her body with his, and that wasn't normal for him either. But when she felt his lips on her neck, she arched her throat and decided to let him lead. Ripples of pleasure followed wherever he kissed. He nuzzled a path down her neck, over her shoulders, and onto her breasts. This was softer than she usually liked, but it still felt good, enough that her nipples hardened, and he sucked one into his mouth, used his teeth and tongue to please her.

Mags moaned and cupped his head in her hands. "Are you trying to make amends? Because it feels like you're...worshipping me." Strange word but it fit.

"Do you not like it?"

She settled back. "Continue. I'm curious what you'll do, given complete freedom."

Gavriel licked and kissed every inch of her body, so slow and thorough that she was soon squirming. It was impossible for her to quell her dominant impulses entirely, and she grabbed his head, shoving his face right where she wanted it. Mags groaned when he settled between her thighs. First, he kissed her there, soft and sweet, then he went to work with lips and tongue, alternating the pressure just as she'd taught him. His mouth on her clit was about the best feeling in the world, and she raised her hips, rubbing her pussy against his face. He made a succulent noise, as if he was truly enjoying this, and cupped her ass in his hands, holding her steady but not limiting her ability to move.

He's so perfect, everything I ever wanted.

Tension tightened her belly, the urgency rising as she rubbed against his mouth. It wasn't easy for her to come on her back, but she might make it this time if he kept going—*yes, just like that.* Since there was nobody to hear them, she could be as loud as she wanted, and she moaned when he found the sweet spot, driving her wild.

"Gavriel, that's *so* good. Keep going. I'm close."

"You like that?" He spoke right into her pussy, sending a gentle thrill through her.

"Fuck yes."

"You want more?"

"Yes!" When he increased the pressure, it was all she could do to answer.

"I love the way you taste. I'm going to suck on you until you come."

"Yes." She'd never been one for dirty talk, but she was starting to like it, especially from him, partly because it was so unexpected.

His mouth felt exquisite, sheer perfection. He knew exactly how and where to use it. Her entire body was hot, the tingles coming in irresistible waves.

"You're about to come all over my face."

"Oh gods, yes." She arched, her body tightening as his

lips sealed over her clit, the pleasure spiking, and she clenched her thighs about his head, muffling his next words.

"...And you're wildly, helplessly in love with me."

"Yes!"

GAVRIEL KNEW THE moment Mags realized what she'd said.

She shoved him away so forcefully that he nearly tumbled out of the tent. "You tricked me, you bastard!"

If she was about to murder him, so be it. There were worse fates than dying by her hand. He knee-walked back to her. "It's true, though. You do. Don't bother denying it."

"That's not the point! You must have a death wish. I *told* you about my curse. You're going to die, one week from today."

He shrugged. "It's fine. I'll have no regrets."

"Easy for you to say, asshole. I have to live with this again—and without you." She was so upset that she couldn't even look at him.

His heart turned over. "Don't think about it. Let's enjoy the time we have."

That was the wrong thing to say. She swore and stormed out of the tent, still naked, but not for long, as in a heartbeat, she was a tiger, heading off to hunt. Hopefully, she'd forgive him for doing it this way, but he'd always been a sneaky bastard. It seemed fitting that he play to his strengths, even in this.

With her gone again, he worried, but not quite as much as he had before. The terror and madness of thinking he'd lost her forever had worn off somewhat. Gavriel occupied himself by attempting to fish with a makeshift rod, but he had no luck. He considered inflating the boat to try farther out, but if something happened to the raft, they'd have to swim out to meet the ship, and after her struggle in the sea, it was better to spare her that.

In the end, he opted to eat another protein bar and do some stargazing. *When was the last time I did anything like this?* In truth, he couldn't recall. His life had been pitifully devoid of meaning and beauty before he met her.

If he'd imagined getting her to admit her feelings would solve the problem, he was utterly mistaken. For the next three days, she ignored him, living as a tiger, sleeping and hunting as one. At first, anger dominated his emotions, but as time wore on, he understood. The only cure for this…was for him to live.

She's acting like this in self-defense.

Mags didn't speak more than five words to him before the boat arrived. In fact, they even packed and took turns blowing up the raft in silence. Respecting her mood, he paddled them out to where Ceras was waiting and let her scale the rope ladder first. Gavriel followed, offering a polite bow to the sailor.

"Thank you for keeping your promise."

"You paid me well, more than I'd make with a day of fishing, and the weather's calm. Did you finish your business?"

He nodded. "The raiders won't bother anyone again."

Ceras leveled an assessing look on him. "I'll be sure to stay on your good side, mate. That wasn't no easy work." Mags stepped past them both, offering only a surly nod to the sailor, who watched her go with a raised brow. "Seems like you pissed her off. With respect, I'll stay out of it."

Gavriel tried to join her in the prow, but when he approached, she stood and made her way to the back of the boat. Sighing, he folded his arms and waited for the trip to end. Part of him feared she'd run, as soon as they hit land. According to the curse's timetable, he only had a few days left to live.

I really ought to be more alarmed by that.

The fact was, when he made up his mind to die on the island, thinking she was already gone, he'd made his choice. Others might not understand the intensity of his attachment, but Magda Versai was Gavriel's reason for living. Currently, he didn't know what a future might look like for them; she had to believe it was possible first.

Aha, that's the solution.

Gavriel bided his time until Ceras brought the boat up to the dock, then he tipped the sailor generously. "You've done more good than you know, sir."

"Eh, if you're talking about eradicating those raiders, then I'm aware how much better off we'll be. Take care of yourself and find a way to appease your lady friend, or you'll have no peace at all." He chuckled at his own wordplay, then went to tend to the lines fastening the boat to the pier.

Mags disembarked while they were talking, and Gavriel sprinted to catch up to her, planting himself firmly in her path. She tried to go around, but every time she moved, he stepped in front of her, and she finally snarled at him, showing teeth.

"Get out of my way!"

"That's the one thing I can never do."

"What?"

"Leave you alone. I won't do it, and you can't make me." He reached for her, wishing like hell that she'd relent and come to him. "If I'm to die for being with you, then let me die. It's better than living without you."

"I can't go through this. Not again. Not if it's you." She stepped back, golden eyes luminous with a pain he wished he could bear in her stead.

"That's my decision to make. Not yours. And you are worth the risk. I'm betting that I'm the one who *won't* be taken."

From the over-bright shine of her eyes, the words appeared to move her. Just not enough. "You can't promise that, shadow warrior. I never wanted to get tangled up with anyone ever again. I hate you for this."

"You love me," he said, and she clamped a hard hand across his mouth as if the gods might be listening for such subversive talk.

He bit her. Gently. That move prompted her to yank her hand away as if his mouth was made of fire, and considering how hard she came, last time he used it on her, Gavriel could understand her wariness.

"Are you trying to turn me on?" he teased. "I'm shocked. It's the middle of the day, but if you don't mind everyone at the public house hearing, then—"

"Stop it." Her voice was weak, and she seemed weary in a way he'd never seen.

He could see how much this resistance was costing her. "Do something for me."

"What do you want, Gavriel?"

"Give me two days. If I'm still around when my alleged time is up, we'll talk about us. Do you promise?"

"There's no point, but sure." Such a hopeless tone. Her shoulders slumped, and she set off toward the inn, eyes downcast.

"I wonder how I'll go out. Pack of wild dogs? Perhaps a building will fall on me."

Mags whirled on him then, eyes snapping fire, which was better than the broken woman confronting despair for the third time. "You're making *jokes* at a time like this? If you say another word, I'll kill you myself!"

In exaggerated motions, he pantomimed zipping his mouth and throwing away the key. She stormed off ahead, though he followed close enough to make sure she wouldn't make a run for it. But no, Mags had too much honor to bolt when she'd promised to stay and witness his grisly demise.

She was playing with Leena when he caught up to her. Gavriel greeted everyone, then he gave her some space, heading to the stable to see how Gray was doing.

The vedda beast was a bit fatter, but he looked good otherwise. He checked his mount's hooves, to be sure. "You enjoyed the rest, hey? What a lucky brute you are. Before she came, you didn't even have a name. I bet you had no idea that I love you, either."

Until he met Mags, he hadn't been able to show such things, not even to the loyal mount who had carried him for years. Gavriel took his time with the brush and comb, then he gave Gray's horns a good polish.

There, that should be long enough for her to calm down. If she loses her temper, we'll end up fucking, and that won't solve anything.

It *would* be fun, though.

As he was about to leave, the boy peered down from the loft. "He's in good health, sir. Once a day, I rode him around town to give him some exercise. Hope that's all right."

"I'm sure he enjoyed it. Thanks for looking after him." He stepped out of the barn, whistling, conscious of a lightness of heart he'd never known. In that moment, he chose forgiveness because Mags would never look at him the same, if he hurt Pru Bristow, and vengeance wouldn't bring his brother back to life.

Not bad for a condemned man.

The weather was bright and clear, and Gavriel had nobody left in the world that he needed to kill. There was just a tiger woman to woo, and she might prove to be the immovable object to his irresistible force.

Only one way to find out.

30.

IF MAGS LET go of the anger she was using as a shield, she might drown in her own tears. *Can't believe this is happening. Again.*

In time, Gavriel strode into the public house, and his ridiculous smile said he still had no idea how serious the situation was. He went over to Haryk. "We'll need the attic room for a few more nights. Is that all right?"

"More than fine." The proprietor sent what he thought was a sly look at Keriel. "It's going well, I think. When the time comes, I'll invite you to the wedding."

The Eldritch woman clearly heard that and was choosing to ignore it on her way to the kitchen. Keriel had already taken Mags's stiff, salty clothes, clucking her tongue over the state of that outfit. She hadn't packed for a long trip, and she'd been gone for much longer than she'd ever anticipated. Sadly, the prospect of returning to her ordinary life in Ash Valley held all the appeal of dental surgery without anesthetic.

Glumly, she ate seven grilled fish and drank more beer than she should, though it wasn't enough to get her drunk. Mags avoided Gavriel until nightfall by devoting her attention to Leena, but the public house was less crowded now, as other families had made space for the refugees, and now that the weather had improved, they were gathering materials to build new houses. That was a happy ending for sure, but she wasn't hopeful about her own prospects.

With a sigh, she finally went up to their room to find the blankets already laid out. Gavriel sat with his legs folded, two candles burning against the dark. "I was waiting for you. Are you calm enough to talk now?"

In answer, she rolled away and turned her back to him. He'd forced her into this situation, and her heart hurt so much at the prospect of losing him that she could die of it. *I won't survive this a third time.* If only she was weak enough to run away, then she wouldn't have to see the end of this, but she'd given her word, damn him.

I don't have to be gracious.

Mags kept the icy facade in place all that night and most of the next day. She could tell Gavriel was getting worried. He flicked her anxious looks, though that could be because he'd realized this was his final day on earth. According to her experience with the curse, he'd perish tomorrow morning, and she couldn't bear it.

Tonight, when he greeted her with smiles and candles, she caved. Mags went to him because it was his last night, and she wouldn't spend it treating him like air. Gavriel wrapped his arms around her and nuzzled his face into her neck.

"I was hoping for this. I've missed you."

She let out a choked laugh. "You win. I can't send you away without—"

"Having me one last time?"

"Wish you hadn't put it that way, but...yes. I'm greedy.

If this is what we can have, I'll take it. At least this time, I'm braced, and I'll be able to say goodbye."

That wasn't what she wanted, of course, but life had taught her that fate wasn't fair. The flash of his eyes hinted that he wasn't resigned to his own demise, and she wouldn't let dread touch them tonight. This attic would be a sanctuary that hid them from all fearful things, allowing only beauty and pleasure to prevail.

"I'm not going anywhere, woman. I'm Death's Shadow, remember? 'Only death' can stand against the shade that haunts you. Your Seer was talking about me in his prediction, don't you see? Perhaps no shifter mate can avoid this curse, but *I* can. Because I'm not Animari. Hell, maybe I'm the penance you have to do to purify your soul."

Mags choked out a laugh. "You're not a punishment, Gavriel."

He went on as if she hadn't spoken. "And even if I'm wrong, even if I drop dead tomorrow, I don't care. You're worth paying any price."

Desire overwhelmed her in a heady rush, and she stopped trying to resist. Never had she wanted anyone this fiercely, this urgently, and she shoved him back, hard. Gavriel's eyes sparked, and he twisted, trying to scramble away, but since he was quiet, she knew he wanted it too.

The word had yet to be spoken.

Breathing hard, he pushed against her hold, and she slammed his hands against the floor, bearing down until he let out a quiet moan. Then she kissed him, biting his lower lip with enough pressure that he had to open his mouth, then she could taste him fully, making him feel how completely he belonged to her. As they kissed, he responded immediately, his cock rising with desperate insistence.

Mags tugged so hard on his shirt that the back split, and he made a helpless sound against her mouth. *Yeah, he likes that.*

"Take off your pants before I wreck them too," she whispered in his ear.

His hands trembled as he rushed to do her bidding. Soon, he was naked, and she wanted to torment him as he had her when he tricked her into confessing her love. Shoving him back onto the blanket, she kept him pinned and used her mouth, her teeth, her tongue, covering him in fierce kisses and bites, until his breath came in ragged pants and whines. She pinched his nipples and he went wild, thrusting against her stomach in compulsive strokes.

She caught the third slide with her mouth and bit down. Gavriel froze. Mags teased him by alternating the pressure of lips, strokes of her tongue with grazes of teeth. He liked a little pain even in this, but from his tormented expression, he was more afraid he would lose control and come.

Mags had no intention of letting that happen. He was already worked up to a fever pitch, and her own intensity was rapidly hitting critical levels. She needed a quick, hard fuck. Now.

Pulling back, she said, "Sit up."

Though he seemed a little confused, he did, and she settled on his lap. This way, she could hold onto him, dig her nails into his back, and he could touch her as well. Tonight, she wanted some reciprocity, though she wasn't willing to yield dominance.

"Ohhh." The sound slipped out of him as Mags sank onto his cock.

So hot. Incredibly hard. For a few seconds, she sat still, just feeling him shiver and throb. It was like she could feel his heart beating inside her.

"Touch me if you want to."

Clearly, he had been waiting for that invitation, because Gavriel wrapped his arms around her as she started to move, rolling her hips against him. It took him a few tries before they got in synch, then it was even better. She sucked hard on the spot he favored, the curve of his shoulder, then she bit that soreness, trying to make it better for him.

Gavriel was panting, pushing into her furiously, and she felt when he lost control. She didn't try to rein him in; she just wanted him to feel, to lose himself in the pleasure that was building in her pussy.

Faster and faster, harder and harder, until they had to be making noise, but she didn't give a fuck even if dust was drifting down from the ceiling. She bit down on his bruise when she came, dug her nails into his back, and his whole body went rigid. Because Mags went first, she luxuriated in his orgasm, stroking his back as he came down.

The way his body jerked at the slightest touch made her smile. They stayed like that for quite a while, before she finally groaned and rolled away, falling onto her back to savor the rush of endorphins.

"You okay?" she asked.

"Remarkably well, all things considered."

She propped up on an elbow to glare at him. "Are you joking again?"

"Not at all. I do feel blessed, as if this is where I'm meant to be. I love you, Mags."

Part of her feared saying the words, like they might make the situation worse, so she stayed silent. She kissed him tenderly, trying to convey it with her lips, so jealous gods couldn't overhear.

THEY SLEPT UNTIL well past noon, judging from the light streaming in the window. Gavriel wasn't surprised to wake alive and in one piece. He'd already decided he existed outside of Animari prophecies, and he wasn't about to lose Mags. Not now, not ever.

For a few seconds, he studied her sleeping face. *Hey, you. Welcome to the rest of our lives.* Then he kissed her awake, taking a slightly wicked pleasure in the way she scrambled alert and locked onto his face, eyes wild.

He kissed her again, just because. "Still here. Still breathing."

"You're not funny." Tears sprang to her eyes, and she swiped them away angrily, refusing to look at him. "How are you still here? *How?*"

"You're stuck with me, I'm afraid."

"Thank you," she whispered.

"For what?"

"For surviving." Then she launched herself at him and hugged him so hard he couldn't breathe. "For existing in the first place. For being so absurdly stubborn and refusing to listen when I tried to be noble. For loving me. For…being exactly who I need."

Smiling, Gavriel wound his arms around her and held on until her desperation diffused into a shy, incredulous joy. She peppered his face with kisses, open and affectionate, as she never had been. The warmth hit him like sunlight. Until meeting her, his life had been a series of requirements, the coldness of duty and obligation. From this point on, there would be only freedom and joy.

He framed her face in his hands, smiling. "I'll wake you like this every day if you wish. Before you stormed into my life, I had nothing. Now I have everything. I have *you.*" He hesitated. "We beat your curse, but I don't know how long I have. I'll limit the use of my gift now, but I used it a lot in the past, and there's no test I can take to predict—"

Mags kissed him to stop the flow of words. "I don't care. Normally, you'd live a lot longer than me anyway, so let's not worry about it. My heart can't take it when you look at me like that."

"And mine can't take losing you." Leaning in, he tilted his head against hers.

"You won't," she promised.

He kissed her forehead, her eyebrows, her temples, then lifted her face so he could gaze into her beautiful eyes. "I truly believe that we make our own fate, Mags. Walk with me. Live with me. Grow old with me."

"Yes, damn you. I won't run. I'll stay. I'm going to…" She drew in a deep breath. "Love you."

"Finally," he growled.

Though Gavriel had said kissing didn't turn him on, Mags soon taught him that there were exceptions, and they rolled around for half the day. Finally, hunger drove them out of the attic, and everyone shot them knowing looks when they emerged.

"Looks like you have some happy news," Haryk observed. "Maybe you'll beat me to the altar?"

"We haven't talked about that," Mags muttered.

Gavriel smiled, unbothered by the other man's speculation into his business. Funny, he didn't mind much of anything these days. Maybe in time, he could even see Thalia without wanting to strangle someone. Probably not soon, however.

They had a meal, provided free of charge, though Gavriel still left a few coins on the table. He made sure Mags got plenty of protein, enjoying the fresh seafood, savory broth, hot bread and salted butter. Keriel finished the service with a platter of cheese, and Mags winked at him, proving she'd been responsible for that. Silly as hell, but it filled him with warmth that she knew—and remembered—how he'd confessed to loving the stuff, during that game they played. These were moments that he'd shared with nobody else, and maybe they didn't amount to much, but that was the beauty of a life together, creating increments of intimacy, a world built for two.

That was something he needed to mention, though. As much as he loved her… Gavriel sighed as they stepped out of the public house—into the cool purple of a dying day. It was the peculiar in-between time, stars just a hint of sparkle, the moon nearly full, but pale against the vivid canvas of the sky.

"What's wrong?" she asked.

"Like you said, we haven't discussed it, but… I can't live among the Animari. I'm sorry, but I can't. I may never fully be able to get past what happened to Oriel. And yes, I blame Thalia too."

He feared how she would react to that, but to his relief, she laced their fingers together, setting off on a course that carried them toward the sea. They walked for a while in silence while she seemed to contemplate what he'd said.

"That's fair. I don't want to settle in an Eldritch town either, really," she admitted.

Carrying her hand to his mouth, he tried to soften his request with a kiss, another sneaky-bastard tactic. Maybe he should be ashamed, but he'd do damn near anything to make this work. "I shouldn't ask you to give up everything for me, but I am."

"By saying I don't want to live in Eldritch lands, I'm asking the same of you," she pointed out.

Fairness forced him to admit, "You have friends. Family. Work that you love. I'm not giving up anything, really. There's nothing waiting for me, only memories I'd rather leave behind."

"Okay, I take your point. Let's put a pin in this for now. Does your phone have any juice left? Mine didn't survive the swim."

"I shut it off to conserve battery since there's no way to charge it here. Why, do you need to make a call?"

"Actually, I do. Two, in fact."

Since she didn't seem like she wanted to explain, he got out his cell and turned it on. "Less than ten percent. You'll need to make it quick."

"Noted."

These were numbers she knew by heart, a fact that made him uneasy as she dialed. Then Mags said, "Ma, it's me. I met someone. When we get time, I'll bring him to meet you. FYI, he's not a tiger, not even an Animari, so I don't want to hear about it."

He stifled a laugh at her bluntness, but her mother was talking, loud enough that he could hear. "I never cared about our line *that* much, you awful child. I just didn't want you to spend your life alone." There was some noise in the background. "Your father says hello and he sends his love."

"Back at him. I gotta go, Ma. Phone's gonna die soon. I won't go so long without calling next time."

"You didn't apologize," he said, as she cut the connection.

"That's not our style. We fight and then pretend it didn't happen and that nobody was wrong."

"If she's anything like you, that must lead a fair amount of conflict." Gavriel smirked, knowing he'd never get tired of baiting her.

She nudged him, hard. "One more call, then I'm all yours."

"I wish I'd recorded that," he muttered, wistful.

This time when she dialed, she put the phone on speaker, as if inviting him to be part of the call. "This is Asher."

She called Ash Valley? He recognized Dominic Asher's voice, though he would never like the bastard. Every muscle tense, Gavriel raised his brows in silent question, but Mags shook her head and put a finger to her lips.

Okay, she doesn't want me to talk.

"I just wanted to let you know…I'm quitting. You need to find a new Chief of Security. Eventually, I'll be back to get my stuff, but I'm not sure when."

"Shit, Mags, are you all right?"

Her gaze met Gavriel's, and she smiled, her heart in her eyes. "Never better. I'll send you my final report regarding what I learned about Slay, the destruction of the loyalist stronghold, and a drug leak coming out of Burnt Amber. What you do with that information is up to you. It was on pause for a long time, but I have a life to get back to."

Dom was silent for a few seconds. "Damn. You have been busy. I don't pretend to understand but I don't have to. You'll always have a place here, got me?"

"Yep. I'm losing power soon. Will send the mission brief ASAP. Mags out." She hung up and switched off the phone, offering it to him with an oddly diffident smile.

"You cut ties," he said wonderingly. "For me. I wouldn't have asked you to—"

"I won't go back until you feel better about what happened at the retreat. I know that'll take time." She paused, watching him with obvious concern. "Will you be okay when we visit my parents? Hallowell is a mixed settlement."

"Of course. Anytime you miss them or want to catch up. I did fine in Hallowell. Before the battle, that is."

Mags smiled up at him. "That's all I want then. I've been settled for a long time. Now I'm ready for our next step, whatever that entails."

They started walking again, ending by the ocean, as he'd predicted. The water was dark and calm, like a promise of peaceful days to come. "Do you have any idea what sort of future you want?"

"One with you," she said at once. "Otherwise, I'm not sure, but... we saw a lot of hardship while we were traveling. I've been thinking on that...and maybe we could make the world a better place. I can be the muscle, intimidate when necessary and *you* have that ability that lets you slip past surveillance..."

A prickle of excitement started at the back of his head. "You thinking what I am?"

"Steal from the rich and give to the poor?" Mags grinned, reminding Gavriel why he loved her. "They need indoor plumbing and running water in Kelnora, not to mention access to the solar grid. We could ask Thalia to budget for it, but..."

"This will be more fun," he finished. "I'll make a list of the estates that can afford to subsidize our charitable efforts. We'll take my murderous skills and make the world a better place. Together."

"And if we ever get tired of roving, we can settle in Hallowell. My family will be yours, I promise."

He didn't hesitate at all over making this offer. "If you

want tiger cubs later, I'm fine with letting Titus—"

"Enough." Mags kissed him hard, the perfect partner, no matter what the future had in store.

Only death himself could love her and live, but only a tiger woman could break the walls around his shadowed heart, so he could give himself wholly to her—tightly bonded, blessed by the gods, and meant to be. Forever.

Author's Note

I'm so thrilled that you read *The Shadow Warrior* and hope you're eager for more in the Ars Numina world. *The Shadow Warrior* is the fourth book in a projected six-book series, as follows:

The Leopard King
The Demon Prince
The Wolf Lord
The Shadow Warrior
The War Priest
The Jaguar Knight

Would you like to know when the next book will be available and/or keep up with exciting news? Visit my website at *www.annaguirre.com/contact* and sign up for my newsletter. If you're interested, follow me on Twitter at *twitter.com/msannaguirre*, or "like" my Facebook fan page at *facebook.com/ann.aguirre* for excerpts, contests, and fun swag.

Reviews are essential for indie writers and they help other readers, so please consider writing one. Your love for my work can move mountains, and I so appreciate your effort.

Finally, as ever, thanks for your time and your support.

Printed in Poland
by Amazon Fulfillment
Poland Sp. z o.o., Wrocław